THE BOY WHO STOLE THE
LEOPARD'S SPOTS

Also by Tamar Myers

THE HEADHUNTER'S DAUGHTER
THE WITCH DOCTOR'S WIFE

Den of Antiquities Mysteries

THE GLASS IS ALWAYS GREENER
POISON IVORY
DEATH OF A RUG LORD
THE CANE MUTINY
MONET TALKS
STATUE OF LIMITATIONS
TILES AND TRIBULATIONS
SPLENDOR IN THE GLASS
NIGHTMARE IN SHINING ARMOR
A PENNY URNED
ESTATE OF MIND
BAROQUE AND DESPERATE
SO FAUX, SO GOOD
THE MING AND I
GILT BY ASSOCIATION
LARCENY AND OLD LACE

THE BOY WHO STOLE THE LEOPARD'S SPOTS

Tamar Myers

WILLIAM MORROW
An Imprint of HarperCollins*Publishers*

P.S.™ is a trademark of HarperCollins Publishers.

FIRST EDITION

Library of Congress Cataloging-in-Publication Data has been applied for.

ISBN 978-0-06-199773-0

12 13 14 15 16 OV/RRD 10 9 8 7 6 5 4 3 2 1

For Ndeke Daniel, tuasakidila—"we laugh and we cry."

ACKNOWLEDGMENTS

Many thanks to the teachers throughout my life who nurtured and encouraged me to write. In particular I remember, in order of their appearance, Miss Anna Entz, Mr. John J. Jester, Mr. J. D. Sodt, Mrs. Seibert, and Mr. Oren Odell, Ph.D.

Notes to the Reader

Unlike in Indo-European languages, the plural forms of words in Bantu languages rely on changing prefixes. Thus the words for the name of a tribe, a single member of the tribe, and the tribe's language will all have different prefixes, although the suffixes will remain constant.

Baluba—name of Cripple's tribe
Muluba—a member of the Baluba tribe, e.g., Cripple
Tshiluba—the language spoken by the Baluba tribe (Note: "Tshiluba" was the spelling in 1958; it is sometimes spelled "Chiluba" today.)

Bapende—of the twins' tribe
Mupende—a member of the twins' tribe
Kipende—the language spoken by the twins' tribe

Almost all of the African words used in this novel are of Tshiluba origin, since that was the predominant trade language for Kasai Province, where the book is set. Because life is so tenuous in this part of Africa, in Tshiluba where we might say "hello," they would say "life to you." A distinction is made between the singular and plural forms of "you." Thus when one is speaking to an individual, the greeting is: *muoyo webe*. When addressing more than one person, one says: *muoyo wenu*. Both *kah* and *aiyee* have no direct translation, as they were merely expressions of surprise and dismay. As such, it is also possible that they were geographically restricted in their use.

This is a work of fiction and, as such, none of the characters are real people. However, many of the incidents are based on my childhood memories. I did, in fact, live among the Baluba, Bashilele, and Bapende peoples, from birth to almost the age of sixteen.

PROLOGUE

It was much cooler in the canyon that lay in front of, and below, the village. Over centuries the crystal clear spring had carved itself a bed two hundred meters lower than the surrounding savannah. Erosion had widened this space enough to accommodate a forest with trees large enough to require buttress roots, their crowns soaring up to neck-craning heights. It was a place of magic, awe, and, of course, much superstition. Women had to go there to draw water, and men to cut the leaves of raffia palms with which to thatch their huts, but no one stayed after dark. Except the chief. One night the chief stayed in the canyon to kill a leopard that had been terrorizing his village. This is the story of what happened, and how it came to be that a boy could steal a leopard's spots, and what that would mean for that boy when he grew into a man.

This was no ordinary leopard, to be sure, but to understand that, one must first understand that the lion is not the king of the beasts; it is the leopard. Lions thrive mostly on the savannahs, because they are bulky creatures, unsuited for slipping silently between, and up, trees. Mature lions—that is to say, the males— have manes that can catch on deep brush. It is true that a lion is larger and heavier than a leopard, and thus can take down heavier prey. (However, the most dangerous of all the creatures on land is mankind, and an unarmed man is no match for a healthy leopard.) At any rate, the leopard has proven to be far more adaptable and its distribution far greater that of the lion, inhabiting both forest and plain, and the dense jungle in between. That is why a chief wears a leopard skin, and nothing else will do.

But again, this was no ordinary leopard. Its first act of terror was to snatch a toddler who had strayed too close to the tall grass that encircled the village. The sun was not yet low in the sky when it happened. The child's mother described an animal of mythic proportions with paws the size of a man's head. Paw marks discovered in a nearby patch of sand indicated that the woman had not exaggerated. They also displayed signs of an extra toe on the forepaws.

That night the leopard returned and set about dispatching every single dog in the village; not one was spared. This was a tragedy of the gravest sort, for the men in the village were hunters and they relied on their dogs to help feed their families. To them a good hunting dog was worth more than a wife.

The villagers mourned the death of their dogs as one would mourn the death of a relative. They shrieked, they wailed, they threw dust in the air, but then, being a practical people, they picked up the torn carcasses and stewed them in palm oil along with hot chilies to eat with the evening's *musa*. One did not waste protein in the Belgian Congo, Africa, of 1927.

After that, the villagers stayed close to their huts, and for a few days and nights nothing untoward happened. And given that the people had done their best to round up their chickens, ducks, and goats and house them indoors, even their livestock went unscathed. But then gradually the villagers relaxed their guard, and one sun-drenched morning the oh-so-patient and very clever cat slipped unnoticed through the shadows of their huts and seized upon a woman as she scraped at manioc roots. Neither leopard nor woman emitted a sound, and the only proof that the leopard had been there was the woman's absence, and the steaming pile of her entrails following her evisceration.

"This is no real leopard," the witch doctor cried. "This is the spirit of the man known as Never Stops Crying, he who took his own life by hanging. He has returned to haunt us. Truly, truly, I say this as one speaking with authority; we are being punished for the way we treated him when he was alive."

"Aiyee!" It was a male who raised his voice to keen like a woman, for that showed the intensity of his distress.

Several people laughed, at which point the witch doctor shook his staff in an angry fashion. "This man has a right to be afraid. You should all be afraid, for I witnessed all of you treating Never Stops Crying shamefully. All of you, that is, except for the chief."

"Yes," they chorused, "except for our beloved chief."

"This means," said the witch doctor, "that our chief is the only one here who stands even a chance of slipping down into the forest unseen and slaying this monstrous leopard."

"Ka!" the chief said. "What about you? Do you not have magic at your disposal?"

The witch doctor shook his head vehemently, causing the long black-and-white monkey fur on his headdress to float in the breeze. "Even I tormented Never Stops Crying as a youth, calling him a girl-boy, and telling him that he was incapable of fathering a child. If I were to descend into the canyon where the leopard lives, not only would he kill me, but most probably his spirit would then forsake the leopard guise and crawl into my body. Then I would return to the village with this evil leopard's spirit inside me, which none of you would see, and I would begin to unleash horrible curses on all of you with my knowledge of sorcery."

"Not so," the man called Stubborn as Head Lice called in a loud voice. "Now that you have warned us, we will simply kill you."

"Eh! Eh!" the people chorused. Yes, yes!

"Simpleton," the witch doctor snarled. "You cannot kill a leopard-man. Even a white man's gun cannot kill such a creature."

No one laughed then. "I see," said the chief. "I suppose then that it is up to me to venture down into the forest to kill this giant beast. Tell me, how do you propose that I do that? With my bow and arrows?"

No one laughed.

"Did you not make a copy of the white man's musket for yourself after you were released from conscription?"

"Yes," the chief said. "However, it will only shoot one bullet, and then it takes much time to reload."

"I will put a spell on that bullet," the witch doctor said, "so that it will find its mark. But you must aim for the left eye."

"Or perhaps you will get lucky," the village fool said, "and the leopard will kill and eat you while you are still walking through the elephant grass that lies between here and the canyon's edge."

The chief did not reply to that; instead he returned to his compound where he said his good-byes to his six wives. Although it was not customary at this time and place for a man to make a show of affection to a woman—even one to whom he was wed— the chief lingered when delivering his parting words to his oldest wife. This was the woman he had married first, and who after twenty long dry seasons, and forty short wet seasons, had yet to bear him a child—although any day that would no longer hold true. As of late, Born Crouching's womb had taken on the shape of a *musa* ball, and her breasts rested atop this sphere like large black papayas. Had it not been for the man-eating leopard, the chief would have taken his first wife into the tall grass for lovemaking, not to bid her farewell.

It has been said that only a man who knows fear and faces it can be called "brave." The chief of this Bapende village was terrified of following the narrowing path, ever descending, through the head-high grass that led to the canyon's rim. Continuing down the steep path that hugged the canyon wall, leaving him utterly exposed, caused his gut to cramp. When at last he reached the place where the forest rose up to meet him, he had so much nervous sweat pouring into his eyes that he could no longer see. To compound his troubles, he'd been leading a large female goat who was herself frightened out of what little wits she possessed. Not only did she bleat incessantly, but along the most treacherous part of the trail, she repeatedly butted the chief from behind. Finally, unable to get him out of her way, she placed her front hooves on his shoulders and shuffled behind him on her hind feet like a deranged human being. Had there been another option, he would have killed her as soon as the trail widened, and cooked her up for supper.

Thankfully, there was no other option. The chief kept walking until he came to a tree of the type known as *Tshimaya*, which has a coarse grain. This particular specimen was about only thirty meters tall—no more—but it did not begin to branch until a point at least six meters above the ground. The chief scanned the canopy to see if the leopard might already be hiding in there. When he was finally satisfied this was not the case, he tied the goat securely to a nearby shrub. Then using the point of his machete, he made a small wound in her left flank so that she should bleed, but only a small amount.

"I am sorry, friend," he said. Then after tying his ankles together, he looped a rope around his waist and the *Tshimaya* tree and climbed up to first branch. There he hurriedly fashioned a sling of sorts from some lianas, in order that he might sit while he safely discharged his homemade musket. Guns such as these were capable of knocking a man flat on his backside, if he was not careful.

Meanwhile the goat continued bleating and thrashing in the bushes. The chief, who was a kind man, cursed the animal softly. Of course he would do his best to save the stupid beast from the big cat, although that was extremely unlikely—suddenly there it was! It was the largest leopard that the chief had ever seen. At the shoulder it stood a palm's width taller than any other, and from nose to tail tip, it was a third again as long as any he had ever seen.

But there was something else about it too, something that he couldn't place until later when he had time to think. It was this: the leopard with the extra toes on both front paws was sick. Only a crazed, diseased animal would place itself so directly in harm's way so many times. This leopard was not in possession of magic. Instead, it had lost the instinct to fear man.

"Look at me, *nkashama*," the chief commanded. "Look up here."

The leopard looked. The chief squeezed off one shot, which passed through the leopard's left eye—an amber jewel of an eye— and the metal slug exploded in its brain. The leopard appeared to shrink like a gourd from the drought. It was a shot chosen because of the opportunity presented and not because of anything the witch doctor had said.

Satisfied that the great beast was dead, the chief untied himself and climbed calmly down from the tree. By this point the goat had fainted from fear, as goats are sometimes prone to do, so the chief gave it a sound kick, which brought it back to life with a bleat. Putting his machete to good use again, the chief hacked off one of the leopard's front paws. After that he used a smaller knife to skin the animal. He worked quickly, but with great difficulty, because the sun was beginning to dip below the canyon walls, and at the level of the forest floor it was already so dark that the fireflies had emerged. And so had the hyenas.

The chief persevered, and when he was done, he dragged the heavy pelt, and the confused and reluctant goat, back up the trail a short way to where there was a small cave high up on a rock face. This was a place to which no man dared to go, on account of its association with snakes. With adrenaline powering both his physical and emotional states, the chief managed to lift the leopard skin above his head and cram it far enough into the recess so that it would not be seen by the casual observer, not even in broad daylight. Then the chief caught the rope tied to his goat and made haste to return to his village.

While they were still a long ways off, the chief's ears were assaulted by the wails of keening women. Someone in the village had died. Or perhaps even some woman had given birth to twins—although only two women were anywhere close to that stage. The chief released the goat and began to run. The goat, eager to be back within the safe confines of the village, needed no encouragement to do likewise. When the chief neared the hut of his first wife and saw the cluster of women outside, and others lying on the ground covering themselves with dirt, his temper knew no bounds.

"Get away, you stupid fools!" he bellowed. "What is the matter that you should behave thus?"

It was then that the witch doctor emerged from the hut, parting the women like clumps of elephant grass. "Your wife has invited evil spirits to inhabit her womb," he said. The witch doctor held aloft his staff, on which was mounted a monkey skull, and also from which hung several small, stone-filled gourds, and a few guinea feathers. "She has given birth to demon twins—boys, both of them. I would have already begun the process of punishing the demon, but out of respect to you, we have waited until you returned from your fruitless attempt to kill the leopard with the extra claws."

As tired as he was, the great chief of the Bapende people raised himself to his full regal height. In one hand he held his homemade musket, but he in the other he gripped a cord of leather, from which hung a blood-soaked object: the leopard's front paw. Even drenched, this paw was of a size never before seen. The chief held it aloft for all to see.

"*E*," he said, in a loud voice for all to hear. "It is true that I did not kill the leopard, but listen closely, my people, and believe me when I tell you that it was one of my twin sons who killed the giant beast. Come look at the paw, which was presented to me by the leopard himself before his spirit was vanquished into the netherworld."

Curiosity, the chief knew, had killed many a monkey; so it was that by and by, the elders could not stop themselves from examining the giant paw and exclaiming over its authentic appearance. And with each new convert the witch doctor's rage grew hotter and hotter. Meanwhile the chief slipped into his favorite wife's hut and examined his twin sons. They were perfect in every way—and *identical*. How could it be that a demon existed in one, and not the other, as witch doctors always claimed?

Then his first wife, the wife of his youth, and wife of his heart, spoke. Her voice was weak and sorrow filled.

"My husband, I beg that you forgive me. I have disappointed you woefully. But if you must—as surely you must—put someone to death, say that the evil spirit has forsaken the babies, and that it has entered me. Then stuff the chili peppers up my nostrils and bury me in the anthill, for these children have done nothing to deserve death."

"Hush, wife."

"Husband," she said, her voice growing stronger, "yes, I remember clearly as the pains of childbirth subside—yes, it was I who made a deal with this evil spirit—"

"Shut up, woman!"

The chief returned to the growing bedlam outside the hut. The witch doctor was still trying to stir up the emotions of the people along the lines of traditional thinking. Everything the witch doctor said made sense; that was the problem. It was normal for women to give birth to one child at a time, just as it was normal for goats to have twins. If a goat failed to give birth to twins, the goat was either too young or too old to do so, or else someone had a placed a curse upon the goat. But when a woman gave birth to twins—well, that could mean only one thing.

The *twin* child was an evil spirit entering this world in a human form, one that had taken advantage of the mother's hospitable womb. The problem lay in discerning *which* one of the infants contained the human soul, and which one contained the spirit from the netherworld. Unfortunately, there was no time to waste, as an evil spirit could wreak tremendous havoc on a village in just a matter of days—sometimes even within hours.

For the greater good, it was therefore necessary to torture and then ultimately destroy both infants. The torture was not an act of unnecessary cruelty; the torture was the only way to make sure that this particular demon (and there were many waiting in the wings) would have no desire to attempt a return visit.

When the husband reappeared in the doorway of his wife's hut, the witch doctor practically shoved his monkey skull staff into the chief's face. "You cannot fool a sorcerer," said the witch doctor. "I will admit that this appears to be the paw that made tracks in our village. But it was you who killed the leopard, not one of the twins. How could a child that small—on the day of its birth—do anything except cry out for its mother's milk?"

The chief was careful to control his smile. "Ah," he said, sounding like a man who had just finished gorging himself at a feast, rather than a father fighting for his infant son's life. "The spirit of my son was able to do so even when he was yet in his mother's womb, for he is the opposite of what you claim. He is a good spirit—a *great* spirit—he is the return of my ancestor, Chief Sends Death Ahead."

The chief waited until the many gasps, whimpers, and much chattering had ceased. Even the witch doctor appeared to know when it was wise to keep silent, for although his eyes flashed, even in the gathering dark of the upland village, he kept his lips pressed tightly together.

Finally it was the chief who clapped his hands. "Behold my people, this is a new day for our village. Soon I shall tell you why. But first I shall tell you this: it is true that when he was yet in the womb—a second time—the spirit of my dead ancestor flew down to the forest, and there the boy beheld me taking aim at this mighty beast. 'Father,' he said wisely, in a voice that only I could hear, 'what good will it do to kill this leopard, for then its spirit will be reborn into another, and when that is killed, it will return as another, and so on it shall go? It is much better, Father, that we do something to stop this animal in this life, than in its next.'"

The witch doctor laughed scornfully. "All this palavering while you were taking aim?"

The chief's smile had long faded. "The words of the spirit are spoken quickly. In the *mind*. Is this not something a man in your position understands?"

The people laughed heartily, which meant his comment could have been a big mistake for the chief and his family, but he was beyond caring. Fortunately, the witch doctor merely scowled before answering.

"Yes, of course. Do not presume to tell me things that I already know."

"Well, then," said the chief, "I asked my unborn son what he suggested that we do. 'We must do two things,' he said. 'You must spare the leopard's life in this world in exchange for one of his paws, and I shall prevent his spirit from returning ever again.'"

The people in this Bapende village murmured in wonder at the unexpected wisdom that this twin's unborn spirit had dispensed to his father, the chief. "Yes, yes," a man cried. "It is well known that a lion with three paws becomes a man-eater, but a leopard with only three paws feels shame and will not be seen again."

The chief knew that this was false information, but he did not correct the man, for he did not wish to shame him. However, a leopard with three paws, if it survives the mutilation, could well become a man-eater. It is only that such animals are rarely encountered. Anyway, what is truth, except those things which the majority of people hold to be true? Besides, the chief knew that this man was not alone in his opinion.

So the new father of twins pressed on with his strange tale. "I then asked my son—who was still in the womb, but whose powerful ancestor spirit stood beside me—how he proposed to stop the powerful leopard from returning from each death time as another leopard? Here is what he said: 'Father, you must cut off his paw slowly. As he is writhing in pain, I shall sneak up on him and steal his spots. Without his spots he cannot die and be reborn as a leopard but is doomed to live perpetually in the spirit world. For all leopards have spots, even the black ones that are known as panthers. Under their blackness—when the sun strikes them just so—one can see spots.'"

"Then where are these spots?" the witch doctor demanded. "Show them to us! And which one of the boys stole them? We must know his identity, in order that we might destroy the other."

"You are a fool and a simpleton," the chief said, "for only the boy who stole the spots is capable of telling you. That can only happen when he is capable of human speech. However, since you claim to be able to understand the speech of spirits, then go back into my wife's hut and ask each boy to speak to you as a spirit. But I say this to you, old man—in front of all my people—if you select the wrong child, then I myself will kill you. And I will cut off your hand that holds your sacred staff, just as I cut off the leopard's paw."

The witch doctor's eyes bulged, and a vein along his neck pulsed. Sweat streamed down his head, following the contours of his prominent brow. He raised his arms aloft and shook his staff so vigorously that the monkey skull flew off into crowd.

"Your chief is lying to you," he roared. "He has consented to having an evil spirit live in our village. Already this evil spirit has begun its work by inhabiting the body of your chief. How else could one possibly explain his ability to make a threat against me—*the* most powerful person in the tribe? Listen well, my people, remember that it is your witch doctor who holds the knowledge of all curses and potions, *not* your chief. Choose wisely whom you will follow."

Yet one by one the villagers drifted away, and for the first time that anyone could remember, they were not afraid to have twins living among them. Their chief had proved to them that he was a brave man, and they trusted him. Besides, was it not more comforting to believe that a twin was a good ancestor, instead of a demon? Yes, of course! And then there was the story of how the spirit child, not yet born, stole the leopard's spots while it was enraged, thrashing about in pain. A story such as this was also of great comfort to children growing up in a land where leopards abounded.

"Father," one of the chief's twin sons asked, perhaps five long dry seasons, and ten rainy seasons, later: "Is it really true, that I, or my brother, stole a leopard's spots? Neither of us can remember where we put them."

The chief smiled. "My son, do not ask the same of our stories as the white man demands of his own tales. Truth and information need not be the same thing. Someday you will understand this paradox. In the meantime, it would be wise if you both claim to be the boy who stole the leopard's spots."

The boy nodded, for he was wise beyond his years.

The Belgian Congo, 1935

The boys were still naked when they attended their first ceremony, which meant that they had yet to grow the hair that would mark them as men. No one in the tribe could remember children so young ever being admitted to the eating-of-flesh ceremony, and it was a matter of much whispered discussion among the women. Even the elders were bewildered by such a drastic break with tradition, but the boys' father was the chief, and he was adamant that his sons should partake in the sacred ritual. Thus it was so.

It was only when the chief agreed to shoulder all responsibility for this particular ceremony that the elders acquiesced—although there are some things that no man, even a chief, can guarantee. If the spirits were displeased, they would punish only the chief. However, should the Belgians discover that the men in this village still practiced the ancient custom of cannibalism, they would hang every last one of the village men until dead, and then string them up to swing from the trees that grew along the road that stretched between Nyanga and the Loange River.

The boys were privy to these discussions, but they were not afraid; only curious. In what manner were the victims prepared? How would they, meaning the boys, feel after partaking in this ceremony? Would it, in fact, right the wrong that had been perpetrated against the one brother?

The Belgian Congo, 1958

Despite the heat Madame Cabochon carried her breakfast of coffee, croissant, and pineapple out to the terrace, where she could watch the baby hippos frolic. Across from the Cabochons' house, the Island of Seven Ghost Sisters divided the Kasai River neatly in two, and the water on the lee side was rife with enormous crocodiles. But nature had armed hippopotamuses, which are vegetarian, with tusklike teeth, as much as eight inches long, and even large crocs are reluctant to tangle with an angry mama hippo.

Today the water was the lowest Madame Cabochon had ever seen it get, so for a change she paid more attention to the island than to the wildlife it supported. According to one legend, the island took its name from the ghosts of seven sisters who drowned while trying to escape from a cruel husband whom they shared in common, when the canoe they were riding in was overturned by one of the aforementioned mother hippos. But the missionaries will tell you that the island was given this name because the natives are afraid of ghosts, and that the island is used by a secret and very wicked society that initiates girls into womanhood.

As much as Madame Cabochon disliked missionaries—they were forever trying to get the Africans to put on clothes—she believed their account. This was only because she had seen with her own eyes the dugout canoes packed with young girls approach the island from the far side, where the shore was unfavorable for hippo calves. At night she would lie awake and thrill to the pulsating drums, as a very drunk, and exceedingly corpulent, Monsieur Cabochon, who reeked of Johnnie Walker Red, would lie sweating beside her, like a volcano oozing magma, and snore.

During those long nights, Madame Cabochon ached to have been born African. Of course she dared not ever share this longing with another living soul, so bizarre was it. Nor dare she even, in the safety of a confessional, whisper that she found the sight of a Mushilele, a headhunter, with his loincloth slung low beneath sculpted abdomen, somewhat stimulating.

Madame Cabochon was a Belgian, born of Belgian parents. She had, however, been born in the Belgian Congo, which was a huge colony sprawled across the heart of the African continent. Therefore, since Africa was the place of Madame Cabochon's *nativity,* did this not make her a native of Africa? Of course it did, Madame Cabochon reasoned.

After all, the sights of Africa, the smells, the sounds, the tastes, had all found their way into the developing fetus via her mother's nervous system. Someday science would prove that; just wait and see. *Someday*—just not today. Madame Cabochon wasn't stupid.

She drained the last of her coffee and then licked her fingertip so that she might dab up the croissant crumbs remaining on her plate. Madame Cabochon was a sensual woman who firmly believed in satisfying all her senses. Since she was stuck being a Belgian, she might as well enjoy everything European with gusto, and croissants were one thing that Europe had gotten right.

Sunday was her cook's day off, so the pineapple had been sliced the day before and kept in the refrigerator. Since even someone who is only pretending to be a European would still eat *everything* with a knife and a fork—even an orange—Madame Cabochon had brought with her from the kitchen a very sharp little knife that the cook used when he sliced uncooked yams and other tough root vegetables.

Madame Cabochon did not believe in luck; she believed in opportunity. It was just as she was picking up the sharp little knife to cut the pineapple slice into bite-size pieces that Madame Cabochon noticed the snake. It was a green mamba, one of Africa's deadliest snakes, and it was coiled around the armrest of her husband's chair—less than a meter away.

Mambas have a reputation for being aggressive; Madame Cabochon had heard Congolese women speak of being chased from their fields by these venomous serpents. Well, there was no point in finding out if these tales were true. Opportunity had also presented itself, so Madame Cabochon took it. Without wasting a second to think about the consequences, she lunged at the snake, her arm fully extended.

When Madame Cabochon clambered to her feet a few seconds later, the mamba's head had been severed, but Madame Cabochon's favorite church dress—the deep forest green frock with the questionably low neckline and slash pockets trimmed in white—was splattered with small flecks of blood. "*Merde*," she said aloud. Then, without giving the matter much thought, Madame Cabochon picked up the severed mamba head using some tissues she kept in her slash pockets and went inside to survey herself in a mirror.

Honestly, one would never guess that this blond bombshell had just celebrated her forty-eighth birthday, and in great style! Every white in town had been invited, and everyone sober enough to walk or drive had shown up although none of them knew her age. Not even Monsieur Cabochon, who was too drunk to find his way out of their bedroom, knew her true age. That was because her uncle had been the marriage registrar in Stanleyville, where they were married, and as a wedding present to his niece he oblig-

ingly shaved a cool decade off her age to match the stories she'd
spun.

But Madame Cabochon really did look good for her fake age
of thirty-eight; one might even believe her to be in her early
thirties. Of course she owed it all to the American cinema.
Jane Mansfield, Doris Day, Marilyn Monroe—all of them were
women with curves. Meanwhile a lot of European actresses
looked as if they were still living on war rations. But not that
gorgeous brunette, Sophia Loren; now there was a woman one
could emulate!

Madame Cabochon tossed her flaming tresses this way and
then that. Oh yes, it had to be the forest green dress! See how it lit
up her hair like a savannah fire? Besides, the flecks of blood were
completely dry now and appeared as tiny newborn freckles, almost
as if they belonged there. Anyway. she would put it to soak when
she returned from church across the river where the blacks lived.

Madame Cabochon, who considered herself to be a native-born
African, despite her flaming red hair, lived in the town of Belle
Vue, in the Kasai Province of the Belgian Congo, which was the
name applied to a vast area of central Africa between the years
1908 and 1960, when it was a colony of Belgium. (Later the name
was changed to Zaire, and eventually to the Democratic Republic
of the Congo.)

Approximately eighty times the size of Belgium, this colony
covered as much territory as the eastern third of the United States
and stretched from a narrow outlet along the Atlantic Ocean
in the west to snow-covered peaks bordering the Western Rift
Valley. The interior portion formed a shallow bowl that contained
one of the world's largest tropical rain forests.

This rain forest was drained by the Congo River, which was
second only to the Amazon in the amount of water that it discharged into an ocean. So powerful was the Congo River that,
after its juncture with the Atlantic, it continued to flow underwa-

ter for another hundred miles, carving out a canyon in the ocean floor that was four thousand feet deep in places. The Kasai River is one of the major tributaries of the great Congo River, but it is also well known for another very important reason: the banks of the Kasai River, and the streams that feed into it, contain alluvial deposits of gem-quality diamonds.

Belle Vue, where Madame Cabochon lived on the day that she slew the little—but deadly—green mamba, was especially famous for its fine gemstones. Coincidentally, Belle Vue, which means Beautiful View in English, was also known for its spectacular scenery.

Not only did the Belgian-owned villas sprawl across the tops of high grassy hills, with just a necklace of emerald green forest along the river, the town overlooked a stunning, horseshoe-shaped waterfall that gave rise to a perpetual rainbow. Surely the rainbow was God's promise that good fortune would always smile upon the simple, well-meaning inhabitants of this town, these 136 brave colonialists who wanted nothing more than to improve their lives, which had been made wretched, even intolerable, by the two wars in Europe.

However, one could not run a diamond-mining operation, even of the alluvial sort, without many hundreds of African workers and, of course, servants to manage the affairs of home because life was so very difficult in the Belgian Congo. And, just as in Europe, the lower class and the upper class did not live side by side, for the two classes shared nothing in common. This was no mean prejudice, merely a statement of facts. After all, a family just in from the bush who squatted behind their house for their personal needs, a mother who went topless, plus a father who slaughtered pigs in front of his door—such a family would not feel comfortable living next door to a housewife who practiced Chopin for three hours every afternoon and who wrote long, poetic letters in ancient Greek to her brother in a monastery back home in Flanders.

Besides, since the Almighty had placed a river at the Belgians' disposal, like a giant moat, and the Divine had seen fit to fill it with hippopotamuses and crocodiles, and then to cap it off with a dangerous waterfall—well, one would certainly be remiss *not* to take advantage of it, wouldn't one? So at the loss of much human life—most of it African, and thus regrettable, but not altogether tragic—the infamous Belle Vue Bridge was built. And directly adjacent to the waterfall, too, if you can imagine that!

Ooh la la, did this ever put Belle Vue on the map! The little town prospered, especially after the Second World War, when the Consortium, the company that owned the mine, built a combination grocery and dry goods store for its employees. No longer did the Consortium's employees need to drive more than a hundred miles over a single dirt track through bush that led through territory inhabited by headhunters. Not only that, but the Belle Vue store supplied milk and cheese flown in via Cessna, and store employees even began baking croissants and bread—sold fresh every morning.

When in 1950 the residents of Belle Vue saw the construction of a clubhouse, with a restaurant, and swimming pool, just for them, they were practically delirious with happiness. Some folks even spoke of retiring to Belle Vue when their productive years were over. Why not? Except for one month a year—the month preceding the big rains—the climate was livable. And anyway, what did Europe have to offer now, except the possibility of more war? (Europe was always at war, was it not?)

It should go without saying that both the store and the clubhouse were for full-blooded whites only. Light-skinned mulattoes and Asians needed to check in with management immediately upon entering the premises, unless they were on business for a white. Just as long as everyone knew their place, it was an easygoing world, one in which nobody wanted trouble.

Shortly after the amenities went in, the Belgians graciously, and inexplicably, announced that they would share them with all whites in the area. Thus it was that the Missionary Rest House was built in record time, high on a cliff top, just above the bridge and the falls. As the missionaries were Protestants, and the Belgians were predominantly Roman Catholic, the Missionary Rest House was built on the African side of the Kasai River, on the "native" side.

Some might say—perhaps herself included—that Madame Cabochon was the femme fatale of the town of Belle Vue. However, Amanda Brown was currently the only female in residence at the Missionary Rest House on the native side of the river—fatale or otherwise. That was because October was the suicide month. No one, not even a lowly, self-sacrificing missionary, wanted to waste his, or her, precious few days of vacation on these, the most miserable days of the year. For three months straight, not a drop of rain had fallen, but now, every day for a month, the clouds had piled higher and higher, like a cotton candy staircase to heaven. At any moment these towering, even majestic, structures could turn jet black and rain would dump down upon the hills—not in buckets, but in barrels.

But in the meantime, the air was so thick with moisture that even the slightest bit of exertion set one to gasping like a fish out of water, although only a very few whites saw the irony in that. The Europeans, who were Catholics and not prigs like the Protestants, swore vehemently at the high humidity while they still had the energy. One common denominator was that everyone, regardless of their religious persuasion, sweated a great deal. Eventually, somewhere in the colony, a person of light skin succumbed to the punishing climate and committed suicide.

One Sunday morning during the suicide month, Amanda Brown left the relative coolness of her cement block house to investigate the commotion she heard behind one of her outbuildings. Laughter, that's what it was, but the fact that she could hear it above the roar of the waterfall—now that spoke to trouble. Upon rounding the corner of her woodshed, Amanda felt immensely relieved to see that the chief instigator of all the noise was none other than her housekeeper, Cripple.

Africans in this part of the Congo, Amanda had soon learned, were most often given names that referred to some aspect of their birth, birth order, or physical appearance. Upon first meeting her, one might think that Cripple, with her bent and twisted body, would hardly qualify as a good housekeeper, but Amanda had never before in her life encountered a mind that sharp, or a personality quite so wily. Amanda would let the cook and head housekeeper, whose name was Protruding Navel, do the heavy lifting; Cripple would serve as her entrée into the mind of the native.

But this, this—whatever it was—was going too far! What *was* this? Amanda asked the same question of Cripple and was ignored. Angry now, Amanda stepped right up to her employee, who was seated on an overturned washtub, which had been placed on top of an even larger tub. Still unnoticed, Amanda clapped her hands directly in front of Cripple's eyes.

"Cripple, answer me!" Amanda spoke in Tshiluba, which was the local trade language and, as such, was spoken by all the Africans living in Belle Vue.

The tiny woman was capable of emitting enormous sighs. "These are my customers, *Mamu*."

"Customers?" Amanda practically shouted. "You have nothing to sell."

Cripple gently pushed the white woman's hands away and began to sway as if she might suddenly be dizzy. "*Mamu,* as you well know, I am swollen large with child. Those enormous white hands of yours have a most unpleasant odor—worse even than that of a jackal that has been dead for three days. At any moment we both might experience a great unpleasantness over which I will have no control."

The gathering—there were over twenty villagers waiting in a queue, and even more standing around just to watch—erupted in laughter. Smelly hands, they mocked. Worse than a jackal that has been dead for three days! Why not just two days? Why not four? Surely a white woman's hands smelled as bad as all that, for they were undeniably a loathsome people.

"Cripple," Amanda said, trying hard to focus only on the woman seated atop a washtub throne. "You must tell all these people to go home—at once! It is Sunday, the Lord's Day, and I will not have you desecrate it with this heathen business of yours. *Whatever* it is."

"But, *Mamu*—"

"Must there always be a 'but,' Cripple?"

"*Eyo, Mamu,* but only because I loathe injustice."

"As do I." The American sighed, just not nearly as loudly as Cripple had. "Okay, you may state your case."

"It is only that I am a heathen, *Mamu*. In my healing business I make no mention of your Lord or his special day. So you see, it is impossible, therefore, for me to desecrate that which you hold sacred."

"Nevertheless, this land belongs to the mission; I cannot have you mumbling secret incantations and communing with the spirits of the dead. My holy book—the Protestant Bible—is very clear about this being wrong."

Cripple was of two minds; the human side of her wanted to laugh uproariously at *Mamu*'s insane suggestion. After all, communing with the dead was the last thing that Cripple would ever want to do—that even came after kissing the thin, wormlike lips of a white man. What about the other side of Cripple's mind? It was all business. Keeping *Mamu* happy was what really mattered if Cripple was going to support herself and the failure she called Their Death (whom she also called Husband).

"Cripple," *Mamu* said sternly, "I said to tell these people to go home."

As can be expected, the crowd that had gathered exclaimed

among themselves and talked excitedly. But Cripple's cheeks burned with shame, and for the first time she regretted her relationship with the young American missionary. Amanda Brown, hostess of the Missionary Rest House, had been always a fair and kind employer. In fact, Cripple had fallen into the trap of thinking that the white woman was her friend. Now *this.*

Cripple thought of standing, but her dignity bade her to remain seated. "You may dock my last week's wages, *Mamu,* because I quit my job—beginning *yesterday.*"

The white *mamu* smiled—just a bit around the corners of her mouth. "*Quit?* You seemed to be happy in my employ. I am afraid I do not understand."

"These people pay me what they can, *Mamu.* Sometimes it is a few francs, sometimes a piece of fruit, and sometimes nothing. Truly, it is all nothing compared to what you pay me. But I have a stomach," Cripple said, referring to the child that stirred within her, "and the stomach asks that I remain seated for much of the day. That is why I have decided to quit this most desirable position of being your humble servant."

"In that case I understand," *Mamu* said.

It was Cripple's turn to smile, for she was both pleased with the outcome of their conversation *and* she had a business proposition. Before Their Death was fired from his job at the post office, he had learned from Monsieur Dupree that Europeans always conducted their business with smiles and handshakes. No doubt Americans, who shared the same unnatural physical attributes, expressed themselves in a similar manner.

"Mamu Ugly Eyes," she said, for that was this white woman's name, "is it not the case that Protruding Navel works like a slave washing your clothes in these very tubs on the day before your Sabbath?"

To be sure, that remark was followed by a great deal of laughter and poor *Mamu's* unnatural complexion turned from white to red. "*Kah!* He does not work like a slave!"

"Nevertheless, for the rest of the week these tubs remain unused, *nasha*?"

"*E*. But—"

"Then why not rent them, and this space, to me? I will pay you real Congo francs, not bananas or eggs."

Amanda, who was only twenty-three, took her first posting as a missionary seriously. True, her job was to run a guesthouse, but during the oppressive heat of the suicide month, the rooms remained empty. Meanwhile, here was an opportunity to show Christian charity to a self-proclaimed heathen, and possibly even in the long run she might be able to convert Cripple. Still, there was a certain protocol to follow and boundaries to be set.

Amanda gestured at Cripple's customers. "This is a place for missionaries to come and rest; it is not a place for crowds to gather. What is wrong with your own compound, Cripple?"

"*Kah!* There are so many children, chickens, and goats running about in my family compound that even an intelligent woman like yourself would find it impossible to think. *Mamu*, how then must a much less clever woman, such as you see before you, be expected to solve the problems of these poor people who have great need."

Amanda bit her lip as she remembered to think twice before speaking. "And *you* can solve their problems?"

"Observe, please, *Mamu*." Cripple clapped her hands and nodded at two men who stood at the head of the line. "The man on the woman's-hand side is a Mupende, and the man on the man's-hand side is also a Mupende."

"They look very much alike," Amanda commented, half to herself. "Are they twins?"

"*Aiyee!*" Cripple said, and the crowd also reacted in a shocked manner. The once orderly queue was now cluster of murmuring anxious people, all of whom seemed poised to run.

"What did I say wrong?" Amanda asked.

Then Cripple remembered that there were times when she had to treat the white woman as if she were a child. In many aspects the whites were children, totally ignorant of how to behave once they set foot in the workers' village, that part of Belle Vue where the Africans were forced to live.

"*Mamu*," Cripple said, speaking with more patience than she had earlier, "they cannot be twins, because the Bapende do not allow such an evil thing to happen."

"I do not understand."

"*Eh*, so I will explain. If a Mupende woman should give birth to more than one child, the infants are lain on a rack in the sun. The same sort of rack that is used for drying manioc roots. Then the parents wait until all the infants are dead but one. Only then may the mother take the live infant to her bosom."

"But that is horrible!"

"*Tch! Mamu*, would you rather have an evil spirit masquerading as a child and perhaps causing the deaths of many villagers before its presence is discovered and then destroyed?"

"No, but—"

"Then we are in agreement; it is better to let the child containing the evil spirit die a natural death so that everyone may live a happy life afterward."

"But—"

"Do not be so argumentative, *Mamu*," said Cripple, who was losing patience again. "Believe me, it is not a natural thing to give birth to more than one baby at a time. This is the something that goats do—and dogs, surely, and pigs, but not people. If this was the natural order of things, then women would give birth to twins all the time. So you see, *Mamu*, again you are wrong. This is why you must think twice before you speak."

Amanda's cheeks burned; she felt like she'd been slapped. As fond as she was of the quick-witted little women with the enormous ego, she hated that admonishment. Both her mother and her mother's mother were forever telling her the same thing. And why? It wasn't like she never stopped to think.

"*Mamu*, are you listening?" Cripple said.

"*Eyo.*"

"Now look at these men again. One can tell that they are members of the Bapende tribe merely by looking at their teeth, which have been filed to disgusting points. It is common knowledge, *Mamu,* that these savages are cannibals, and therefore are in need of your salvation. Would you turn them away, and by doing so, condemn them to your hell?"

"Enough of this nonsense, Cripple! Let us see how you settle this dispute—whatever it is—before you start preaching to me."

Cripple took a deep breath. "Mupende man," she said. "What is your name?"

"Surely my name is of no importance to you; I have not come here to be your friend."

You should have heard the bystanders laugh at the young man's impudence! Or were they laughing at Cripple? Either way, such behavior was quite unacceptable; after all, Cripple was both his elder *and* a possessor of special powers.

"He is afraid to give you his name," said the other fellow involved in the case, the one on the hand of the woman. "This one fears that if you know his name, you will be able to place a curse upon him."

"That is not so!" cried the young man. "My name is Lazarus Chigger Mite. There, mock me if you will!"

But no one dared.

"Lazarus Chigger Mite," said Cripple thoughtfully. "That is a powerful name, for in the village the mites are plentiful. Does possessing this name offer your feet protection from this terrible scourge?"

Chigger Mite held out his left foot, the foot of the woman's side. Cripple saw that it was remarkably smooth and showed no sign of infestation.

"*Yala!* Your name has served you well."

"Yes, and perhaps I owe some of this good fortune to my god Jehovah, and his mother, the Blessed Virgin Mary. I am a true

Christian, you see, a Roman Catholic, not a *Protestant*, like the *mamu* for whom you work." Chigger Mite used the appropriate Tshiluba terms for religious references, of course, for he too was fluent in that language.

Cripple was careful to roll her eyes discreetly. "Please, just tell me your side of the story."

"It is very simple, O great wise woman. Just this morning, while hunting in the forest along the stream that runs nearest the village, I came across—and killed—the largest of all rock pythons."

Cripple smiled and help up a hand signaling Chigger Mite to stop. "I am curious," she said. "How large is this snake?"

"Truly, truly, *Mamu*, it is the largest of all snakes, for I do not exaggerate. Do you see that bush with the yellow flowers?"

"Yes, I see."

"If the head of the snake is here, then the tail of this fearful monster extends all the way until it reaches that other bush over there—the one with red flowers?"

There were many gasps, as might be expected from a crowd that large. Even the white *mamu* expressed great surprise, and no doubt she had seen many strange things where she came from.

"Where is this snake now?"

"But wise woman," the second man complained loudly, "you have yet to even ask my name."

"*Tch!* In that case, tell me your name—but hurry, for I wish to see this snake."

"*Mamu*, my name is Jonathan Pimple. I am a *true* Christian, a *Protestant* like yourself."

Before Cripple could protest and proudly proclaim her hea-thenness yet again, the man named Chigger Mite chimed in. "*Mamu*, it is the Roman Catholics who are the true Christians. For ours is the same faith practiced by Jesus and his mother."

At this the white *mamu* stepped forward. Her face was red,

which is a clear sign that a *mukelenge* is angry or that you have surprised her on the toilet.

"Jesus and his mother were not Roman Catholics," she said. "They were Jews. When Jesus was alive, there were no Catholics and no Protestants, either."

"Are you sure, *Mamu*?" Jonathan Pimple said. "For I have seen Jesus's idol, and that of his mother, in Chigger Mite's church."

"*Tch*," said Cripple as she folded her hands across her belly. "This white *mamu* is an expert in these things. Why else do you think she has come all the way from America? If it is religious facts you have come for, then you could do no better than to listen to her. But Protestant, Catholic—these things I care nothing about, for I am a staunch heathen. However, if it is some other bit of advice you seek, Jonathan Pimple, you best get on with your story, for I grow weary and impatient."

He nodded. "*Eyo*. Well then, what Lazarus Chigger Mite does not tell you is that this grandfather of all snakes—this *muma*—is now in possession of my finest goat."

Cripple leaned forward with great interest. Given the restraints of her condition it must have appeared comical, for there were those who laughed. Of course, a wise woman knows when it is useless to lose her temper.

"Was it a full-grown goat?"

"*Eyo*. A ram, even—with horns like this." Jonathan demonstrated, much to the crowd's continued amusement. "Now the *muma* has a bulge like a pregnant woman. Like yourself."

"With twins!" Lazarus Chigger Mite said.

The crowd roared.

"You simpleminded men," Cripple said crossly, "you have yet to tell me the nature of your palaver."

"*Aiyee*," said Jonathan Pimple, clapping his hands to his cheeks. "It is this. Wise woman, to whom does this goat now belong? To Chigger Mite, who slew the *muma*, or to me, the rightful owner of this fine white goat? I was saving this goat for my dowry in order that I might purchase a fine Protestant bride and raise children who would be law-abiding citizens and leaders for the new Congo when independence comes."

Cripple ignored the people who repeated the word *independence* and who simultaneously raised their hands, their fingers forming a V for victory over their Belgian oppressors. When she shook her head, the message was meant for Jonathan Pimple and Chigger Mite.

"From what I have been led to believe, the answer to your question is very plain for all to see: the goat belongs to the python, and the python belongs to Chigger Mite. Now, if someone will please help me down from these washtubs, I will go and see this wonder for myself."

Both men nodded, clearly accepting her wisdom, and the murmurs from the crowd were indeed quite edifying. However, a truly wise woman understands that there can be no public displays of pride, for hubris begets hatred.

The Belgian Congo, 1935

Both men were bound—hands and feet—with lukodi vine. They were naked as well. It was a moonless night, and with just the fire to illuminate their bodies, the boys at first mistook them for goats that had been shaved and set aside to await their turn at the spit. Perhaps there was something in the eyes of the men that helped give this impression of intelligence, for that night they gleamed, dark, wet, and much larger than either boy remembered.

The men were not gagged and were therefore capable of speech. Because their knowledge of the Kipende language was limited, whenever possible they tried to make themselves understood in French. They spoke a third language as well: Latina. It was this third language that they had resorted to when they had engaged in their witchcraft.

Every day the two white men would entice the village boys to draw close by means of food. Then they made the boys sit in rows, smallest to largest, with no thought given to age or status, so that free boys sat between slaves. When the boys were seated, the men forced them to mimic the sounds employed in their white witchcraft, bizarre incantations requiring much repetition. The boys who did the best job of mimicking *these sounds received extra morsels of food, but those boys whose lips and tongues did not cooperate were actually struck—struck, if one can believe such a thing! But struck only by the man with hair the color of flame. He had even struck the smallest of them.*

Much palaver was made then in the council hut of the men. As a rule, one did not strike children; surely one never struck the children of others. Here was a man who was not the mother's brother, or of the clan, or even merely just a member of the Bapende tribe. Here was a white witch doctor who reeked of the scent of wild boar, and whose hair was the color of those who suffered badly from worms. It was his loathsome hand that drew blood from the nose of a child still young enough to grab hold of his mother's teat when he needed comforting.

The Belgian Congo, 1958

Madame Cabochon loved going to Sunday mass. It was not because she was religious, but because she adored dressing up for church. Full circle cotton frocks with tightly cinched waists, in the American style, the deeply scooped necklines just a blush away from being indecent. But no stockings, of course, because this was the tropics. No woman, no matter how devout, would think of wearing stockings.

There could be no denying that Madame Cabochon was a beautiful and voluptuous woman. Unfortunately she was married to Monsieur Cabochon, who was a drunk, and a surly one at that. So each Sunday morning she was driven by chauffeur across the river that was the great divide between white Africa and black Africa, for Saint Mary's Catholic Church was planted firmly among the heathens, the people who needed it the most. Upon arrival, Madame Cabochon and her gaily colored frock would separate from the chauffeur, for they used different entrances and sat in segregated sections. After all, one could hardly expect a native who bathed in the river daily to sit next to a Belgian who bathed just once a week—and even then, was content to sit in his own filthy stew.

Madame Cabochon cherished each minute of the spectacularly scenic drive to Saint Mary's Catholic Church and back. When she arrived at church, Madame Cabochon saw it as her duty to keep a tally of who among the white employees of the Consortium was in attendance, and who was not (bimonthly attendance was compulsory). She also saw it as her duty to critique the outfits of the other company wives, so that in case any of them should wish to stop by her house later in the week for a spot of gossip, she would be equipped with the truth. Hers was not an acid tongue, mind you; she was merely gifted in the art of dressing with panache, in a tropical climate wherein even chain mail would wilt and hang like a sodden rag.

At any rate, at Saint Mary's Catholic Church a wooden screen separated the races, and platform seating ensured that the colonists said their prayers positioned closer to God than did their subjects. From her customary window seat in the front row, Madame Cabochon was assured of receiving her Communion wafer first; that way she was free to observe the others as they filed up to feast on the Savior's body.

Precedence was always given to the Europeans, of course. Not only that, but it was Consortium members first, then any other Belgians in attendance, followed by visiting northern Europeans, then North Americans (of Caucasian descent)—if Catholic—and last, Europeans of decidedly Mediterranean appearance. After a suitable pause, the mulattoes—who sat in their section behind the whites—were ushered forward. This wasn't racism; ask any of the Europeans there. This was merely ensuring that order was kept. *Order*: Wasn't that what human beings craved the most?

Unlike their Protestant neighbors, Roman Catholics cared about such things as modesty in their houses of worship; therefore, bare breasts were not tolerated, not even among those heathens attending church for the very first time. Also, women were required to cover their heads. Because of these rules Madame Cabochon was invariably treated to a parade of colorful scarves and African wrap dresses. (Although to be sure, Madame Cabochon, who had been raised in the Congo and who had glimpsed many breasts other than her own, was above such petty judgments.)

However, as a woman of high spirits, discriminating taste, and strong sexual appetites, Madame Cabochon was not afraid of judging a book by its cover. To Father Reutner, a disheveled old priest from Berne, Switzerland, she gave the grade of F-. It wasn't just his rumpled and stained vestments, his thin greasy hair, or his frizzy beard, streaked bile-brown from years of dribbling tobacco juice that she found off-putting; it was the priest's heavy German accent. Father Reutner sounded just like a male version of Madame Cabochon's mother-in-law back in Brussels. Madame Cabochon thoroughly detested her husband's mother, who was not only German born, but also a secret supporter of the Third Reich during the recent war.

At any rate, on that especially hot Sunday morning during the suicide month, the day that Madame Cabochon slew the deadly poisonous green mamba, the woman realized that she had just had all she could take of church for one day. For one thing, Father Reutner looked particularly disheveled, and for another, his crude accent sounded exceptionally grating. Mass was not yet over—the closing benediction not yet sung—but if the lady in the fetching emerald green dress, with the slash pockets trimmed in white, tarried just one second longer, she might explode like a stick of the dynamite, the kind that her engineer husband used when he blew up streambeds in search of diamonds.

The most obvious way for her to get outside—the *only* way outside—was to slip past her husband, skim over the knees of the lecherous (but unattractive) Monsieur LaBoeme, and around the stomach of his corpulent wife, genuflect in the direction of the altar, and then pivot left through the side door of the nave. This was assuming that neither the deacon nor Father Reutner did anything to stop her. While Africans came and went with some regularity, their passing precipitated a good deal of clucking and grunting on the part of the frustrated holy men. Madame Cabochon had never beheld a European attempt to escape before, and her heart raced with joyful excitement to think of the consequences.

Monsignor Clemente resisted the temptation to dab at his temples with the monogrammed handkerchief that he kept concealed in a secret pocket beneath his snow-white cassock. The beastly heat outside was amplified by the metal shell of the black automobile in which he rode. An oven on wheels, that's what the car was, and his was the goose getting cooked. In the long run, this familiar discomfort didn't matter; what mattered was that the cardinal's orders be carried out.

Yet despite feeling like a piglet on a spit, the monsignor, fresh from the Eternal City—that is to say, Rome—possessed an uncanny ability to appear as cool as a gelato. Perhaps this was his greatest gift, this ability to appear at ease in his environment. There were those, his *mama* in particular, who thought he should have been a film star, so regular were his features, so broad his shoulders, so clear his eyes and strong his chin, and that hair— those thick black curls, inherited from the Sicilian side of his family. But to the handsome priest, now nearing middle age, these outward gifts had never been anything but curses. Not only did women throw themselves at him, but sometimes men as well— seminary had proved to be a trial by fire for someone as beautiful as "Pretty Boy Clemente."

It was his feelings of worthlessness, however, that drew Monsignor Clemente to religion—to a God—at such an early age, and ultimately to the priesthood. What went on inside the perfect shell was anything but. The real Monsignor Clemente was ruined; he had been from an early age. The real Monsignor Clemente was like a rotten soft-boiled egg that, if opened, would emit a sulfurous odor even stronger than Satan's.

As always, Monsignor Clemente was determined to keep his shell intact, although it was a decision he had to make daily—like an alcoholic's fight against the bottle. Today would be the hardest day of the struggle. If he could make it through vespers—

"Stop here," Monsignor Clemente said to his African chauffeur. He spoke in French.

"Yes, Father."

Monsignor Clemente watched dumbfounded as a white woman suddenly appeared in the window of the church just ahead, turned, then dangled helplessly for a few seconds, before dropping to the ground. He could almost hear the breath being knocked out of her, and then a soft moan. The priest still played soccer on a regular basis, and some of his regular opponents claimed he had the reflexes of an alley cat, but by the time he'd jumped out of the black sedan, the woman was up on her feet and running. Reflexively, Monsignor Clemente hitched his cassock up around his ankles and ran after her.

The route she chose took her through one of the most densely populated neighborhoods in the village. Goats bleated, chickens squawked as they scattered, and the startled cries of the women and children—the *heathen* women and children not in church—were bliss to the visiting priest's ears. Since Monsignor Clemente took care to follow well behind the fugitive from God, he went unnoticed by her in the din.

It was only gradually, however, that Monsignor Clemente became aware of the fact that the narrow, crooked lane was beginning to fill with people, all of whom appeared to be chasing the white woman. No—some were passing her! Yes, now he was caught up in a rapidly flowing stream of humanity; now he saw the woman's bobbing head, now he didn't.

"What is it?" Monsignor Clemente called out in French. "What is happening?"

"Someone killed a giant python. It is said that it swallowed a goat."

It was only afterward, when the man who'd answered his question had melded into the burgeoning torrent of people, that Monsignor Clemente realized that he'd been spoken to by the man in Tshiluba. What's more, he'd understood every word.

Police chief Pierre Jardin was not a particularly religious man. If asked about his beliefs, he would admittedly give you the runaround, because he didn't see how such information was anyone's business but his own. This was especially true when it came to the nosy inquiries from the American missionaries, none of whom would accept no for an answer. To be fair, it must be remembered that these people were merely concerned about his soul because, without an exception, they believed that, as a Roman Catholic, Pierre Jardin was headed for eternal damnation and the flames of hell. Even the modern young woman who ran the Missionary Rest House was of that opinion.

Despite his lack of interest in spiritual matters, Pierre Jardin was a regular attendant at Sunday morning mass. It was, after all, his duty to set a good example for the citizens of Belle Vue— maybe even more so for the whites than for the Africans. Pierre always arrived early, along with three of the men assigned to work for him, black soldiers all of them. They were always dressed in freshly washed and pressed khaki uniforms—but they too had to split up and use separate entrances. No one minded, of course; no one even gave it another thought. This was the way it had always been.

That particular Sunday, as usual, Pierre's mind wandered after he'd received Communion. In fact, it wandered over to where Madame Cabochon sat, and there it loitered. His few feeble attempts to rein it back in were in vain. So entranced was he by her comely appearance that he was slow to react when the object of his admiration hoisted her shapely hips into the open window well and slipped effortlessly to the ground.

Capitaine Pierre Jardin jumped to his feet. *"Excusez-moi, s'il vous plaît,"* he said to the woman he'd sat next to. She just happened to be Madame Fabergé, the wife of the new operations manager.

"Certainement," she said. Her golden brown eyes were too large and round for her face, giving her the appearance of a lemur. This slight disfigurement was most unfortunate because Hélène Fabergé was a woman of exceptional intelligence and fierce loyalty; she would have made someone—or some people—at Belle Vue a first-class friend.

"Is there a problem?" Monsieur Fabergé demanded.

Apparently no one else had seen the incredible—*merde!* The entire congregation was bolting. Father Reutner and the deacon were shouting at them and waving their arms—even the acolytes were getting into the act—but the worshippers were like horses escaping from a burning barn.

"Yes, monsieur, there is a problem," Pierre said, for at the very least there would be a problem if he did not follow the crowd and help see that order was maintained.

As Pierre passed the altar rail again on his way out through the side door, he felt the thick calloused fingers of Father Reutner digging into his collarbone from behind.

"You Judas," the old priest growled. "This is all your fault."

"My fault?"

"Oui. You are far too lenient with these people. They are like children, but you treat them like equals! Blow your whistle, Captain. Order your men to arrest them. Do something! They cannot be allowed to bolt from church before the final benediction."

"Au revoir, mon père," Pierre said. Then he ran from the church. He ran on legs that were better nourished than any of the Africans. Soon he overtook all the parishioners except for the youngest and strongest. These he followed through the town's winding lanes, past entrances to frail bamboo courtyards, where even

frailer elderly citizens sat to catch a glimpse of the world passing by. Pierre jumped over puddles where children and Muscovy ducks splashed happily. He dashed through newly planted fields where already the cannabis-like leaves of the cassava plants grew waist-high in the tropical sun.

At the edge of the forest Pierre caught up with the runners. In fact, jostling about along both sides of a narrow ravine was the entire adult population of the Belle Vue workers' village, excepting those who had been the attending the late mass. However, it would only be a matter of minutes before these people too joined the curious throng. Across the cassava field, like a dark surging tide, was the leading edge of the congregation he'd left behind.

As a police officer, Pierre had every right to investigate something of this magnitude, but for once, on a Sunday morning, he wished to be a private citizen. A private *white* citizen, that is, which is something quite different from a being native African. On one hand, Pierre *was* tempted to pull rank as a white man and demand to be let through to see whatever it was that had drawn such a crowd. On the other hand, he had always believed that he owed a great deal of his success as a police captain— especially in these difficult political times—to the fact that he did not demand to be treated any different than he was willing to treat others. This was a lesson that he had learned from his father; it was the only good thing he ever got from the senior Jardin. It was more than enough; it was worth Pierre's weight in gold.

There was a third approach, one that Pierre knew would work, and which wouldn't be held against him. He began by greeting everyone in atrociously accented Tshiluba, even though he was quite capable of speaking fluently and sounding like a native.

"*Muoyo wenu,*" he shouted over the din. *Life to you.*

It was immediately clear to everyone within earshot that a white man had joined their ranks. The throng parted like the

Red Sea in the Bible story, giving Pierre unimpeded access to the bizarre scene at hand. What he saw was undeniably African, yet totally preposterous.

Even though the young white man had been raised in the Congo, Captain Pierre Jardin had never, ever, seen anything like this before. Nothing like it had even come close.

The Belgian Congo, 1935

S'il vous plaît," the dark-haired man said to them. Pleading. He said more words in rapid French, which neither boy could understand. Then the dark-haired man tried Kipende. ". . . big mistake . . ." He repeated these words over and over again, growing louder each time. Meanwhile the man with flaming hair was whimpering like a hungry puppy.

Although the boys were young, with not even the hair of a man, they instinctively knew that neither of the white men was behaving in his own best interest. If the men were to put up a brave front, there was a slim chance that the chief would respect them and grant them a reprieve. If one, or both of them, were to suddenly exhibit lunatic behavior—hooting like monkeys, growling like lions, flopping about in their bonds like stranded fish—there existed an even higher likelihood that they would gain their freedom. After all, to kill someone possessed by an evil spirit is to then invite that spirit to take up residence inside you or your abode.

Despite the fact that the younger of the twins had been unspeakably wronged—for it was not just hitting that the other priest was guilty of—the boy felt sorry for the men. The boy grieved to see a goat slaughtered, or even a chicken. This way of feeling was unnatural—he knew that instinctively as well, and so he kept it hidden. The boy lived entirely within himself, and it was this ability that would help him survive to adulthood. His brother, on the hand, was a fighter who struggled always to keep some measure of control; it was this characteristic that would see him survive to adulthood.

The Belgian Congo, 1958

Being a witch doctor is an honorable profession. It is an occupation passed down from uncle to sister's son. In many tribes, the eldest brother of one's mother takes precedence over the mother's husband when it comes to rearing the children. After all, how can one know that the offspring are really her husband's? But the mother and her brother did emerge from the same *bisuna*, of that one can be sure.

Many whites dismiss the witch doctor's craft as so much hocus-pocus, or collusion with the devil, but those attitudes are the result of ignorance. It takes years of intense study to become a practitioner of tribal medicine, and a special personality. Cripple's husband, whose given name was Their Death, certainly had the intelligence to absorb the vast amount of jungle lore concerning herbs, barks, fungi, and insects. Some of these ingredients aided in healing a patient, while others contained lethal amounts of poison, and still others put one in a comatose state that resembled death, but from which one could spontaneously emerge relatively unscathed.

However, despite his wealth of knowledge, Their Death lacked the most crucial component required to be a successful witch doctor. Their Death lacked salesmanship. Even the best herbs produce only modest results on their own. To be truly effective, the healing power of the herbs must be accompanied by the patient's power of belief in them.

But healing is only a small part of any witch doctor's practice. It is the placing on of curses and countercurses that one depends on for a livelihood. Their Death was well aware of this fact, but he was a man with a kind heart; he was born with a twinkle in his eye. How can such a man place a curse of death upon another and have it *seem* true, much less have it actually come to pass?

The answer is that one cannot. Therefore, Their Death was a failure as a witch doctor. Never before in the history of the Baluba tribe—and it is a very large tribe of many millions—had there ever been a hereditary witch doctor who was such a failure at his profession as Their Death, nephew of the great Many Deaths, at whose memory people still quake.

In truth, Their Death was an educated man. He had attended the Roman Catholic mission school and was a graduate of the sixth form. In addition to that, his former boss at the post office had lent him many books on a variety of subjects. And one of the things that Their Death took away from his education was the notion that it was disgraceful for a man to be supported by his wife—even if that man was as incompetent in his craft as Their Death was. This was especially true if the wife was a semi-invalid like Cripple.

It was because of his high moral principles that Their Death risked his life in his second career: that of maker and seller of palm beer, *maluvu*. To make the beer one simply needed to find an oil palm tree that was flowing, cut off the inflorescence, capture the sap that oozed forth thereafter, and then let nature run its course. There were always enough airborne yeast spores to immediately start the process of fermentation in the sugary liquid.

In fact, so quickly did the sap ferment that often by the day's end it would be rank, having turned to vinegar unless the liquid was tightly sealed in a gourd.

As for selling the brew, that was never a problem. Although Captain Pierre and his soldiers kept a watchful eye on the citizenry—for their protection—they pretended not to notice the consumption of the *maluvu,* so long as the imbibers did not harm one another or unduly disturb the peace. In 1958, life for an African was short and often brutal; if the edge could be taken off with a sip or two of palm wine, then Their Death, who was after all in the business of healing, felt obligated to do his part.

So it was that every day he went into the forest and searched for an oil palm (*Elaeis guineensis*) that was in flower. Having located one, he fastened a special rope called a *luku* around his waist and around the trunk of the palm. Next he tied his ankles together so that they wouldn't slip apart, in order that his legs might function as a brace. Then, while leaning back into the rope, he scooted his feet up the trunk, inches at a time. After that it was the rope's turn. Next it was his feet. Now so on, until he was fifty feet into the air.

At any moment the rope could break, or his feet could slip, but the real danger awaited him when he got to the crown of the tree. Up among the fronds lurked the possibility of a wide variety of poisonous snakes, but most especially feared was the green mamba. If he was bitten by *nyoka wa ntoka,* then death was certain to occur within minutes. Rather than face the agony of asphyxiation as his organs shut down, he was prepared to hurl himself to the forest floor, and hopefully in such a way as to break his neck.

As he neared the crown, Their Death slowed his ascent, his eyes furiously scanning the canopy of ferns and frond bases. Mercifully, it felt much cooler up out of the sun; at the same time the air was heavy and stagnant with mold. Bees and flies were buzzing around the inflorescence and Their Death foolishly swatted himself several times before tying safety ropes around the petioles of two sturdy fronds that forked above his head. At last he set to work cutting a gash in the base of the flower stalk itself.

There it was, for all Belle Vue—black and white—to see: the largest *muma* ever to be killed in the history of any of its beholders. Surely this was the case. African rock pythons can grow to be twenty feet long, but this one was closer to thirty feet in length. And its girth! It was as big around as a man's thigh, except for its extremities, and of course where the goat lodged; at that point the snake was as big around *as* a goat!

Chigger Mite laughed happily and reenacted the moment of truth for the ever-expanding crowd. "I was returning from the bush," he said, "having completed my needs, when I heard the sound of thrashing nearby. I took only a few steps off the trail and there it was—this monster. Protruding from its mouth was the rear half of a goat. Clever man that I am, I prayed to the Roman Catholic gods—Jesus Christ and his *baba*, Saint Mary—and they directed me to a tree overgrown with *lukodi* vines. These I cut and tied securely around the hind legs of the goat, and the other ends around that tree. You see?" He pointed to a sturdy young *tshinkunku* tree, and then he paused to let the villagers murmur their appreciation of his bravery and resourcefulness.

Not until the crowd grew restless did Chigger Mite draw a deep breath before continuing his monologue. "I knew at once that the goat belonged to my friend here, Jonathan Pimple, because it was white, and only Jonathan Pimple had a white goat. That is why I immediately sought his help in killing this *muma*. However, Mister Pimple did not respect the laws of the forest, so together we sought a ruling from the little wise woman known as Cripple. It was she who gave the following verdict. The goat belongs to the snake, and the snake belongs to me."

Then, for the first time, Chigger Mite noticed the headman's presence. Suddenly the day had taken a turn for the worse. The workers' village was not a traditional African village; the people represented many tribes. Although they were all black skinned—with the exception of the Flemish mulatto and his children—at least half a dozen families came from other African countries. Because of the potential problems this ethnic mix presented, the headman was appointed by the OP on a rotating basis. Because the headman ultimately had the police and the army to back him up, he had a great deal of power—indeed, even more so than the traditional chief of a very large village.

The current man in charge of overseeing the village was from the Bakongo tribe. He came from the capital city, Léopoldville, and he was supposed to be an expert on generators. It was also said that Belle Vue was to be only a temporary posting for him. What was for certain was that he loathed living in the provinces and that he disdained everyone not belonging to his tribe. He disliked the citizens of Kasai Province in general, but he particularly loathed members of the Bapende tribe. At least these were the thoughts that filled the mind of Lazarus Chigger Mite on that hot Sunday morning in the suicide month of 1958.

Indeed, Lazarus Chigger Mite did not as much as glance at the snake before waving his arms expansively at the crowd. "*E,* I shall keep what remains of the white goat—for believe me, my brothers, its flesh will be foul both to your eyes and to your taste. But to all of you, I give this *muma,* the meat of which is said to be among the tastiest in all of the Kasai."

"*Kah!*" the headman bellowed. "We do not eat snakes in the city where I come from. We are not uncivilized like *Bena Kasai.* However, we do eat goat—especially goat that has been properly tenderized."

The crowd roared with laughter at Lazarus Chigger Mite's expense.

"Therefore," the headman continued, obviously quite pleased with himself, "you will deliver a pot of goat stew and a fresh ball of *fufu* to my dwelling tonight for the evening meal. *Shala bimpe.*"

Stay well. After delivering the traditional Tshiluba salutation, the headman—who was not even a Muluba—turned and stalked imperiously away.

The crowd hushed. Even the babies stopped whimpering while Lazarus Chigger Mite approached the great African rock python with his sharpened machete raised high over his head. With one swift downward motion, he intended to sever the serpent's spinal cord at the base of the skull. With two or three more vicious whacks, the body and head would be forever parted and Lazarus Chigger Mite would be the stuff of legends.

But wait. Now Lazarus Chigger Mite emitted a wail that was both louder and more aggrieved sounding than that of any bereaved person that Pierre Jardin had ever heard—and in the Belgian Congo he had heard many piercing cries of mourning.

"Who killed my snake?" Lazarus Chigger Mite eventually managed to say. He dropped his machete and held up the head for all to see.

A python does not need a large head in order to swallow a goat; its jaws dislocate and the mouth stretches to accommodate the prey. In the back of the mouth a pair of backward-pointing teeth prevents the prey from escaping, but these teeth also make it impossible for the snake to disgorge the victim once the process has begun.

In at least one case, two pythons attempted to swallow the same antelope, starting at opposite ends. When the reptiles met in the "middle," the larger snake had to continue swallowing the antelope *and* the smaller snake—either that, or else starve to death!

At any rate, the head that Lazarus Chigger Mite held up was the size of three fists—no more.

"*Wa kafue, mene mene!*" he said.

"Truly it is dead," the crowd chorused.

Lazarus Chigger Mite tossed the head up the embankment. Whether he meant to toss it at the Belgian woman, Madame Cabochon, even he could not say. Although it landed right at her feet, it did not stay, but rolled back down the steep gulley.

"We laugh and we cry," Madame Cabochon said, which is the proper way of expressing one's thanks.

"*Tangila, muana etu!*" Lazarus Chigger Mite said. Behold, one of our own!

"*E,*" some said, although many said nothing.

"Our own do not oppress us," a bold young man said.

"Friend," Madame Cabochon said, "I oppress no one. As a woman, I neither possess power, nor do I wish to have it."

The young man snorted derisively. "And yet you speak such words openly. Do you think that an African woman could speak thusly? If so, you know nothing about our culture."

Madame Cabochon did not appear to be intimidated by the stranger. "Friend, you are wrong, for I am not stupid; I know that it is ignorant men such as yourself who keep the intelligent women of this country from speaking openly about their thoughts. But there are countries where women sit in judgment on men. And did you not know that in even in Africa—in Kenya to the east, and Rhodesia to the south—a woman is the queen?"

"Ah yes, Elizabeta!" the young man said. "She is a *white* woman—an oppressor. But listen to me, people of Belle Vue; the Prophet Kibangu came to show us the way to rid us of tyranny. We must begin by killing all the whites—even the unborn, who sleep in their mothers' wombs. For like this *muma*, they too will grow up to be dangerous snakes."

"You speak treason," Madame Cabochon said. Each word cut through the heavy wet air like a sharpened knife. "Captain Jardin," she called the police captain across the gulley, "you should arrest this man."

Captain Jardin shrugged, but did nothing to apprehend the stranger. Apparently, like men everywhere, he did not appreciate being given directives by a woman.

"Yours is a false prophet," Madame Cabochon shouted recklessly. "I have heard those silly tales of the Prophet Kibangu's death and resurrection, and they are lies. Just made-up stories that mimic Christianity. There is not a shred of truth to them. I have heard also that Kibanguists believe that they will not have to plant crops in the year of independence, for then all that the European has will be theirs. Well, I am telling you; those that believe this are fools! For you will get nothing of mine but a bullet in the forehead!"

Never, in all the history of Belle Vue—in all the history of the Belgian Congo—had a white woman spoken thusly to a throng of Africans. It was truly a moment of such importance that Lazarus Chigger Mite temporarily forgot about the great *muma* that someone else had slain in his absence.

Perhaps he would encounter another enormous snake someday, but never, ever, would he be able to arrange for a white woman to stand up and tell everyone within earshot that they were a fool for believing in Joseph Kibangu. This was something that had to be savored—like the freshest palm beer. In fact, he could practically smell freshly collected palm sap at that very moment.

Then just when he thought it could not happen, the moment got even sweeter for Lazarus Chigger Mite. The young stranger leaped through the crowd with the agility of a colobus monkey until he was face-to-face with Madame Cabochon.

"I am a true follower of the great Prophet Kibangu," the stranger said. He spat each word as if it were a bit of gristle, a hazard to choking. "He is the Great Prophet; I am but a lesser prophet—a seer of near events, but not of great truths. Still, I tell you people gathered here—*all* of you, whether African or European—that this wonder of a bridge that my African people have built to span the mighty Kasai River over the waterfall—just in order that the white man might have his view—this bridge will the great Prophet Kibangu strike down in the next great storm. Then will the village with its African inhabitants—its human beings—be severed from the white colonialists in their town that they have arrogantly named Belle Vue."

"*Kah!* What nonsense," Madame Cabochon said. She laughed

right in the face of the so-called lesser prophet, causing Lazarus Chigger Mite to cringe inside, for he bore her no ill will, and had no wish to see her die—either then or later, when all the whites were to be massacred.

And *then*—oh, this truly cannot be believed unless one sits in the palaver hut with a gourd full of palm wine, of the strongest sort, and hears the same story repeated by more than three friends. For then Madame Cabochon reached into her pocket and removed the severed head of a *nyoka wa ntoka*—the head of a deadly green mamba! This she practically jammed into the stranger's mouth, causing him to scream and fall over backward.

"I pronounce a curse on you," she said. "I call upon the spirits of all the whites who are buried in the Belle Vue cemetery. I ask them to weave a net of death that will ensnare you and pull you down to them in their underworld before the rains bring forth new grass."

The silence that followed these words was like a leopard running upon stone. Not even a suckling babe dared breathe, nor an old man break wind.

One could only hope that this would be the time when the gendarme, Captain Jardin, would intervene, but then one would be wrong. Monsignor Clemente had heard that the young police chief had been born and reared in the Belgian Congo, and thus he was more in tune with how the natives thought. However, his impassivity at the moment smacked of cowardice; it came nowhere near hinting at wisdom.

The first lessons drummed into prospective missionaries to Africa at seminary is that the natives are like children: "It is a waste of time to try to reason with the African. If you cannot persuade him outright, then fear is your only other option." This was sound advice for both the government and the church.

Although the monsignor represented the one true God, there was no time for a homily. He certainly lacked the power to arrest anyone, although he would if could, and—God forgive him—he wouldn't even mind roughing this young fellow up a bit. To be truthful, as long as he was being honest, he would very much like to beat the *merde* out of the young black revolutionary.

He cupped both of his tanned hands, with his long, exquisitely shaped fingers to his mouth. "*Attention!*" He switched immediately—automatically—to Tshiluba.

"The woman is correct; the bridge that spans the mighty Kasai River will never fail. It was built with the strongest of metals. It is the same metal from which hammers are made. As long as the earth remains intact, so shall the bridge remain in place. But as for you, you so-called lesser prophet of a greater false prophet, I predict that on the new moon, a one-eyed she-leopard, with three cubs, will emerge from this very forest and bring with her a terrible hunger. Her need for sustenance will be so strong that it will infect you with insanity, and you will tear off your clothes and run into the bush, where she will leap upon you and devour you."

When it was clear that the monsignor had finished pronouncing his curse, at least a dozen voices rose, wailing in terror; however, that of the young militant was not one of them. This man, whom the monsignor had now come to think of as the Lesser Prophet, stood in place just as solid and immovable as one of the tall red anthills that dot the savannah.

Lazarus Chigger Mite did not recognize either man. As a faithful Roman Catholic he would, no doubt, soon learn all there was to know about the new white priest. It was the identity of the other fellow that had him worried. He could tell by the speaker's accent, and lack of tribal markings, that he was a civilized man of one of the Baluba clans, but nothing more than that.

Quite possibly this fellow was a rabble-rouser, brought in from the capital by the headman expressly to make trouble. He could even be a Communist. Lazarus Chigger Mite had heard from his white boss at the mine that if the Communists got control of the country come independence, then every person would have to share what was his. In a society such as that, Lazarus Chigger Mite would be forced to cut his *muma* into thousands of bite-size pieces and feed even the undeserving. Just the thought of that caused him to seethe with rage.

"Now I will show you the goat that awaits liberation by my machete," he shouted. He acknowledged the crowd's laughter before going on. "You will all get a chance to see this delicious creature, which by now has been marinated by the juices of the *muma*'s stomach. However, you will not be permitted as much as a taste, for—as you undoubtedly heard—I am being forced to hand this delicacy over to our headman, he of the Bakongo tribe."

Lazarus Chigger Mite pushed against the heavy carcass of the reptile so that he might roll a section of it over, thus exposing some of the belly. That way it would be easier to slice it open with his machete. After all, it would be foolish for him to do battle against a sturdy rib cage in front of so many people. But even as the snake yielded and exposed its soft under parts, a terrible reality was revealed: the python's belly had already been slit open for the length of a man's arm.

"*Kah!*" cried Lazarus Chigger Mite as he jabbed at the scaly gash.

"*Kah!*" echoed the astounded villagers, for they too had never expected to see such a sight. In response to each thrust of the machete blade, out pushed branches with leaves and vines, so much foliage altogether that a man could not easily carry a pile that large from one spot to another without dropping a great deal along the way.

The bold young man, he who might well have been a Communist, pointed at Lazarus Chigger Mite accusingly. "This man has deceived you—all of you, no matter what your tribe. He has made a mockery of you. You have become like children who must run and see the latest attraction, regardless of how preposterous the claim. This *thing*—this thing he calls a *muma*—is not even a snake; it is a sorcerer's invention."

Despite the fact that he was a real Christian—a Roman Catholic, and not a Protestant—Lazarus Chigger Mite stepped back in alarm. It was not only a serious accusation the stranger had made, but a frightening one. A creature this large—if indeed it had been created through witchcraft—could be very powerful, and potentially wreak havoc with him and his village. What was he to do now?

Then the most astonishing thing happened. Madame Cabochon, his Belgian oppressor, dropped the mamba's head so that she might clap her hands. As she did so, she called loudly out to the crowd, imploring them to give her but a moment of silence.

"Residents of Belle Vue," she said in Tshiluba, "people of Kasai, do not listen to this man. He is not one of you. I ask you, does anyone here know the name of his mother's clan? *Anyone?* No? Then let me suggest that it is this man—an obvious *foreigner*—who is the sorcerer who planted this *muma* here—in *your very own* forest—so that *one of your own* should find it, and that one of your own should appear foolish. For I ask you now, does anyone here know who Lazarus Chigger Mite's people are?"

"*E,*" half the people yelled as one voice. "He is a Mupende from the Nyanga-Yanga clan."

"And how do you know this?"

An ancient woman with bare breasts that drooped almost to her wrap cloth pointed at Lazarus Chigger Mite with a crooked finger. "This man's hearth is next to mine. I have known Lazarus Chigger Mite since the days when I still possessed all my teeth." She grinned broadly, displaying only three brown stubs, and the crowd roared with laughter. "I tell you, *mukelenge,* that this man does not lie."

Madame Cabochon turned to the man who might well be a Communist, and who most certainly had no business being at the Belle Vue workers' village. "Go away," she said. "You are not wanted here. Go back to your own people if you wish. But leave us alone!"

Lazarus Chigger Mite could not believe such a thing was happening. Furthermore, neither could the people, for they were apparently shocked into silence.

The Belgian Congo, 1935

***B**oth boys cried. This surprised the father, until the boy's uncle reminded him with sharp words that his twin sons were yet just small children, and that no other children before them had ever witnessed this ceremony. It is one thing to slaughter and dress a goat in front of a child, but quite another to put a human being—even one such as this—on the spit.*

Despite the boys' tears, all were in agreement that it was necessary for them to watch the proceedings. Thus they did. Likewise, it was necessary that the other white man, the one who had not harmed either boy in any way, must be forced to watch.

It has been said that the real test of one's manhood is the moment of one's death. A real man—or a real woman, for that matter—will choose to die with dignity. A real man might utter sounds of pain, but never of fear. Using this test as a guide, one could instantly conclude that the white man with the flame-colored hair was a man in body only. Even as the sharp, pointed stake that was to be the roasting spit first came into view, he howled as loud as ten keening women. In fact, it might well be said that it was precisely this man's intense fear that kept his companion alive.

That is to say, compared to his friend, the dark-haired man appeared to be carved from stone. He did not pull back from the raised machete, nor did he flinch at the sight of the stake. He did not whimper, nor did he throw his arms up to protect his face and head.

"I will not remember your badness," he said in tortured Kipende. Imagine that if you can. The crime of this man's friend was of the sort not to spoken of, and yet this man dared to forgive his executioners! Was this cheek, or was it bravery? Was this man playing the elders for fools? Perhaps he was hoping that they would spare him on account of his effrontery—for surely these words were said in order to shock the governing council. No matter what truly lay in the dark-haired man's heart, the end result was that on account of his bravery, it was decided that he should be given a chance to live.

Of course there would be certain conditions.

The Belgian Congo, 1958

Amanda Brown had loved Sundays back in Rock Hill, South Carolina. Homemade pecan rolls for breakfast, young adult Sunday school classes, stimulating sermons in a language that she could easily understand, lazy afternoons visiting with family and friends—or, in recent years, suitors—these were all fading memories. Sundays in Belle Vue, however, were the loneliest days in the week.

To Amanda's knowledge she was the only white Protestant for fifty miles in any direction. That is, if one did not count the Greek Orthodox manager of the Consortium's commissary and his family, which of course Amanda didn't. Her duties were to run the Missionary Rest House as if it were a full board hostel for those Protestant missionaries of cooperating denominations who might be passing through town, or who might need a short vacation in what passed for civilization. However, most of the guests checked in on Monday and checked out on Saturday, leaving Amanda utterly alone for the Lord's Day.

Yes, there were a few Protestant natives (some fortunate souls who had somehow managed to escape the clutches of the Roman Catholic Church), but it would have been unseemly, if not unpleasant, for a lone white woman to attend the small Methodist chapel on the far side of the village. For one thing, those workers spoke the Lunda dialect, and for another, the children would have pestered her to death begging her for handouts.

Thus it was that most Sunday mornings Amanda spent reading her Bible and praying. Quite honestly, Cripple's claim to have the "second sight," or whatever it was, was more of a distraction than it was an irritant. As long as the Mission Board didn't hear about the housekeeper conducting her unholy business on their property—particularly on the Sabbath—then Amanda didn't really object. About this snake, that was definitely something worth checking out (just think of the letters home if it turned out to be true). Besides—just being brutally honest again—the serpent might well have been sent by God in answer to one of Amanda's many desperate pleas for something, anything to break up the tedium of Sundays spent alone.

So it was that while the crowd surged toward the main road that would lead them up the steep hill on which the village perched (only then could they beat a path to the forest), Amanda made up her mind to journey as far as she could in the mission's battered old Land Rover.

"Cripple!" she called to her employee who, despite her handicap, had hobbled a fair distance and was almost out of earshot by then.

"*Mamu?*"

"Wait! I too am going. I will pick you up in the machine."

"But, *Mamu*," Cripple protested through cupped hands, "this place is in the forest. Your machine cannot go there."

"Then how can you, one who is lame?"

Cripple, who was panting heavily by this time, stopped to catch her breath. "Do you mock me?" she asked between gasps.

"Truly not," Amanda said. She was both taken aback and

deeply offended. "The machine will take us as far as it is able, but I have my wheelbarrow in the back. I will push you the rest of the way."

"*Aiyee!* Now surely you mock me. Poor Cripple, you say to yourself; she has only the brains of a monkey."

Amanda could feel her right temple twitching, which was sometimes a precursor to a migraine headache. At the moment, it was more "poor Amanda" than anything else.

"I do not mock you. Now, do you wish to see the largest snake ever to visit the Kasai, or will you sit by the fire when are you are old and whisper with shame to your descendants that you are the only woman of your generation who did not witness this great event?"

"But you are white, *Mamu!*"

Amanda feigned surprise. "No, such a thing is not possible!"

"*Kah!*" Cripple smiled. "Never have the people of Belle Vue seen such a sight: a white woman pushing a black woman in a wheelbarrow. I shall become an even greater heroine to my people, *nasha?*"

"Without a doubt. I, however, will be known as a traitor to my people. Perhaps Captain Jardin will throw me in jail."

Cripple scrambled to get in alongside Amanda, all the while shaking her head vigorously. "The captain must not arrest you, *Mamu;* for if he does, who then will pay my salary?"

That night the drums of the Belle Vue workers' village talked incessantly. They spoke of the *muma,* this ancestor of all snakes, that had been slain before it could enter the village and swallow a child—or two! But by whom had it been slain? Surely not by the fool Lazarus Chigger Mite! That man could not tell the difference between a live beast and dead beast, between a goat and a bundle of foliage.

The drums sang loudly the praises of the little Muluba woman named Cripple, she who had the misfortunate to be married to the failed witch doctor, but who, nevertheless, had triumphed over her adversity. Cripple, a bent, no-account black woman, heavy with child, had ridden triumphantly into the forest, pushed in a wheelbarrow by her white oppressor. Surely the woman Cripple was a symbol for what was to be: a new Congo where the black man was to be waited on by the white man.

Cripple is our hero, the drums said over and over again. Lazarus Chigger Mite is a fool. Of the odious interloper from Léopoldville, the talking drums had nothing to say.

Their Death speared a chunk of succulent goat meat with a sharpened sliver of bamboo and held it out to his beloved Cripple. "Is this not sweet and tender, wife?"

"Indeed it is. Their Death, this is by far the finest-tasting antelope you have caught in the forest. Tell me again how you came by it."

"There is nothing to tell. I was high up in a palm tree cutting nuts as I do on a daily basis, when suddenly far down below I could see something thrashing about in the bushes. Of course it was this poor little fellow. Cripple, I know that you do not like to hear such talk, but I wonder if perhaps it was the God of the Christians who sent this antelope to us, such as he sent the ram to our father, Abraham, when he was on the verge of sacrificing his only son."

"*Nasha!*" said Cripple. "Abraham is not our father; he is the father of the Jews, and I am a heathen. Besides, this antelope was white, and he went *maaaa* when he ran around the village breaking into people's vegetable patches and stealing their chicken feed."

Their Death laughed. "Do not think ill of me, Wife, for liberating this poor creature from the confines of a *muma*'s stomach. Truly, I heard it protest mightily, and although the monkeys also possess arms, they did nothing to help. When I finally got there, Lazarus Chigger Mite was gone and the goat had already been swallowed. What I did, Cripple, I did for the child that grows in your belly."

Cripple was silent for a long time. "*E*," she finally said, and belched happily.

The next morning, before the cocks began to vie for mates, Cripple was awakened by the sound of persistent coughing just outside her hut. In her morning dream-state she at first supposed it was Their Death, perhaps fanning the fire into life in preparation for the morning meal. Then, with a start, she realized that Their Death lay beside her, and it was another person whose presence waited acknowledgment without.

"Sister Wife?" she called softly. "Have you returned?"

Their Death's Second Wife would have been welcomed at that moment, despite her jealous and complaining ways. She was, after all, young and strong, and quite capable of stirring the morning's mush without aid, no matter how far along with child she was.

"It is only Jonathan Pimple," a low voice said in reply.

Cripple made quick to grab her day wrap before stumbling out into the compound. For once she was grateful for the heavy fog that sometimes rolled up from the river. She would have been decently covered in any case, but now she felt doubly protected from a man's curious stares.

"What do you want?" she hissed.

Jonathan Pimple bowed his head as if he were addressing a European. "I must speak to you in your capacity as a wise woman, as a leader of our people."

Cripple cleared her throat, which is something that everyone should do first thing in the morning. She did this several times. Then she picked up a large stick and jabbed it at a hen that was pecking too close to the coals in the hearth. The chicken squawked, as it is supposed to do, and ran in a zigzag fashion for some weeds that separated Cripple's clearing from her neighbor's. The hen ran even faster after Cripple threw the stick at it, purposely missing it, but coming very close nonetheless. All this gave Cripple time to think, for she was, indeed, a very wise woman.

"Jonathan Pimple," she said, "much was made of me last night by the talking drums, but in truth I am just a crippled woman who was in need of a means of conveyance. I did not subdue the white woman; to the contrary, she is my employer."

"*Eyo*. I am aware of this. But I sense that our Heavenly Father has bestowed on you special qualities. He has given you wisdom, *Baba*. I can see that; everyone can see that. This is the reason the drums sing your praises."

Cripple felt the life within her react sharply to his words. "I am a heathen; I am not ashamed of my heritage."

"Nor am I ashamed of mine, but now my eyes are open."

"Good. Then you will have no trouble seeing through this mist on your way home."

"But, *Baba*, first, I beg you, give me of your wisdom. I am prepared to pay you."

Although she had yet to do any work, Cripple felt the need to rest. She waddled over to Their Death's chair, which was the only one they owned, and lowered herself carefully into it. After having endured many years of weather, and the weight of Their Death plus his beloved children, it was a wonder that the home-made chair remained standing.

"Do you know how to make *bidia*?" Cripple asked.

"*Bidia*? Our mush? Of course, *Baba*. I am a bachelor."

"Good, then stoke the fire—please—and get the water boiling. We will surprise my husband with a nice hot breakfast. And as you work you may share with me your *dikenga*—your problem."

"These things I can do," Jonathan Pimple said. He built a perfectly respectable fire, and it was while he waited for the water to boil that he began to speak from the heart. "I wish to become a Roman Catholic," he said. "Like Lazarus Chigger Mite."

Cripple, who had begun to doze in the comfort of Their Death's chair, jumped. "What? Why do we speak of spirits again? I find this most annoying."

"Because this is my problem; I wish to become a Roman Catholic, but in order to do so, I must confess my sins to the priest. But *yala*, there is one sin so awful that I cannot say it, even when I am alone inside that box of wood—which smells of the sins of a thousand others."

Cripple yelped with glee. "Truly, it might be worth the price of conversion just to smell this box. And you, Jonathan Pimple, what is your gravest sin? I have heard that Roman Catholic bachelors are forbidden to tug on their pleasure sticks."

"*Aiyee*," said Jonathan Pimple. "This is not speech of women; talk of this nature is reserved for the man's palaver hut."

"Then state your problem now, for the water begins to boil."

"Very well. Did you know, *Baba*, that I am not a native Muluba like yourself?"

"This knowledge comes as a relief, for the thought of a Muluba with his teeth all filed to points for no reason was almost more than I could bear."

"*Baba*, do you poke fun at me?"

"Of course. Were you not jesting as well?"

Jonathan Pimple gave Cripple a blank stare.

Then it was that Cripple realized, both with compassion and embarrassment, that Jonathan Pimple was not the shiniest palm nut in the bunch. "Perhaps you should tell me about yourself," she said.

"I am a Mupende, the son of the powerful chief Nyanga-Yanga. Perhaps you have heard of him?"

"I have not," Cripple said.

"When I was but a young boy I was taken in a raid by the Bajembe tribe. I am told that the purpose was to get my father to pay a ransom, but he would not. The Bajembe then sold me to someone of the Baluba tribe to be used as a street cleaner and a keeper of goats."

"That is a sad story."

"*Eyo*. When I was still with my people, the Bapende, I was

privy to a ritual ceremony where—it is a ritual that has not been performed for many years, of that I am certain."

"What sort of ritual? And please, Jonathan Pimple, put some fire under your story so that it boils like my water. Soon there will be none of the water left with which to make the *bidia*."

"*Tch*," Jonathan Pimple said, "there is no pleasant way to put this; it was the ritual of consuming human flesh for certain purposes."

"Cannibalism?" Cripple had heard that the Bapende had a history of cannibalism, but she had never had the opportunity to speak to one who had actually practiced it—or even just witnessed it as a child.

"*E*. But as I said, I was just a child; surely I was a boy of no more than eight long dry seasons in age. That would be eight years as the white man—"

"I know how frequent the dry seasons are." She couldn't help but snap. Their Death's chair was now getting to be uncomfortable, for it was made of hard unforgiving wood. "Then again," she added, "where you come from, the seasons might be very different than they are here."

"No, *Baba*, they are the same. But as for the ritual, it varies depending on the tribe's needs. If it was speed that we needed in order to chase down game, then one of our warriors would lie in wait and catch a well-known runner from another tribe. Then the men from our village would share in feasting on his legs. If it was skill at shooting arrows, then a famous archer would be caught, and his arms would be cooked and the meat distributed at the ceremony."

"This is disgusting," Cripple said. "Tell me more."

"Thus it went with all parts of the body. The brains to gain wisdom, the stomach to aid digestives troubles—"

"And what if your women were infertile?"

"Our women were never infertile," Jonathan Pimple said.

There is more than one way to skin a forest rat, Cripple told herself. "What if one of your men was limp like yesterday's ma-tamba leaves?"

"Yes, yes," Jonathan Pimple cried, "then I suppose he ate the *lubola*."

Cripple laughed. She laughed so hard that the child within her awoke and laughed along with her. However, she did so with her hands over her mouth so that Their Death would not hear and awaken. But Their Death did hear her—or perhaps he heard the child.

"What is this racket?" Their Death said, appearing in the doorway of the hut. "And why is this goatherd tending to our cooking pot?"

"This goatherd goes by the name of Jonathan Pimple," she said. "He is of no account; he has come for advice. In exchange, he will make us breakfast. Go back to sleep, Their Death, and I will wake you when it is ready."

"*Bimpe*—good," Their Death said, "but be careful, Wife. This man has the look of a Mupende, and is it not a fact that in the past they were known to be cannibals? It would not go well for anyone if it were you that he served as my breakfast."

Cripple could see that Jonathan was made especially angry by Their Death's remark, and when Their Death closed the hut door behind him, she tried to make light of it for Jonathan's sake. "I am afraid that a crippled body such as mine would be useless for ritual purposes, and from a practical standpoint—well, I have seen Bashilele chickens with more meat on their bones."

"*Tch*," Jonathan said and hung his head.

"It must be difficult to be a minority," she said.

He nodded. "That is why I am here. The Roman Catholic Church will soon be the new majority—for all of Congo."

"But it is a white man's religion."

"Do you think that I care? I wish to succeed, *Baba*. The church can send me abroad to study."

Cripple tapped her head to signify that knowledge and wisdom were forthcoming. It was her own symbolic gesture, and it had quickly become her trademark. Clients were often disappointed if she did not do this.

"Your problem is really not so difficult; you must immediately confess that you ate another person—"

Jonathan Pimple jumped to his feet. "*Aiyee!* I did not say that!"

"But it is the truth, is it not? Anyway, the Roman Catholics will understand, for I have heard that they eat their Jesus every Sunday. By having the truth out in the open, you will not have to live in fear of exposure or blackmail. Life without fear; that is life with true power. Besides, as you said, you were but a child. One forgives a child everything but the murder of his parents."

"*Tch, tch, tch,*" Jonathan said, shaking his head in wonder. "Truly, you have the gift of knowing."

"*E,* but not to such a degree that I know which part of the man it was that you consumed. It was a man, I assume."

"Yes, of course. At no time was a woman or child ever a part of the ritual. Tell me, who would want to acquire a characteristic that was weak or simple?"

"Only a weak, simpleminded person, I suppose."

"Exactly. But, *Baba,* there remains one detail that might still be a complication."

"What is that?"

"The man whose hand I ate was a white man—a Roman Catholic priest."

"*Kah!*" cried Cripple. She began to tap her head furiously and unconsciously. "Jonathan Pimple, you must never speak of this to anyone. And if anyone asks me what you were doing here this morning, then I will tell them that you were still upset about your goat—which was delicious, by the way."

"That is my goat I smell? How can that be?"

"Jonathan, do not be distracted! You were never here; we did not talk about your backward tribe or its disturbing rituals. Do you understand?"

"But, *Baba*, we did speak—"

Cripple struggled to her feet. The life in her belly seemed to resist, pushing back with the strength of a boy child.

"*Ya bimpe*," she said. Go well.

"My confession; what do I do about that?"

"Do not confess! Do not become a Roman Catholic. Remain a poor Protestant, a man without power. At least you will be a live Protestant."

"*Aiyee yi–yi–yi*," Jonathan moaned. "My problem defeats me."

Cripple watched as poor Jonathan Pimple, former child cannibal, adolescent slave, and would-be politician, left her compound brokenhearted.

The Belgian Congo, 1935

The boys' uncle urged them to eat the ritual feast because they would not partake voluntarily. Then the chief, who was also the twins' father, commanded them to eat, but the younger would not until the older set the example. For the older boy it was equally repugnant to partake of this feast, but he did so in order that he and his brother might be obedient to their chief, and also that his younger twin, whom he loved, might reclaim that which had been stolen from him.

When the boys had finished eating their small portions, the men gave up great cries of victory on their behalf, and on their behalf the women in the village—perhaps a kilometer distant—responded with cries of victory on their behalf as well. It was chief's number six wife, who was also the twins' mother, who led the women in their response. Upon hearing the women, both boys trembled alike, for they knew the strength of their mother's love, and they could imagine the depth of her feeling.

The Belgian Congo, 1958

When Monsignor Clemente stumbled into the rectory at four twenty-six in the morning the following Thursday, he wasn't drunk; he was exhausted. And, damn it, it wasn't his fault that the stingy ass OP, Marcel Fabergé, insisted on turning off the generator that supplied all the electricity to Belle Vue, both the European and African sides of the river. Well, not that he could really bitch about that considering the fact that the last time he was posted here as a common priest, there hadn't even been the luxury of electricity. Those were the days of Coleman lanterns with fragile wick globes, and also the type of lanterns with thick cotton wicks that had to be trimmed every Saturday.

Mon Dieu, but that Father Reutner was a loud snorer. No doubt he could be heard all the way down in Angola, a good sixty kilometers away. It was because the man was fat, let's be honest about it. That wasn't judgment; that was merely an observation. Father Reutner indulged in the sin of gluttony—and gleefully so, one might add. What's more, the Swiss priest didn't even bring up gluttony in the confessional booth.

But you had to give the man credit for maintaining his vow of celibacy. Monsignor Clemente had steeled himself to find an African concubine sharing the old man's quarters—such was often the case in overseas postings where loneliness could become overwhelming. However, despite the appalling squalor in what was supposed to pass for a rectory, there was to be found absolutely no sign of a female. Monsignor Clemente was sure of that; ironically, he was gifted when it came to sniffing out the female scent. In fact, he could tell a number of things about a woman just by smelling the air that she had breathed.

"*Alors!*" said Father Reutner as he fumbled for a flashlight. "Who is it?"

"It is only Monsignor Clemente, Father. Go back to sleep."

"No, no, my alarm will ring in just—uh, three minutes. This is the time I always rise on Thursday mornings."

"At half past four?"

"*Oui.* The early mass is scheduled at five, so that the women can get to market by six."

"You are veritable saint, Father."

"Forgive me, Monsignor, but feeding Our Lord's sheep, as he asked, does not make me a saint."

"No, forgive me; it was a joke."

"You joke about spiritual matters, Monsignor?"

What a dreadfully dull, irritating fellow this Father Reutner was turning out to be! If Monsignor Clemente had found himself posted with a priest like this when he first came to the Congo, he never would have lasted even a week.

"Father, you may dress and excuse yourself for Mass at your earliest convenience," the monsignor said.

"Will you not be joining me?"

"At the moment I find myself more in need of silent prayer."

"The benefit of the holy sacraments—"

"*Bonjour,* Father." It came out as a growl.

* * *

Madame Cabochon tugged first on the left side of her bosom, then on the right. The kelly green blouse, which showcased her burnished hair to its best advantage, fit so tightly it looked as if it had been poured over the molded cups of her brassiere. She was a terrible automobile driver, and she knew it, but still she'd risked life and limb crossing the Belle Vue Bridge, and then there were all those pigs, goats, chickens, and children to contend with once she got to the village.

Yet it was imperative that she speak to Monsignor Clemente; after all, he was leaving to return for Rome the following Monday. If one was going to throw the party of the year, then one had better throw it while there was a genuine celebrity in town: in this case, a handsome man of God just a few steps away from—well, from *what* exactly? Perhaps being appointed a cardinal? A prince in the church? One dare not think higher than that—yet in a place like Belle Vue, where there was truly nothing to do, what sin was there in daydreaming that she could one day lay claim to having entertained the successor to Saint Peter himself?

How truly awful that on weekdays the whites-only pews were given over to the market women in order that they might have a better view of the Eucharist and possibly learn something about this foreign faith to which they'd subscribed—many of them rather late in life. The caveat with this line of thinking was that occasionally—okay, so rarely as to be statistically unimportant—whites *did* attend weekday services. When they did, they often found themselves sitting next to tattooed heathenish tribal women who smelled strongly of wood smoke, or a plethora of other disturbing things that were peculiarly African, and which made it nearly impossible for any European to concentrate on the words of the mass.

Thank heavens Madame Cabochon had not come to concentrate on Latin words or, for that matter, to connect with the Lord on any level. As soon as Father Reutner's gravelly voice began to chant the last amen, she was out of her seat and headed for him with all the determination of a tsetse fly.

"Father," she said, grabbing the sleeve of his cassock from behind.

"*Merde!*" he said, and then abruptly turned to genuflect in the direction of the crucifix as he made the sign of the cross. "You see what you made me do," he said, turning back to Madame Cabochon. "Fortunately the monsignor is still with us, so he can hear my confession."

"You see?" Madame Cabochon said. "No harm meant; no harm done. But speaking of the monsignor, where is he?"

"I'm afraid there was a death in the village last night, Madame. Monsignor was summoned to administer last rites and has only recently returned. I thought it best to let him sleep in."

"Perfect then," Madame Cabochon said and, without another word to the hardworking Swiss priest, practically skipped from the church.

What a lovely morning it might yet turn out to be. Although the fog was still as thick as leek soup, it gave the churchyard a delightful—almost European—air of mystery about it. Between the church and the rectory was a row of classrooms, but it was far too early for school, so there was no one to be seen, or to see her. Besides, given the poor visibility, she could have been any white woman—or even just a ghost. The irony behind this last thought made Madame Cabochon laugh, for she was deathly afraid of ghosts herself, having seen one as a child.

Upon arriving at the rectory apparently unseen, Madame Cabochon became even more emboldened and tried the screen door. Finding it unlatched, she slipped into the cool, dark reception room—the living room, the Americans called it.

"Monsignor," called softly. "Monsignor, I am Colette Cabochon. I wish to extend an invitation to you." There was no response, so she waited, but just a few seconds, and then called again.

"*Oui, madame?*"

Colette whirled. Somehow the monsignor had managed to sneak up behind her without making a sound. While he wasn't dressed in pajamas or a nightdress as she half expected, the monsignor's more formal black robes had been replaced by a simple white cotton cassock. His salt-and-pepper hair, which he normally wore so manicured that it looked carved from marble, now stuck out in all directions from beneath his skullcap.

Madame Cabochon was so thrilled that she forgot protocol. It was only after she had begun to curtsy that she realized her mistake. Well, what was it that the English said anyway? *In for a penny, in for a pound?* That was her, all right. Madame Cabochon could feel the color rushing to her cheeks as she curtsied so low that she came within a stitch of splitting the back seam on her new pencil sheath dress (said to be all the rage in Brussels that year).

"Forgive me, Monsignor," she said. "I trust that I did not wake you."

"You are forgiven, madame, for indeed you did."

Ooh la la. The man was not making this easy. However, he was still a man—and a virile one at that. Madame Cabochon had a knack for smelling things as arcane as a man's sex drive. Some very young, muscular boys she'd dated had scored a zero in that department, whereas one very scrawny bookish type she'd met on a trip to the Left Bank in Paris had made her bells chime like a Mozart concerto played on a carillon. And just because a man wore the collar didn't mean he didn't give off that certain smell. That smell wasn't something one's vows could eradicate.

"You do not attend matins?"

He smiled sleepily. "It should surprise me if this was your business."

Madame Cabochon recoiled at his bluntness. By now, surely, there was no point for her to state the purpose of her visit.

"Again, I apologize. I will see myself out, Monsignor." She backed away, head down, and was about to turn when he said her name.

"Colette?"

"*Naughty Boy Albert?*"

"Ah, it *is* you! *Little Colette Underpants* from Stanleyville."

Madame Cabochon alternated between laughing and gasping. "I can't—uh—believe it. Naughty Boy Albert, the boy who made me play the Underpants Game every time I visited my cousins in Belle Vue."

"*Oui,* but it was your cousins who taught me the game. How old were we, four? Five at most?"

"Six," she said, "Albert—may I call you that?"

"I insist."

"This is unbelievable! How did you recognize me?"

"Father Reutner said that you were living here. He described you for me; I must say, his description did not do you justice."

"That comes as no surprise to me. And of course I knew that *a* Monsignor Clemente had come to visit, but I had no idea that it was the naughty little boy who lived up the street from Cousins Jacques and Marie. You know, back then I never even knew your last name. Twenty years later, and just look what happened to you! You're all grown up."

He laughed. "Funny, Colette, how twenty years for you somehow became forty-five years for me."

"It could be that you're just hopelessly bad at math. Although I must say that you're very good at remembering names. Surely I've changed a bit since you saw me last." She couldn't resist two more tugs on the kelly green blouse.

"One could not exaggerate the difference."

"Does it please you?"

"Colette, I too have changed. I've taken the vow of celibacy: I am no longer Naughty Boy Albert." At least he had the decency to wink as he said this.

"Of course, Monsignor, I was only joking. Life is very boring here, as I'm sure you must remember."

His dark eyes twinkled. "I seriously doubt that life anywhere within one hundred kilometers of you is boring. Madame, I was there at the scene of the monstrous snake. I watched as you stood up to that tyrant with all the bravery of a resistance fighter. I can only imagine what you must be like the rest of the time with all that spunk—that energy. May I be so bold as to say: your husband is a lucky man?"

Mon Dieu! The man of God might not intend to do so, but he was igniting some very dry, flammable kindling. Very well, she would continue with her mission, and let his Boss sort it out! But first she had a thing or too on her mind that needed to be aired.

"You were pretty brave yourself," she said. "Maybe too brave."

"How is that?"

"Well, you've been gone a long time; you've missed out on a lot. The rate things have been heating up—young men like that mean what they say. Some of them really are out for blood. I can smell it in the air. It isn't even 1959 yet, and already some whites with young families are sending their children back to Belgium. By the end of next year there will be a full-blown exodus; just wait and see. Oh—but you won't be here, will you?"

"Colette, my superiors—"

"*Oui,* the fat old men in Rome in orange capes; what do they care about some poor Belgian housewife living in the heart of darkest Africa? Perhaps if we shipped them some altar boys—"

"Enough!" he said.

His sharp tone surprised her. "*Bon.* Believe it or not, the purpose of this visit was not to offend you. I am here to invite you to our home—that of Monsieur Cabochon and myself—for a dinner party Saturday night at eight P.M. I realize that you have your own chauffeur with you, but to minimize the scandal on your part, I will send my chauffeur to pick you up at half past seven."

He said nothing, merely regarded her under long dark lashes. Those lashes would be the envy of any woman.

"There will be plenty of other people there," she added, "so you needn't worry. But our cook is fairly new, so I can't promise about the food. However, I assure you that the conversation will be absolutely scintillating."

"Wonderful. Does this mean then that the American will be there?"

"*Pardonnez-moi?*"

"I could not miss seeing her at the great *muma* event—she with the native woman in the wheelbarrow. Tell me, Colette, do you still remember your Tshiluba?"

"It was never my language," she snapped. "I was only visiting my cousins. But yes, I speak it now."

He merely smiled; it was the irritatingly benevolent smile of a man who had mastered his emotions. Self-righteous smugness, that's what it really was.

"Have you even met the American?" she asked.

"*Oui.* Like you, she is an accomplished linguist—altogether a very intelligent young woman. Colette, on the surface the two of you are very different; but I think that if you gave each other half a chance, you would find that you really have a lot in common. Who knows, you could even become fast friends."

Madame Cabochon felt like retching. How could Monsignor Clemente, aka Naughty Boy Albert, compare Belle Vue's most brilliantly colored sunbird, one with iridescent feathers, to a common house sparrow? An *American* house sparrow?

"I don't think that the American would feel comfortable at my dinner party. I will be serving alcohol, and people will be smoking. To the Protestants those are both evil things."

"Hmm. Well, I shall have to have a talk with whoever passes as their pope. Perhaps I can get her special dispensation—Protestant style."

"She can come," Madame Cabochon said. She turned and left the rectory without as much as inclining her head. Naughty Boy Albert be damned.

* * *

The suicide month was not a popular time to vacation at the Missionary Rest House. Topographically speaking, Belle Vue was not situated high enough to provide relief from the humidity, which, combined with the temperature, made it feel like you were breathing through a hot wet washcloth. As a consequence, Amanda Brown was without any guests for the first time since her arrival in the Belgian Congo three months ago. This gave her the luxury of taking her meals when she pleased; it did not, however, guarantee that she could eat undisturbed.

"Mamu Ugly Eyes," a male voice said, "may I at last get your attention?"

Amanda looked up from a July issue of the *Saturday Evening Post*. It was one that she had brought with her and that had miraculously managed to survive the plane crash that was her introduction to this diamond-producing town. She read it now not for information, or to be entertained, but for the connection to home as she scanned the familiar words.

"Protruding Navel," she said to her head housekeeper with remarkable patience, "why did you not simply say '*Excusez mois,*' like the other houseboys in Bell Vue? I do not possess eyes in the top of my head."

He snorted. "*Mamu,* I am the son of a chief, and you are but a woman. It is you who must take into account my presence and inquire as to my purpose for standing here."

"I see. Very well. In my country, the men are also in charge. They are the chiefs and in most cases their wives are told to obey them."

He nodded with apparent approval.

"Of course then a silly woman like me knows nothing about money. Therefore I am afraid, Protruding Navel, that before I can pay your salary I must write off to America and make arrangements for a man to give me specific instructions. After all, I would hate to make a mistake. At any rate, it may take a couple of months; I thought you might like to know this."

Amanda had often heard the expression "like a deer caught in the headlights," and now she knew exactly what it meant. Was she lying to Protruding Navel? Perhaps—although she preferred to think of it as misleading; anyway, it was to make a point.

"Mamu Ugly Eyes," he said quickly, "there is someone at the door who wishes to see you."

"Oh? Why did you not say so?"

"Because you did not ask."

"Who is it?"

"A man."

"What sort of man?"

"It is the *Bula Matadi, Mamu.*"

The man in question was the Rock Breaker—the white police captain, the handsome young Belgian whom Amanda was sweet on. Just the mention of him sent a tingle of pleasure running up the young woman's spine.

She glanced at her image in what remained of her coffee: unfortunately, the inky liquid was not a flattering reflector. Where did those jowls come from? And how long had she had that pimple on her forehead? It was the humidity that was to blame. In South Carolina, even in the height of the summer, she had never experienced anything like this.

"Show him in," she said. "And then please bring another plate."

But when Pierre strode in a moment later, he refused to sit. Neither did he kiss Amanda—not even on the cheek. Well, that would certainly have been career suicide if he had, but still, a girl can always dream. After all, a Belgian girl would—a Belgian woman would surely have been kissed. Why must missionaries—Protestant missionaries in particular—always be so proper? Yes, Protruding Navel would have gossiped like nobody's business, but what would the harm have been in that?

"Good morning, Mademoiselle Brown," he said and shook her hand. A handshake? Ugh!

"*Bonjour, Capitaine,*" she enunciated crisply.

He scanned the room in all the directions, including both open doorways and what lay beyond. Then he waited.

"Protruding Navel," Amanda called. "Please bring some coffee and a croissant for Captain Jardin."

A loud snicker was heard from the short hallway that led to the kitchen. Protruding Navel stepped from the shadows where he had hidden, pressed up against the wall.

"*Mamu*, you know very well that there are no croissants to be found in this American palace. From you one often hears the complaint that this silly variety of French bread is too messy, too messy even to be eaten in a pig's house. Is this not the truth?"

Amanda could feel the color rush to her cheeks. "That will be quite enough," she said. "You are dismissed. Now please go outside and gather fallen mangoes."

"*Tshinyi?*"

"You heard; now go."

"*Tch*," he said, but he sauntered off.

"Now please, Pierre," Amanda said, "don't keep me waiting a second longer. What is it? Is it news from home? What brings you here so early?"

Pierre scooped up Amanda's slender hands and held them between his. "There was a murder in the village last night," he said.

Amanda gasped softly.

The Belgian Congo, 1935

The chief held his ceremonial staff in the air, signaling silence. The wood was smooth and dark from generations of hands and hearth fires; it was impossible now to tell the type of tree from which it had come. From the top of the pole dangled the skull of a rhesus monkey, the flowing black-and-white tail of a colobus monkey, and a cluster of porcupine quills. A topknot of bright red feathers from the tail of an African gray parrot had been glued to the tip of the rod, just for show.

Immediately the men fell silent; it is quite possible even that some were afraid that ill fortune might befall them next. For at a feast such as this, where one man falls upon the other, only the fool would not be so dull as to think that he was entirely safe from mischief.

The Belgian Congo, 1958

Father Reutner had noticed the lone man enter the rear of the church. He couldn't help but keep an eye on the fellow throughout Mass if only because he was taller than all the women, and because his white shirt stuck out like a poultice among their colorful wraps. When it came time to receive the Eucharist, however, the stranger remained in his pew, his head bowed.

There was something about the way this man glanced around wildly, like a yearling horse, then bowed his head intently during the prayers—too intently, in fact—that gave Father Reutner the distinct impression he had another Protestant on his hands. Well, a convert from Protestantism was better than none. Lately, for every convert he was able to get on the rolls, the church lost two communicants to the cults.

Ach, the cults! They were getting more and more ridiculous. Why, this latest one was said to revolve around the figure of an African prophet named Kibangu, who, like Jesus, had conquered death. Supposedly he had died in a fire, in a locked house, and had been seen walking unharmed among the flames. His followers numbered among the thousands and called themselves the Apostles. They dressed in white robes and carried staves. But instead of preaching love and redemption, they walked from village to village preaching vengeance against the Belgians.

Three weeks ago this coming Sunday his sermon was interrupted by one of their firebrands shouting that when independence finally came, those Congolese with enough faith to have built a "garage"—a *tshitanda*—would magically receive an automobile. Of course, driving an automobile would require knowledge of European technology, and the best way to get that was from European brains—literally. Osmosis for the masses.

"We will kill you, white man," the interloper had shouted. "Then we will take your brains and mix it with palm oil. This salve we will then rub on our heads. After one night's sleep we shall wake the following morning with all the knowledge that you, the white devil, keeps secret from us so that we cannot progress."

"But I keep nothing secret from you—or anyone," Father Reutner had answered. He later decided that his tone had been that of a beggar. He'd been a coward in his own church. How could he expect more souls to convert, to stand up to the old ways, if he, the supposed shepherd, wanted nothing more than to bolt from the flock before the wolves closed in entirely.

It would be different now. For one thing, he'd been praying for strength over the last three weeks. Besides, now there was just him and the lone man in the back pew: it was somehow different if the congregation wasn't there to watch him lose face.

"*Muoyo webe,*" he said cautiously. Life to you.

The African jumped to his feet and extended a calloused hand. "*Eh, muoyo webe, muambi.*"

"What is it that you want?"

"Want, master? I do not want anything—but to know your God."

Father Reutner reared as if by chance he'd encountered a poisonous snake laid across his path. A direct conversion request like this, especially one coming from a man, was highly unusual.

"Who put you up to this?" The words had tumbled out unbidden.

"*Kah!*"

"*Toh, toh, toh!*" No, no, no! "That is not what I meant to say. Please sit and we will discuss this matter."

The African was clearly agitated, but he sat anyway. Father Reutner had seen the same look in a goat's eyes just before the animal's throat was slit. If this was a genuine request on the man's part, the priest was prepared to assign himself a substantial amount of penance for having been so quick to judge.

"*Muambi,*" the African said even as he sat, "my name is Jonathan Pimple. For many years I have been a Protestant, and I have believed that I was a Christian. However, recently I have heard from others that only you Catholics are the true Christians. Is this so?"

As tired as he was, Father Reutner still felt his heart beat faster at the prospect of snatching a soul away from the competition. "Ah—Monsieur Pimple, a Christian is a follower of Jesus Christ, and so I cannot in good conscience make the claim that the Protestants are not Christians. But I can say most emphatically that if it is entry into heaven that you seek, then you have come to the right place. Only a person baptized as a Roman Catholic is eligible for entry into heaven."

"E, *muambi*, I desire your heaven very much."

"Is that so? What is it about our heaven that you desire, Monsieur Pimple?"

"I have heard it is a place of peace. And rest. And where I will at last get a house that will not fall down in the next big storm."

Father Reutner laughed despite his reservations. "Very well; I will convert you. It will involve much study—unless, hmm. Let us hope that this situation does not arise."

"Unless what, *muambi*? You must tell me so that I can be prepared."

"Unless the Protestants try to win you back. Then I will convert you at once. Now then, I suppose we can begin our first lesson right here. Tell me everything you know about the One True Faith."

The African shrugged.

"Well, what did they teach you about God in the Protestant faith?"

"That he had but one son whose name was Jesus Christ, and that Jesus died so that everyone might go to live in heaven with him, even the Catholics—but only if they repent of their sin."

"*Gott in Himmel!*" Father Reutner felt all the blood in his face rush to the one big vein in his forehead. "What sin is *that*?"

"It is the sin of being Catholic. But, *mukelenge*, this I find very confusing as I can see that Jesus Christ and his mother, Mary, live there"—Jonathan Pimple pointed to a pair of statues flanking the dais—"and they would not do so if this was truly as evil a place as the Protestants claim it is."

"*Nein, nein,*" Father Reutner shouted. "That is not true! Jesus was not a Protestant; he was a Catholic!"

"I am sorry, *muambi*. You see, I truly am an ignorant man in the ways of your church."

Father Reutner took some deep, calming breaths. It would be a grave sin indeed if he let his temper get in the way of snaring this lost sheep and returning it to Christ's fold—especially since, just by looking at the man's mouth, he could tell that the man was a Mupende. Around Belle Vue, they were like the Samaritans of the New Testament: despised.

"Monsieur Pimple," he finally said, "we all make mistakes. That is how we learn. Fortunately Mother Church has given us a process through which we can be forgiven of our mistakes. You recite your mistakes to me, and I will give you spiritual advice on how not to repeat such and such a mistake. In addition, I will give you a small punishment that will help you to remember. This is called confession."

"*Muambi,* if it pleases you, could you give me an example?"

The old man nodded. Indeed, he was quite pleased to do so.

"Let us say that you tell me that you beat your wife too hard upon occasion—"

"*Aiyee,* this I do not do!"

"No?"

"I have yet to take a wife, *muambi.*"

"This is not good, for a man without a wife is a man who will entertain impure thoughts. He will then search out the village prostitutes, or he will *ditongesha.*" Masturbate.

"*Muambi,* never has a white man spoken to me so directly!"

"*E,* but that is the nature of this ritual called confession."

"*Mukelenge,*" said Jonathan Pimple—Lord, "are these things— these mistakes that I have made—do they stay with you? For I am told that they do."

The old priest was shocked. "So someone has already been speaking to you about conversion?"

"Absolutely not! Except for this matter of confidentiality. As a Mupende, I had reason to be concerned."

It was truly like a lightbulb went on inside the cleric's head. "Ah! You were perhaps a cannibal in your youth?"

"*Eyo.* But I was just a small boy, you see, son of the powerful chief Nyanga-Yanga."

Father Reutner rubbed his hands together, as if washing them. "Cannibalism is a grave sin, my son."

"Even for you who are a Catholic?"

The priest raised one of those leathery hands. He wished to strike the impudent Mupende. He had heard this sacrilege more times than he cared to remember: What was so wrong about Africans eating other Africans, if once they converted, they would actually be eating Jesus Christ? Perhaps their question wouldn't be quite so infuriating, if Father Reutner had a pat answer he could give them, something that their simple minds could grasp.

When Jonathan Pimple didn't even have the decency to flinch,

Father Reutner resumed symbolically washing away the blood of some anonymous Mupende victim. "Tell me about the man you ate. What do you remember?"

"*Mukelenge,* I remember very little."

There were certain questions about the practice of cannibalism that Father Reutner had always wanted to ask a Mupende tribesman, someone old enough to remember that barbaric custom. Someday when he retired, if his mind still held up, and the termites hadn't succeeded in eating his copious notes, Father Reutner intended to write a book. It would be a sociological profile of the Congolese tribes among whom he had served. His working title was *Bringing Light to the Heathen Lands,* although during the process of collecting this valuable information, the good priest discovered that very disturbing thoughts had arisen in his own head.

"But the person you ate—it was a man, yes, and not a woman?" Father Reutner was ashamed of himself for thinking thus, but it seemed to him that eating a man was a worse sin than eating a woman.

"*E,* it was a man; of that I am sure."

"How can you be sure after so many years?"

"Because there is no reason to eat a woman unless one is very hungry, even starving. The flesh of a woman does not bestow special powers upon one; to the contrary, by consuming a woman one might even take on those characteristics that are female. Tell me, *Mukelenge,* would you wish to develop breasts and the place from which babies emerge?"

"*Silence!* You are in the house of God. Tell me, do the Protestants show no respect for God?"

The savage was quiet a moment. "They do not," he said at last. "Not in the least. This is yet another reason why I must convert to your way as soon as possible; those wicked Protestants have corrupted me and set me on the broad and winding road to hell."

"And yet you have the nerve to sit here and quote that Calvinist John Bunyan to me."

"*Aiyee!* I do not know this John of which you speak. Does he live in the workers' village?"

Father Reutner took a deep breath and tried to visualize the cover of his book. The photo would depict a traditional Mupende tribesman, one who still wore mud in his hair and filed all his teeth into sharp little points—like a fish! Or a kitten. *Yah,* a cover like this was guaranteed to make the book a bestseller.

"Monsieur Pimple, I am told that the most tender—and flavorful—part of a person is the hand. That part of the palm which is at the base of the thumb. Is that not the piece traditionally reserved for the chief?"

"Yes, Lord, that is so. But I remember neither the taste, nor the texture of this piece, for the morsel my father shared with me, his heir, was strictly symbolic. It was so small that a mouse would scarcely have noticed this sample of flesh passing down its gullet."

"What a shame," Father Reutner cried, "that a mortal sin of such weightiness left so faint a memory. Can you remember nothing else concerning this horrific event? Nothing at all? Did the victim cry out in pain? Was he boiled alive in a large pot? Did he beg for mercy? Please, you must remember more details."

The silly Mupende shook his head. "We were merely cannibals, Lord, not savages. We did not boil anyone alive. The man was first decapitated with a machete and *then* chopped into pieces. Five pots were filled with the offering of his meat."

"Did you say *offering*?"

"*Eyo.* If this man did not intend for us to eat him, then he and his friend would not have first appeared to our women as they bathed along the banks of our river."

Father Reutner had heard enough. It wasn't just enough of *that* conversation; it was enough African conversation ever. It was exactly this kind of logic that was going to keep Africa—Congo, in particular—perpetually locked in the Dark Ages. The savages bathed naked, were spotted by outsiders, so the outsiders were eaten!

"*Ya biebe,*" he screamed, his gravelly voice rising two octaves.
Go!

The man named Jonathan Pimple rose, with his chin jutting
out defiantly. "It was a *white* man," he said. "That much, I remember. He was a Catholic priest just like you."

In Amanda's mind, the words *murder* and *village* immediately
conjured up the image of Cripple. Today was only Thursday; it
wasn't laundry day, so the tiny Muluba woman should already
have checked in with her. In a panic she spoke her thoughts aloud.

"Oh God, please don't let it be Cripple!"

Pierre pulled her close to him, wrapping his strong tanned
arms tightly around her neck. "Amanda, no! The murder victim
was not Cripple!"

Amanda pulled free. "Then *who*? And how dare you scare me
like that?"

His look of bewilderment restored her equilibrium.

"I'm sorry," she said. "I didn't mean to sound like that. It's just
that I care a great deal about Cripple."

He took her in his arms; gently this time, and she went softly,
willingly. "The victim of this horrible crime is the same man who
laid claim to killing the python last week. His name is—"

"Lazarus Chigger Mite."

"You *knew* him?"

"No, but he and another fellow were here seeking arbitration
from Cripple. I don't normally watch her play magistrate, but it
was Sunday morning, and I was at loose ends."

Pierre released Amanda from his embrace and sat rather heavily across the table from where they'd been standing. He shook his
handsome blond head.

"That Cripple! Sooner by later she is going to get herself into
much trouble."

"*Or,*" Amanda said, feeling surprisingly defensive.

"*Pardon?*"

"The idiom is 'sooner *or* later.' You said '*by.*'"

Pierre, bless his heart, was so annoyed by the impromptu language lesson that his growled response was something that Amanda would have found quite embarrassing at a dinner party back home in Rock Hill. Surely Mama and her book club friends would have been scandalized.

"Forgive me," Pierre said, raking his strong brown hands through his thick mane of hair. "My boys—my sergeant—woke me at a little past three. Do you have any coffee left?"

"I thought you didn't like the way we Americans make coffee."

"Ah, but there is an old saying: a wise man would do well to eat turnips rather than starve to death."

Amanda laughed. "Is that saying African or Belgian?"

"It is neither; I just now made it up."

She rang the little brass bell that she kept near her at all times while she ate. "One cup of black turnips coming up. Protruding Navel," she said, without raising her voice a single decibel, "I know that you are listening, so please bring Captain Pierre a cup of coffee."

"*I am not listening, Mamu.*" His emphatic words were followed by a great deal of inexplicable clattering in the kitchen, but by and by he appeared bearing a mahogany and ivory inlaid tray, upon which was a blue enamel mug, filled to the brim with steaming, freshly brewed coffee.

Amanda and Pierre waited for several minutes after he disappeared again before resuming any serious conversation. It was Amanda who spoke first.

"That man is impossible," she said wearily.

Pierre nodded silently.

"I would fire him if I didn't have a hundred guests scheduled to arrive next week."

Pierre's eyes widened, but then narrowed when he saw that Amanda was smiling and shaking her head. "Back to Cripple," he said. "That's why I'm here. And, of course, to see you."

"Of course."

"There are rumors circulating about the village that the night the python was killed—and for the following day—Cripple and her husband feasted on goat stew."

"So? I mean, I pay her a competitive salary, don't I? And it's only goat; it's not like it's filet mignon."

Pierre chuckled. "I love how you Americans pronounce that word. Like you are putting gas in your car, no?"

Amanda flushed. "Perhaps it is just I who mispronounces it; I haven't had a lot of practice ordering that particular cut of steak, mind you."

"And permit me to remind you, Miss Brown, that I was raised in this country, where good beef is a rarity—no pun intended, yes—but please, permit me once again to apologize. I do not mean for us to get sidetracked. I wish only to convey the information that some of the villagers suspect Cripple and her husband of—well, of stealing the goat from under the nose of Lazarus Chigger Mite."

"But that is ridiculous! You saw for yourself: Cripple arrived riding on my shoulders, and as for her husband—why, he was off in the forest collecting sap for palm beer."

"That is his story, and *c'est vrai*, I did not see him in the crowd. But the rumors have it that he extricted"—he paused and shrugged—"is that how you say the word?"

"I don't know," Amanda said. She wasn't being difficult; she really couldn't tell what he was driving at.

"To remove. The snake's belly was filled with bushes, no? This means that someone extricted the goat and replaced it with the bushes."

"*Extracted*!"

"Excuse me?"

"Never mind. Listen, Pierre, the fact that the python's belly was filled with branches doesn't mean anything. For all we know, Chigger Mite could well have put them in there himself before summoning an audience. How do we know he didn't take his precious goat to another village the day before and sell it? To pin this on Cripple's husband is nothing but superstition."

"*Oui*, but it is very good for his business, no?"

"Come again?"

"Then you have not heard; those same people who believe that Cripple's husband can magically transfer a goat from a snake's belly to a cooking pot are now flocking to him to buy potions and pay to have spells cast on their behalf. It seems that Their Death's career as a witch doctor has been revived."

"Lord have mercy!" Amanda said. It was surprising how much she felt betrayed—but by whom?

Perhaps it was by Their Death, whose career might make it unnecessary for Cripple to work, and then she would seldom see her friend—her only friend in Belle Vue—again. On the other hand, maybe it was simply the fact that Cripple had been holding back from her. Friends are supposed to share news. Then again, what hubris to think that she and Cripple were such good buddies. Given the world they inhabited, where they occupied opposite sides of such an uneven power structure, true friendship wasn't even possible.

Yes, she'd carried Cripple in the wheelbarrow through the cassava field, all the way to the forest's edge, to where the great *muma* lay slain, a modern-day dragon. However, just a few months ago she'd witnessed Cripple being carried on the shoulders of angry young men shouting "*Independence!*" at the top of their lungs, when what they really meant was "*Kill the whites!*"

The Belgian Congo, 1935

The chief beckoned to one of his younger warriors. This was a man who knew the Bula Matadi *quite well, having been caught by soldiers and pressed into physical labor for building a road. During this time—which was almost double the time it takes a woman to grow a baby—this man had learned a great deal of the French, for he was a clever man, and skilled as a mimic as well. The chief bade this man speak to the remaining captive, and so he did. Although the words were those of the great Mupende chief, the voice was that of a white man—a Belgian overseer of low social rank.*

"Look at me, you stupid monkey," the clever Mupende said, "for I am about to make you a very attractive offer."

The white man turned his head slowly. "Mon Dieu," he said quietly. "I thought you were—"

"A white? Like you?" The clever man laughed. Few among the assembled cannibals understood what was being said; nonetheless, many other men laughed as well.

"You have no accent," said the white man.

"*Oui, I am like a parrot. Now listen up, you filthy bastard, here is our offer: the chief has decided to let you go.*"

"*Go?*"

"*Yes, go! What an ignorant bunch of savages you are; jungle bunnies, really, not understanding even any basic French.*"

The white man with the dark hair lowered his dark eyes. "*I never called your people those names. Not ever.*"

At this point the chief started waving his staff and speaking in rapid Kipende. "*He says I should get on with my offer,*" the clever man said. "*So anyway, you must surely be aware—even a baboon like you—that this offer comes with a condition.*"

"*This baboon understands,*" the white man with the dark eyes said. He spoke calmly and without fear.

The Belgian Congo, 1958

When the drums announced that Lazarus Chigger Mite was dead—murdered, in fact—Their Death forbade Cripple to leave the family compound. Even to use the communal privy, he said; for the time being, the night gourd would have to do for her needs.

"Their Death," Cripple said, not fully awake, and thus not fully comprehending the complexity of the situation, "what does Lazarus Chigger Mite's unfortunate death have to do with me? Or with you, for that matter?"

Their Death looked lovingly into his wife's eyes, and then down at the growing belly that contained their ripening child. "Wife," he said, "the headman has been here twice to see me since the day that Lazarus Chigger Mite killed the great *muma*. Both times were to purchase my services.

"The first time he wished to buy a spell to be put on a relative in Léopoldville who was healthy but who does not work. This man lives in the family compound of the headman and has been a financial drain for many years. The spell is only to cause this young man to seek employment."

"And the second spell?"

Their Death shook his head. "*Tch*," he said, and spat just outside the door of the hut. "He asked me—no, he ordered me—to cast a spell on the dead man, Lazarus Chigger Mite. For that one, he said he would pay me nothing until the man was four days dead in his grave. Longer even than Jesus Christ—those were his very words!"

Cripple was as fully awake as she had been the night savannah fires burned right up to the eastern edge of the workers' village and ignited their huts with wayward sparks.

"*Aiyee!*" she exclaimed. "Those were awful words; and this I say as a heathen. Tell me, Their Death, why would a powerful man from Léopoldville, a member of the elite, want Lazarus Chigger Mite dead? The *muma* slayer was but a lowly Mupende. When the headman's ancestors, the Bakongo, were kings, feted by the king of Portugal, Lazarus Chigger Mite's ancestors were serving up their enemies for dinner."

Their Death laughed heartily. "Wife, you joke, but it is the truth. As for what his motive could be, think back to the first murder in Mukanda wa Nzambi." The Holy Bible.

"Not only am I a heathen, but I have never been to school."

"How could I ever forget? But did you not say that you sat outside on the grass while your brother was in school and learned his lessons faster than he did?"

"That is so," Cripple said.

"*Ne?*" Husband said.

"Aha!" Cripple said, nodding as the spark of knowledge lit up her eyes. "Jealousy was the motive."

"*E*. The headman was envious of the fact that Lazarus Chigger Mite was getting praise for killing the mighty *muma*. As you know, this would give him great standing in the village—even if there was no goat." Husband paused and sucked loudly on his teeth. "But perhaps there was, and that goat was indeed stolen by me using my special powers. I am once more a powerful witch doctor, *a muena tshihaha*."

"*E*, but Their Death, you know that your powers—" Cripple grabbed the center pole of the hut and pulled herself clumsily to her feet. "Unh! Their Death, he will kill you next!"

"No—but perhaps he will try."

"This is terrible; you must go to the police! You must speak with Captain Jardin. You can trust him."

"Yes, in good time. Do you know this thing called irony, Cripple?"

"I am uneducated, Their Death; I am not ignorant!"

"Indeed, you are not. The irony is that at first the headman probably hoped that I *could* cast a spell on Lazarus Chigger Mite and thus do his dirty work for him. But of course I refused. You do believe me. Do you not?"

"Their Death, do not my waste time with foolish questions, for the night gourd calls." Cripple did not speak harshly, for she loved Their Death, and of course she knew a woman's place—that is, she thought, unlike the white *mamu*, for whom she worked.

Pierre Jardin hated sleeping during daylight hours. It not only messed up his circadian rhythms, but no matter what time he awoke, there always followed a period of disorientation and lethargy, sometimes even a massive headache. Therefore, when Pierre finally toppled into bed late that Thursday morning, he left strict instructions with his head houseboy not to disturb him. One can understand, therefore, how it might be that Captain Pierre Gerome Jardin was not his most pleasant self upon being roused merely two hours after his head hit the pillow.

"*Muambi!*"

"*Sacré-coeur! Alors*, Man with Birthmark, did I not leave strict instructions for you not to bother me?"

"Yes, *muambi*, you did, but the Belgian woman is here to see you. She will not listen to a black man, even a head housekeeper such as me. She said that she will count to one hundred before coming back here to get you yourself."

Pierre felt his headache get even worse—if indeed that was possible. At the same time, he could feel the corners of his mouth start to tug upward at the thought of Madame Cabochon clicking her way down his cement hallway in her stiletto shoes, her flame-colored hair flowing behind her as if her proudly held head were the Olympic torch. One certainly didn't have to like the woman to think that she cut quite a sight. By the same token, one could be quite smitten with another woman—a far more innocent type, a lady even—and still appreciate the feminine wiles of Madame Cabochon.

"*Which* Belgian woman is it?" he asked, just to be sure. God forbid it was the new OP's sweet, and very religious, young wife.

"Monsieur," said Man with Birthmark, "it is the woman with big breasts."

Pierre chuckled. The houseboys, the yardmen, the night watchman, all had crushes on Madame Cabochon—at least on her breasts. Because they could see only the tops of them bobbling above her provocatively low-cut dresses, there was much discussion as to whether or not the rest of the breasts existed out of line of sight.

"*Katuka we!*" Get out!

The speaker was none other than the woman with big breasts herself, and Pierre had to admit that she was justifiably indignant. Therefore, he did not complain when she strode into the room, threw open the wooden shutters, pushed her way through the mosquito netting, and sprawled across the end of his bed. One of the breasts for which she was so famous came dangerously close to spilling out of the deeply cut scoop neckline of her tightly fitted bodice. It was virtually impossible not to look at it; it was like watching a truck teeter on the edge of a cliff, half its wheels on, half off. There was nothing you could do about it, but you would never forgive yourself if you turned away before the big finale.

"Pierre," she snapped, "eyes up here."

"Then perhaps, madame, you would be so kind as to sit up.

Might I even suggest that you take the chair in that far corner of the room?"

"Don't be such a silly boy, Pierre! I am almost twice your age. You couldn't possibly be bothered by my presence on your bed." At that she tugged the other side of her bodice down so that both her breasts bobbled on the threshold of premature liberation. She also pulled back the sheet.

Pierre leaped from his bed, pulling his top sheet with him. As a bachelor he had no need to cover up the slumber suit that God had given him at birth. In fact, wearing pajamas during the suicide month was an act of stupidity. The only reason he'd been covered at all was that there was a small hole in the mosquito net in need of mending, and despite the heat, he wasn't about to have the most sensitive part of his anatomy bitten.

The young police officer was tall and muscular, but he wasn't particularly graceful, and one foot caught in the netting and delayed his departure. Madame Cabochon laughed wholeheartedly. She had a surprisingly deep laugh, considering that she was not a smoker.

"Why, Captain, I didn't know that you were Jewish!"

"What?"

"Never mind, it was a small joke about a large item; I forgot that the *Bula Matadi* have no sense of humor."

Pierre wrapped the sheet tightly around his waist and stumbled backward to the chair. As both he and his would-be seductress were fluent in English, and the houseboy wasn't, Pierre switched languages.

"Look, what is it that you want? This better be good. And anyway, you are not almost twice my age; I'm twenty-eight, and you are thirty-eight. Your age is a matter of record, as is that of every other white in Belle Vue, since each of you is registered with me at the police station. Madame, I even have your weight."

In a flash of blue, Madame Cabochon sat up, pulling her knees in front of her chest. The peep show was over.

"You are a cruel man, Captain Jardin. I have half a mind to leave you off my guest list."

"Frankly, madame, my dance card is full. I shall be content to sit out on my balcony and contemplate the river."

"But you haven't even asked the occasion? What if it is that King Baudouin and Queen Fabiola have decided to tour the Congo one last time before this dreadful impending thing called independence? My grandmother was the youngest daughter of a viscount, so I do have a royal connection, you know. I'm sure it's more than anyone else in this shitty little hellhole can claim."

Pierre smiled; the only thing he knew was that Madame Cabochon read too many American novels. That, and if he wasn't already falling head over heels with the young American, Amanda Brown, and if Madame Cabochon was not already married—albeit to a horrible little Nazi—he would surely throw off his towel and leap back into his bed. After all, *Petit Pierre*, as his private part was known only to him, was certainly ready to get down to business.

"Well, *should* Their Majesties wish to visit our little town—then their security would be rather tight, especially now, precisely because of this impending thing called independence. As I am the chief of police of this 'shitty little hellhole,' I would be the first to be contacted. But since I have not been contacted, I can safely assume that the most royal ass to be seated at your function will belong to you."

Madame jumped off the bed, all the better to express her indignation. Again the mosquito netting got in her way, bringing yet another smile to Pierre's face.

"Damn you," she said. "Must you always be so—so—*mon Dieu*, I cannot think of a word bad enough in this English!"

A shift in her tone had informed Pierre that it was time to

stop teasing her. "All right, Madame Cabochon, what is this occasion?"

She tossed her auburn mane and snorted—quite like a filly, he thought—while she stalled to regain just a little power. "It is a dinner to honor Monsignor Clemente," she said.

"Is that so? Does he know this?"

"What sort of impertinent question is that? Of course he does! The monsignor and I were childhood friends—right here in Belle Vue. Everyone who is anyone will be there, including that plain little American girl whom you are so fond of."

"Miss Brown?"

Now Madame Cabochon smiled. "*Capitaine* Pierre," she said, switching back to French, "must you be so disingenuous? You know quite well who I mean; there are no other Americans here at the moment."

"Yes, but what makes you think that I am especially fond of this plain little girl?"

This time the auburn-haired filly stomped the floor with impatience. "What do you think I am, a cabbage? Do you think I'm incapable of observation? Or at the very least of listening to gossip? All everyone talks about is how you've been stumbling about like an elephant bull in musk. Don't you think it's about time you quit thinking up excuses to visit that dreary Missionary Rest House and escort your little girl out on a real proper date. Who knows, she might even take to Belle Vue's high society, and they to her. With any luck, she'll defect from that heretic Protestant cult and the two of you can get married and produce lots of little Jardins. Imagine that—a *jardin* of Jardins!"

Pierre hoped that his deep tan hid any signs of blushing. "Madame Cabochon, if this were a proper city—such as Luluabourg—your deportment would not be considered necessary entertainment, so I would have tolerated far less of you just now. Here in the bush, however, we must take our amusements whichever way we can. But as all good things must come to end, so must your unwelcome visit. *Au revoir, madame.*"

The beautiful redhead, however, remained rooted to his cement floor as securely as the granite-embedded pilings of the bridge that spanned the Kasai River. She was nothing but trouble, this one.

"Birthmark!" he called. "*Lua, angata mukashi.*"

Even though Pierre had suspected that his manservant was lurking about, Birthmark's reappearance was disturbingly quick. Pierre glared at the man, who didn't even have the sense to avert his wide-eyed stare. No doubt these crazy Belgians and their highly sexualized ways were going to be the subject of a few hearthside discussions tonight.

The impertinent housekeeper had once asked him how it was possible that such a decadent and fallen race as the whites could have conquered the more numerous Africans with their higher moral values. Had they somehow first managed to cast a spell on all of Africa? he'd asked. If it was indeed true that the airplanes that he saw taking off and landing from Belle Vue's small commercial airport could fly over all the continent, then perhaps it was from them that the unctuous powders that supported this nefarious spell were unloosed upon his people.

At any rate, Madame Cabochon was even less pleased to witness the speed with which Birthmark materialized. "Boy," she said in French, although she knew Tshiluba like the native she practically was, "if you worked for me, today would be your last! How dare you spy on us?"

"Madame," Birthmark said slowly, perhaps insolently as well, "my master has asked me to take you from the room."

"And what if I refuse to go?"

"Madame Cabochon," Pierre said quickly in English, "that's not playing fair, and you know it."

"Oh, what the hell do I care about playing fair anymore? They're talking about kicking us out in two years."

At that point Captain Pierre Gerome Jardin had had all he could stomach from any one person in one day. He leaped to his feet, grabbed the exasperating seductress, and threw her over his shoulder. Unfortunately, somewhere along the way to the front verandah to drop her off, he stepped on his sheet.

The Belgian Congo, 1935

The younger brother slept, but the older brother could not because the clever man and white man would not shut up. Whose god or gods were better—what nonsense when one had a terrible headache.

"You people are barbaric!" the white man said.

One might question how a boy so young—or anyone for that matter—could remember so much, but this was no ordinary boy. All that he witnessed and heard was carved into his memory. Of course he did not understand every word that was spoken by these men, but surely the gist of what they said was seared into his young soul.

So exceptionally clever was he that already he could recite his clan's complete lineage, beginning with the great flood seventy-two generations ago and extending, unbroken, down through his mother's side to this very day. On his father's side, it was nearly the same, but for the fact that in the sixty-third generation past his father's people were said to have been slaves captured from the primitive Bakuba people who kept no records.

"You *are* barbaric!" said the clever Mupende. "Do you not partake of your God on a regular basis? We, the Bapende, do no such thing. To consume our gods would be abhorrent to us."

The white man laughed foolishly. "Your gods? Your gods are made of wood and animal bone. You would break your pointed teeth consuming them!"

"Those are not our gods, Barbaric One. Those are merely representations that remind us of our gods. Our gods are invisible; they are spirits that inhabit trees, rocks, and rivers. They cause the clouds to rain and the sun to shine. They drive the animals to our arrows and spear points when we hunt. Believe me when I say that we would never eat our gods!"

"That is still idolatry. There is only one *God; not one god for—for everything that you see."*

"Yet you have three *gods, do you not?"*

"You cannot offend me, Mupende."

"Good. Nor is it my wish to offend you when speaking of your gods. In fact, never has a Mupende approached a white man and asked him to change his belief concerning his gods." The clever man paused. "Why do you think that is?"

"Because your beliefs are wrong," the white man with dark eyes answered without any hesitation.

The clever man's nostrils flared.

"What did he say?" the chief demanded.

"He said that he has observed that you are a chief who is greatly admired by his people. He said that your leadership qualities are of such high caliber that you deserve to be chief of not only this little village, but in fact, you should be made a king—like the one that Bakuba people have!"

The chief frowned. "Eh? I did not hear him say the word Bakuba; *surely it is not so different in the language of Belgique."*

"Truly my king, it is very different." He turned to the white man again. "Tell me, did you also perpetrate this crime upon the one boy?"

"Mon Dieu, I did not! It is not in my nature."

"That is what the boy said; that is why they did not kill you so far. However, it was something that I needed to know for myself. Listen, white man, is it important to you that you live? Perhaps you might

wish to preach about your god to other Congolese? I hear that the people in the Zappo Zapps tribe are very easy to persuade."

"Yes, I would like that," the white man said without any hesitation.

"In that case, and since you have lived up to the condition set before you, then you are free to go."

"But how? Where? I am naked. I can't even find my way back to your village in the dark."

Unlike the Bula Matadi, *the boy's father was a man of his word, but he was not a man of unlimited patience. Sensing that the clever man had given the captive his freedom, the chief pointed at the thick bush with his staff.*

"It would be wise to hurry, white man, before my elders change their minds."

Instead of dashing for freedom, the strange, bewitching man stood tall and straight, and although he was quite naked, nonetheless he possessed an air every bit as regal as that of the boy's father. If it were not for the unbelievable color of his male parts, one might have thought him to be totally human.

"Every one of you, with the possible exception of the boy—but only if he is baptized as a Roman Catholic*—will surely burn in a place of eternal flames, yet you will not die. Your bodies will feel horrible pain, and you will scream out in your pain. You will beg to die, but you will not. This will be your punishment for what you have done tonight to my friend."*

"You must go now*," the boy said and pointed to the bush. Not only was he clever, but he was also wise beyond his years.*

The Belgian Congo, 1958

Jonathan Pimple had yet to take a wife, so he was often alone. But unlike many men, Jonathan Pimple was seldom lonely, for he needed to be free to ponder whichever matter struck his fancy at any particular time; after all, Jonathan Pimple was a thinking man.

Why, he wondered, did some people eat human flesh just as easily as if it were goat meat, yet others were horrified at the very thought of it? On the other hand, the same people who were the most repulsed by the custom of consuming human flesh were the Catholic priests. Did not these men dispense small bits of a white man's body in their services to their faithful each week?

True, it was flesh like none other that Jonathan had ever seen, but the white man was full of surprises, was he not? Therefore it was necessary that Jonathan Pimple, who had an inquiring mind, examine a piece of this flesh closely.

A woman named Firefly was Jonathan Pimple's next-door neighbor. She lived beneath the giant mango tree that was infested with red ants, and which, therefore, no one could climb to harvest its ever-bountiful crop of blushing fruit. Firefly was a faithful Roman Catholic, as well as a good friend. A woman friend is an unusual thing for a man to have, but Firefly had a keen mind; this is what qualified her as one of Jonathan Pimple's many blessings.

So it was that when Jonathan Pimple expressed his strong interest in examining a piece of flesh, Firefly only pretended to swallow the host. Instead she deftly managed to palm it before it made contact with her tongue. Just how she accomplished this, she would tell no one, not even Jonathan, lest anyone else attempt— and manage to succeed—at what was surely a desecration.

For Firefly knew that taking a wafer home with her would be considered a grave sin—maybe even an unforgivable one, *if* the priest ever found out. Yet how could a just God condemn her for such an action when it was Jonathan Pimple who had put the idea in her head? He had also raised several other questions that needed answering.

This is how Jonathan Pimple convinced his good friend. "Consider," he said, "that this Jesus Christ lived almost two thousand years ago, yet the missionaries have been here less than one hundred years. Now then, they insist that *unless* we believe that this Jesus Christ became a ghost after he died, and that he lives now somewhere above the stars—but in a place that they have never seen—when we die we will burn in a great fire. There we will be consumed by unbearable pain for all time. But *if* we believe, then when we die, we will be given unimaginable riches—although we will no longer have a yearning for women, so we will not be given women."

Firefly had a most pleasant laugh. "Nor will I be given any men. But yours is the Protestant view, I think—although the Catholic view is somewhat similar."

"*E.* No matter the interpretation of their book, why should *they* be the ones who possess the truth? Perhaps it is *our* witch doctors and *our* elders who should be instructing *them* in the path of the unseen world."

"*Aiyee!* Enough of this foolish talk, my friend. I, for one, am not about to give up my unimaginable riches."

Jonathan Pimple smiled and grunted his agreement. He was all for unimaginable riches; too bad that they were not promised for this life. He had a secret desire to study medicine at the university in Brussels. Even if the Belgian government sponsored him, the cost for "incidentals" was staggering. In fact, Jonathan Pimple had never even heard of most of the items: *deodorant, toothpaste, shaving cream*—the list went on and on.

"So then let us now examine this bit of flesh that you have stolen from the white man," Jonathan Pimple said.

Although he had spoken lightly, with amusement in his voice, Firefly was much aggrieved. "No! Do not say that I have stolen this," she cried. "It was merely borrowed."

Jonathan Pimple took the wafer from her trembling hand and held it up to the sun. "This does not resemble the white man's flesh that I ate," he announced.

Firefly gasped softly. "Tell me more, Jonathan Pimple."

"I was just a boy, Firefly, I remember very little. But it was the same as eating any other kind of meat that walks on the earth or flies through the air. Only fish is different—fish and insects."

"I am a *Muluba*, Jonathan Pimple; my tribe does not eat the flesh of others. There must be a reason for that fact." She laughed her pleasant laugh. "Ah yes! There are many more *Baluba* than there are *Bapende*. Perhaps that is the reason!"

Jonathan laughed as well. "That would be a result, not a cause, Firefly. Besides, we never ate members of our own tribe; we only ate captives taken during war, or people that we captured who were trespassing in our territory—and that includes the white man."

"*E.* Tell me, confidentially, does a white man taste differently than a black person?"

The truth was not nearly as much fun to say as a good story, and probably not what she wanted to hear anyway. Therefore, without any guilt whatsoever, Jonathan Pimple gave in to temptation.

"A white man is very bitter to the tongue." He shuddered dramatically. "He is like a tart, unripened guava. One must add the juice of ten long stalks of sugarcane to the pot, or he is virtually inedible. Salt as well."

"Salt?"

"*Eyo.* Salt intensifies the flavor of all that it is added to, and in addition to being bitter, the white man is essentially flavorless. What little flavor he possesses can be accessed only with salt. But never be fooled by the leg made from wood, for it will leave splinters in your mouth."

"*Kah?*"

It was a story that had been a favorite of his when he'd been a small child. He had heard it many times, and he had always assumed it was true. Then again, perhaps like many other tribal tales, this was a story, the value of which was in the entertainment—and not because it contained some great eternal truth.

"A great many years ago, long before I was born, a white man—a great explorer—"

Firefly clapped her hands, which were long and delicate, despite being rough from her toil as a wife who performed her chores well. "Wait! How can this be? This has been our land since even before the great flood; at no time has a white man set foot on even as much as a grain of sand that has not been seen by one of our people."

"*Bulelela,* Firefly." Truly. "Nonetheless, that is the title by which this man went. When he was taken captive by my people and shown the pot in which he would be cooked, he became very much afraid."

"It is only natural," Firefly said.

Jonathan Pimple pretended his face was carved from wood. Firefly had a soft heart, which meant she would make a good mother, but she already had a husband. For her sake—and for his—he would be careful to remember that.

"Yes, fear is natural, but at that point some men in that situation simply give up; they cry out for mercy as if they were—"

"Women?"

"*Kah!* Small children! Or else they struggle until their last breath, which is most unfortunate, as it causes nodules to form in the muscle tissue and gives the meat a most unpleasant taste. It is the same with pigs."

Firefly looked up at him with wide, innocent eyes. "*E,* it is so with pigs. My father beat me once for running too close to a sow that was tied beneath our mango tree. Truly, the meat was full of nodules, and I was beaten again and again."

"Now what was I about to say—yes, this man behaved in neither of these two ways; instead he smiled! Yes, Firefly, you heard me speak the truth! This white man smiled and then asked the chief to cut off his leg"—he gestured—"right here, just below his manhood. Not only that, but the white man indicated that the chief must cut the leg off right through his pants!"

"*Aiyee!* But that is such a waste of good pants! If this happened as long ago as you said, it must have taken a tailor a very long time to sew them. Perhaps the *machine* for sewing was not yet discovered by this time."

Jonathan Pimple was deeply offended. "Do you mock me, Firefly? Ask around to the other Bapende in this village, for I am sure that you will find more than a few who have heard the story of the white man's leg that tasted of wood."

Firefly gave him her full attention. "Was it of a different flesh? One that tasted of wood?"

"*Eyo;* it was in fact wood. Just like that tree over there, so that no matter how long it cooked, wood it remained. Then the chief ordered the white man stripped of his clothes and it was discovered that his second leg was indeed real flesh—such as that of a human, but belonging to a white. Then the white man confessed that his leg had suffered disease and had been removed and replaced by the wooden one."

"Was the chief angry to be deceived in this manner?"

"No, the chief was a simple man and he marveled at the stunt. In the end, he let the white man go free."

"And what would you have done, Jonathan Pimple?"

He shrugged. The chief had lost face, had he not? And what business did a white person have in Bapende territory anyway except to look for slaves, or perhaps force new beliefs upon the people. Besides, a one-legged white man had no chance of surviving on his own. Would not even a white man prefer a few quick whacks of a machete over being mauled by a lion?

He was still thinking over his answer when the sky opened and began to dump the first rain of the season on the residents of Belle Vue's workers' village. It was the likes of which no one had ever seen. Jonathan Pimple and Firefly parted without speaking another word.

Those white residents of Belle Vue *not* invited to the Cabochon dinner party were missing out on an occasion as grand as anything the town had ever seen. That is the mantra Madame Cabochon repeated to herself as preparations for the evening went from bad to worse, and then descended into the realm of disaster.

Rain was to be expected during suicide month, but the lightning that accompanied this storm blew out the transformer that supplied electric power to the homes on the European side of the river. Not even a year earlier Madame Cabochon had, in a great show of modernity, been the first housewife in town to dispose of her wood-burning stove in favor of an all-electric model. One could not be any more modern than that!

When her new electric stove stopped working, Madame Cabochon had an undercooked pork loin in the oven, two pans of yeast rolls yet to bake, potatoes to boil, and vegetables to simmer— completing dinner was impossible! *Impossible!* What was she to *do*? She couldn't ask anyone for help; none of her nearby neighbors had been invited.

However, Monsieur Cabochon, who had at first been against the idea of entertaining a clergyman, turned out to be surprisingly helpful. He drove his half-German derriere over to the Club Mediterranean, where he drank Johnnie Walker Red by the light of a Pullman lantern.

There were two things Madame Cabochon did not lack: a sense of drama, and—as a Jewish friend of hers back in Co-quilhatville once described it—chutzpah. When the guests were dropped off under the portico that evening by their uniformed chauffeurs, they found their car doors opened by a colossal Suda-nese man dressed in a starched white jacket bearing gold epaulets. His left earlobe sported a large hoop that appeared to be gold as well. Appearances are everything, are they not?

This giant ushered the guests to French doors that were opened by a pair of servants, similarly outfitted. Only then did one get a glimpse of the divine Madame Cabochon, arrayed in a swirl of pink chiffon that was more toga than it was gown, and which was held together by antique cameos, some spit, and a bit of luck. As to the whereabouts of Monsieur Cabochon: it was murmured that he had crossed the river to deliver some much-needed medicines to some poor child stricken with malaria. At any rate, continuing the grand deception that this was a grand evening—one for the record books, even—was the fact that every candle in the house was lit, and every kerosene lamp and lantern pressed into service.

Somewhere—perhaps it was at her Swiss finishing school—the hostess had learned a little decorating tip involving alumi-num foil. When used as a backdrop for candles, it multiplied their presence, and so although the metal wrap was scarce as snow in the jungle, and had to be ordered months in advance, Madame Cabochon used every roll she had and turned her dining room into what she imagined the tsar's winter palace in Saint Peters-burg might have looked like—in miniature, of course—for a gala event. *Those* were but just two examples of Madame Cabochon's flare for the *dramatique*.

As to her legendary chutzpah—well, displaying that was just plain fun. Really, she had no choice, so why not pull out all the stops? The only item on her original menu that she could still serve was some canned baby green peas. These, however, would have to be served cold. Madame Cabochon, who had ever so cleverly hand lettered ten paper menus, gently folded some *real* mayonnaise, a bit of chopped red onion, and some thinly sliced celery into the legumes and served them atop leaves of fresh Bibb lettuce. She titled this dish: *Petits Pois Americains.*

"*Alors,* Mademoiselle Brown," said the OP, Marcel Fabergé, without either a hint of playfulness or irony, "how does Madame Cabochon's interpretation of this dish compare with the way it is prepared in your native America?"

The OP was a swarthy little Walloon—a French-speaking Belgian—with a neck like a sink drain, and ears that stood at right angles to his head, and with cartilage so thin as to be translucent. A more ridiculous-looking little man for the job, Madame Cabochon could not imagine. Yet there was something crafty about this man—perhaps even devious—that kept all his European employees on their toes. That was the only reason he'd been included on the evening's guest list. One wouldn't want to snub this OP, no matter how much one despised him.

Madame Cabochon was just opening her mouth in order to prevent the missionary from answering when the question was answered for her. The plain young American, who was seated beside the OP, touched his arm lightly and flashed him a toothy smile. Those Americans were all teeth: strong, straight white teeth that they were quick to display frequently, and almost arrogantly, as if it were their birthright.

"My compliments to the chef," she enthused. "In America, especially in the South, this is a very popular dish. My grandmother—may she rest in peace—was famous for her pea salad, but I must say, Madame Cabochon's is even tastier."

Madame Cabochon beamed.

"*Salad?*" said the OP. "So this is merely a salad, and not some fancy national dish?"

"Marcel," whispered his wife. She was seated across the table from him, and unless she was able to reach far enough with her foot to kick him in the privates, she was essentially quite powerless.

"No, no," Amanda Brown protested, her face growing Contadina red. "We most definitely do call it American-Style Peas. It's in all the cookbooks and everything." She turned to Madame Cabochon. "I just love your table decorations. They are so clever—what with the foil reflecting back the candlelight. It looks so professionally done."

As much as Madame Cabochon hated to do so, she knew there was wisdom to be had in making a public show of civility to the Philistine from the New World. Imagine that, a woman born and bred in Africa looking down her nose at an American! But yes, that was exactly the case. Madame Cabochon may have been reared in the Congo, but she was descended from good *European* breeding stock, and she had been to finishing school in Switzerland. She was cosmopolitan in her outlook. She had a worldview, and she was no longer a virgin. That about said it all.

That and the fact that she simply could not stand that the mousy missionary seemed to have instantly captured the heart of Belle Vue's most eligible bachelor, a man who was unquestionably a heartthrob. Of course, Madame Cabochon was nobody's fool; she didn't for a minute envision a future with the uneducated police chief. The man had no ambition, no plans to advance himself. What's more, he probably wanted a family, whereas the very idea of babies made Madame Cabochon's skin crawl—at the very least babies gave one stretch marks and sagging breasts. Besides—and this was a closely guarded secret—Madame Cabochon was beyond the age of breeding.

"Mademoiselle Brown," the hostess said, expertly feigning warmth, "you have an interest in decorating, perhaps?"

"*Oui, madame.* Some of the furnishings at the Missionary Rest House are truly outdated. In fact, if I might speak frankly—"

"By all means," Madame Cabochon said. She was quite ready for a juicy bit of gossip; but then, who wasn't?

"The entire place could use a facelift."

"Facelift? *Qu'est-ce que c'est?*"

"*Mon Dieu,*" the OP moaned, "is there anything more dreary than two females discussing—how do you say—matters *domestique?*"

Then, much to Madame Cabochon's immense satisfaction, Monsignor Clemente came to life for the first time that evening. One moment he was barely more than a statue: cold to the touch, his eyes blank. He didn't seem to notice her at all, whereas the next moment he was all man. His chiseled features, made all the more handsome by the infusion of Latin blood, were wasted on a man of the cloth. What a pity!

"Perhaps we *should* talk about more serious subjects," he said in his educated British accent. He turned to Captain Pierre Jardin. "Last Thursday I learned from the talking drums that the great python hunter, Monsieur Lazarus Chigger Mite, had been murdered. Yet there seems to have been scarcely a word about it spoken in the white community, and no funeral that I am aware of. Was Monsieur Lazarus Chigger Mite a Protestant perchance?"

"He was not a Protestant," the American chirped. "He was a Roman Catholic."

Everyone turned to look at her, as if she could possibly know the answer. Then again, she was young, American, and potentially pretty—the three things that the men of Belle Vue valued the most, regardless of their vocation.

"How do you know this, Amanda?" Pierre asked. His mouth was still full of Madame Cabochon's cleverly prepared meal.

"Because the subject of Lazarus Chigger Mite's religion was discussed behind my woodshed the day he killed the great *muma.*"

"What is this *muma?*" asked the OP irritably.

"It is a Tshiluba word," Pierre said. "It means python—that's all."

"Then please, can we not stick to just one language at a time? It is enough that we must speak English tonight!"

"Marcel!" said his mousy wife, before clamping her hand over her mouth and looking down at her lap.

But Monsignor Clemente was favoring the American with a devilishly handsome, but much unappreciated, smile. "Mademoiselle Brown, what lies behind your woodshed?"

"My washstand, sir. You see, Cripple—she used to be my assistant housekeeper, but now she is in the family way—has a little business enterprise going on back there."

"She's a fortune teller," Pierre said, and winked broadly.

"No, sir, she is not! Why, that is against our Bible, and I bet that is even against y'all's!"

The monsignor's smile broadened.

Madame Cabochon smiled as well, but somewhat ruefully, and to herself. Clearly the monsignor hadn't had many dealings with the deceptively charming Americans known as "Southerners." They were a species unto themselves. That is exactly what made them so dangerous to European men; men were linguistically unequipped to spot the snares these women laid. A woman, however, didn't need a dictionary to interpret another woman's intentions, even an American's, because the game never changed.

A woman—herself excluded, of course—wanted a strong protector, and a provider for her children. It did not matter if he was a priest of the Holy Roman Church, because there was not a woman alive who did not believe she could change man's allegiance. A man, on the other hand, desired only two things: a fertile woman through whom he could pass on his seed, and someone with whom he could find sexual pleasure. These two aspects did not have to occur in the same woman by any means.

"For God's sake, mademoiselle," the OP shouted, "tell us what is going on behind your washing stand!"

Madame Cabochon glared at the OP. She had watched help-lessly as her father physically and mentally abused her mother. She had also been the victim of an older brother's bullying. When she was in third form and François in fifth, he and his friend Jacques once made her swallow a live grasshopper. He would often steal sweets—treats of any kind, really—and even money from their mother's purse and blame it on his sister. It was Madame Cabo-chon who took the beatings for that.

When she at last began to grow a woman's body, he pinned her to the bed one day in an attempt to rape her. Fortunately she was able to grab a pencil from the bedside table and stabbed him in the right eye, permanently blinding it. However, for the sin of disfiguring her father's "only heir," Madame Cabochon was sent to a convent in Elizabethville for a year, where she learned a life lesson that was to color her worldview from then on: there is no such thing as reality, only one's perception of the way things are.

The Belgian Congo, 1935

*T*he clever Mushilele did not translate the white man's words as they were spoken. The chief and his elders had been very generous with their gift of life, and it was not right that they should be repaid with insults. Besides, is not the bearer of bad news likely to be confused with the person, or persons, who really are responsible? Nevertheless, the clever Mushilele gave the boy a threatening look, as if to warn him never to speak of this matter to anyone on pain of death.

The clever man need not have concerned himself with trying to frighten a small boy. After the white man ran into the bush, in the black of night, he was not followed. Instead, the chief nodded to his drummers, and everyone present began to sing and dance.

It was a good time; it was a happy occasion. The younger twin's innocence had been restored, and those men seeking special attributes from the victim had been given a chance to feed on the corresponding limb or body part. Now it was only a matter of "wait and see." In the meantime, the drums would beat and the people would celebrate, for life was short, and every heartbeat was an occasion to celebrate.

"Uncork all the gourds of palm wine," the chief said. "We will feast *and drink until we are so drunk that we cannot hear the women conducting their celebration."*

It was then that the older twin realized just how much of a boy he still was, for he longed to be back in the village with the women and the other boys his age. Some of the men—he knew this from how they acted in the village—became mean-tempered and picked fights when they were drunk. A couple of them even sported nasty scars. And truthfully, the scent of his mother—wood smoke, breast milk, and sweat from a day in the manioc fields—these and others combined to tug at his heart and his eyes filled with tears.

He wandered to the edge of the light ring, and just a bit into the bush, because he felt queasy. He was the chief's son and would not bring shame to his father by throwing up in sight of the elders. Besides, he had just successfully completed his first tasting. If he was seen vomiting, would they tell him to eat again? If so, he would refuse! Then what would become of him? What would become of his weaker brother, who now still lay sleeping despite the great noise?

The Belgian Congo, 1958

The OP was a reasonable man. All Marcel Fabergé desired out of life was to make it through to the end as comfortably as possible. Wasn't that what any normal human being desired? Even the savages who worked for him? So what if in Marcel's case being comfortable meant retiring to a seaside villa in the south of France? Few men could say that they had worked harder than Marcel to get to where they were.

When Marcel was ten years old, his father, a Rom (a member of France's Gypsy community), sold the boy to a bricklayer. It wasn't a legal sale, of course, but it just as well might have been. It quite possibly saved Marcel's life, because although the lad was immediately put to work carrying bricks, eventually he was adopted and given the family name. When Europe's Gypsies, like her Jews, were rounded up by the Nazis and shipped off to be exterminated, nobody gave Marcel Fabergé a second thought. Okay—perhaps a second, and a third, but never more than that.

"Why is Uncle Marcel so dark-skinned?" That was a frequently asked question among each new crop of Fabergé children.

The Fabergés, you see, bred like rabbits; they were almost as prolific as the Flemish. Mama Fabergé, a great believer in Walloon efficiency, delivered her babies in litters—always twins or triplets—until eventually there were eighteen, including Marcel. All seventeen genetic heirs were male, and all seventeen eventually joined their father's construction firm: *Fabergé et Fils.*

As one might imagine, the boy couldn't wait to strike out on his own and become self-sufficient. And when he did, it was as if the Fates had been waiting and were all aligned and on his side. In scarcely more than a decade, the young man went from mail room clerk to operations manager in one of Africa's most lucrative diamond mines. That an abandoned Gypsy boy from such a large adoptive family could rise so quickly in his chosen profession, that of administrator for the Congo Mining Consortium, was a marvel for everyone in his working-class neighborhood back in Brussels.

But just because the OP had a working-class background, and pressed into his soul were ancient, long-forgotten memories of Mother India, these things did not make him in any way less a Belgian; and most certainly no less astute than his predecessor. There was, however, one huge difference between him and the miserable fool who had held his position before him; namely that Marcel Fabergé lacked the capacity to learn foreign languages while the aforementioned had possessed a moderate ability in that regard.

Now this American woman with her English that was not quite English was about to drive him crazy. "Mademoiselle," he roared again, "I demand that you tell me what is going on!"

"*S'il vous plaît, monsieur,*" Madame Cabochon said, wagging a finger at him as if he were a schoolboy, "your manners, please. No shouting at my table. This is a dinner party, not a flamenco performance! Now apologize at once."

How dare the bitch! Madame Cabochon was known for speaking her mind, but this—this flamenco reference was a racial slur. He'd never told a soul at Belle Vue about his Gypsy ancestry. Only his wife, Hélène, was privy to that information, and that little lemur had enough skeletons in her family tree to worry about. Besides, Hélène adored Marcel in her own way, and he her. If outsiders didn't understand the dynamics to their relationship, so be it.

Thank God then that Hélène screwed up the courage to defend him. "Forgive my English, please, for it is very poor. But it is my husband who is owed an apology," she said softly. "It is she who must make the forgiveness. Always he works very hard for the people of Belle Vue—European and African, and always they make for him only much trouble. Is that not so, Marcel?"

"Your English is fine," the American said, "and I am very sorry, sir, if I have I contributed to your distress."

"Do not be sorry," Madame Cabochon snapped. "When Monsieur Fabergé took over as OP, all the whites working for the Consortium were promised a raise. Ha! My husband's pay packet has not increased even by one franc! But the Africans—now that is a different story, is it not, Monsieur Fabergé?"

"My housekeeper is a wise woman," the American said quickly, picking up her story. "A *mumanyi*. The people come to her for advice."

"*Attention, mademoiselle*," said Monsignor Clemente, "a wise move on your part would be to stay clear of witchcraft."

"Oh, but Cripple is not a witch!"

"Is not her husband a witch doctor?"

"*Oui*, but not a very good one. In fact—Pierre, will you help me explain?"

This reliance, of the silly young missionary, on a Belgian police chief was as absurd as it was irritating. The OP was about to speak his mind—social consequences be damned—when someone knocked on the front door with such force that Madame Cabochon's very attractive derrière literally parted company from the chartreuse silk pad that covered the woven raffia seat of her chair.

* * *

The large golden brown eyes of Madame Fabergé also observed her hostess's dramatic reaction to the rapping at the door. Hélène Fabergé was a big admirer of Madame Cabochon, whom she thought of as strong—at least for a lady. Yes, Hélène was a keen observer of all the qualities that made up a lady, for like her husband, she too was a Gypsy. A *Roma*: it was a word meant to be spit from the lips of a real Belgian.

"*Garçon!*" Madame Cabochon barked to her head table boy, although everyone knew by now that his name was Weak Eyes. "Open the door."

"*Oui, madame.*"

Hélène expected to see Monsieur Cabochon stagger through the massive French doors, for he was a known drunkard. Instead, she had the pleasure of being utterly shocked by the sight of a very drunk villager: the headman! After all, there were so few things that were truly amusing in this staid little European enclave. One would have thought that a gathering of expats so far from home would be living it up.

Well, that was certainly not the case here, whereas it was rumored that in British East Africa, particularly Kenya, the whites were having the time of their lives. Already the exploits of Baroness Blixen and Denys Finch Hatton were legendary. Even certain male members of the British Royal Family were said to have availed themselves of their hard-drinking colonialists' most prized possessions.

Hélène Fabergé missed nothing of what happened that evening in Madame Cabochon's home. Hélène's eyes and ears recorded everything and imprinted the events on a mind as sensitive as celluloid film.

"What do you want?" Madame Cabochon had demanded of the uninvited visitor. She spoke in French, and it was quite clear from her tone that she had purposefully omitted the use of an honorific.

The headman swayed slightly as he slowly fixed his stare on Madame Cabochon. "*You* are what I want."

"Madame," said the OP. "You forgot to say *Madame.*"

The headman turned. "I did not forget"—he stopped, as if carefully searching through his bag of verbal insults—"*whitey.*"

"Get out of my house!" Madame Cabochon ordered. Now there was a lady worthy to be admired. Of course if you are just another dirty Gypsy, just about anyone was a step up on the scale—*c'est vrai?*

The headman didn't budge. "On the morning of Independence Day, this will be my house—oh yes, I can see that it is a fine one even from where I stand. And you, madame, will be my fourth wife. But you will not speak to me then like you speak to me now—unless you want a fine beating. Because if you sass me, madame, I will sit upon your neck, and beat you about your back and buttocks with a wire that will leave thick welts upon your skin."

Perhaps a lesser Belgian housewife would have backed off at this point. It is doubtful, however, that a prewar Gypsy woman would have even flinched; but Nazis had been just as successful in their campaign in exterminating the Gypsies as they had been in getting rid of the Jews. Most Romany these days tried to remain in the background as much as possible. This translated to accepting their role as second-class citizens, so of course Madame Fabergé said nothing. She even lacked the courage to talk back to an African.

"You do not frighten me," Madame Cabochon said, although her tone might have been interpreted as saying something altogether different. "Because now we Belgians are still in power. Unlike many of my fellow whites I try to be fair in my dealings with you Congolese—go ahead, ask my houseboys—but you, monsieur, you are nothing but a savage."

"And you are a whore!"

Mon Dieu! Hélène saw the vein in the police captain's temple begin to twitch as he squirmed in his seat. She fancied she saw the hate streaming out of the savage's eyes. She sensed from her husband's heavy breathing that his blood pressure was climbing to dangerous levels. The monsignor, however, sat expressionless and absolutely still, like a buddha in a black silk dress.

When Madame Cabochon rose to her feet, she was magnificent. "For the last time, monsieur, get out of my house!"

It was only then that the three so-called white men—cowardly little boys all of them—had the nerve to also stand and square their shoulders. As for the American girl—pff!—always so entitled they feel, no? She remained seated as if she were the queen of *L'Angleterre*.

"I have changed my mind," the headman roared. "I do not want you for a wife, only to take you as my woman. After that I will kill you—with a machete—chop, chop. But the young woman"—he pointed straight at the American, despite his drunken state—"she will be my next wife. But the other one; she is not so white. I will take her as my woman and then pass her around. Maybe then we will chop, chop, chop."

Hélène screamed.

Only then did the pitiful European men advance on him, but the headman managed to escape into the darkness and rain, leaving only the stench of palm beer behind.

The Belgian Congo, 1935

*I*t happened so quickly that the boy did not have time to scream. So dark was the night, however, that his first thought was that the hand over his mouth belonged to the white man with the dark eyes and hair. But then he was lifted off the ground—plucked like a chicken hawk might seize a fledging from its nest—and literally carried some great distance from the men's camp. How far, he was never to know, but long before he was set down again, the sounds of celebration emanating from both the place of his abduction and his home village had long faded, and all he could hear was his own heartbeat and that of his abductor.

At last the man set him down in a clearing, but not before tying the boy's hands together behind his back, and then his feet. "Boy," he said in Tshiluba, "do you understand this language that I speak?"

"Eyo," the boy said, "for I am not a monkey like a Mushilele. Not only is Tshiluba the language of the Baluba and Bena Lulua, but of the entire region."

The man struck the boy, knocking him to the ground. "Perhaps it has not occurred to you that you are now my slave."

"I am a chief's son; I am no one's slave."

The Mushilele kicked the boy just under the sternum, knocking the breath out of him. The boy had once almost drowned in a small pond, his legs hopelessly tangled in water lilies. The feeling now was similar. His captor yanked him to a standing position again, which helped somewhat with his breathing.

"Do not think, boy, that you can win favor with me by acting brave. I know that you are only barely past the weaning stage, for I saw you cry for your baba, *and later I observed as you took no more than two sips—three at the most from that gourd—and then fell promptly to sleep."*

The boy said nothing in response, for he was much relieved to think that this Mushilele did not realize that he was a twin. The Bashilele, like the Bapende, did not suffer their twins to live. If his status as a twin were known, then he might not even be seen as fit for slavery. In that case—well, never mind; he would keep up the deception.

Still, he was deeply troubled by the revelation that this man had observed his twin brother crying. How long had they been watched, and by how many? What about the village? He knew that each Mushilele youth was sent out to retrieve an enemy skull at the time he wished to prove his manhood, but this Mushilele was a full-grown man. Plus, he intended to sell the boy into slavery, not use the boy's skull as his trophy drinking cup.

Could there have been an entire war party hiding in the thick bush surrounding the men's ritual camp? Were they at that very moment all being slaughtered? Then after the men were killed, the Bashilele were sure to invade the village proper and capture all the women and girls of breeding age—or soon to be of that age—and carry them off with them. The old, the infirm, and all male children would be summarily slaughtered. Even in the boy's eyes this was neither right nor wrong; this was the way things were—the way things had always been, although that did not make it any easier to think that you might never see your mother and twin brother again, unless you ended up in the same village

*someday as a slave. Or perhaps you might even have to wait until you
entered the spirit world to be reunited with your family.*

*But he must stop thinking, because his Mushilele captor seemed ca-
pable of reading his face just like his father could read the paw prints
along the marsh.*

The Belgian Congo, 1958

Cripple wrinkled her nose. "Their Death," she said, "I smell the approach of much trouble."

Their Death grunted. As was often the case at night, especially those nights when the kerosene lantern had to be lit, Their Death's thoughts left his head to enter a book. Once inside the book Their Death's thoughts would journey to faraway places, sometimes even over the Great Water to the white man's land known as *Mputu* in the Tshiluba language (although no one is quite sure why it is named thus). Perhaps it is a corruption of the word *Portugal,* although it also means "a child born just after twins." Change the word to *mputa* and it becomes an "ulcer," a "weeping abscess."

Cripple loved it when Their Death read to her aloud from his books, when he would take her along on his mental journeys, but as of late he had begun to read at an exceedingly slow pace. Like a snail his eyes moved across the page. The problem was that the source for these special books, the ones that were capable of taking Their Death and Cripple on journeys far beyond Kasai District, this source was no longer available to Their Death.

If one guessed that the source had been a bookstore or a library, one could not have been further from the truth, for such a thing did not exist at Belle Vue—certainly not for the Congolese. No, the source had been a white man, a Belgian, but he had come to no good.

This Belgian supplier of books, who was also the postmaster, admitted to having another man as one would have a woman—if one could imagine such a thing. But that was not all; this man also attempted to steal a very large diamond from Their Death's hand. The only thing that prevented this from happening was that Their Death wears a very strong potion around his neck. The heathens claim that this potion is even stronger than the *luhingu* fetish of the dead man called Jesus that the Roman Catholics wear around their necks.

"Their Death," Cripple said again, "even as this boy, Huckelbelly Finn, and his *Lulua* friend, Niggelo Yimma, must tie up their watercraft for the night, so must we stop with our story, because we are surely about to receive visitors. Even now they enter our compound."

And it was so. A moment later six sodden heads, atop six dripping bodies, crowded around the fire, each vying for a position that offered warmth without smoke. Although strictly speaking that could not be said of the baby, Amanda, as he was too young to be vying for anything except for a position at his mother's breast. However, his mother, Second Wife, did enough shoving and pushing for the two of them. Cripple had to remind herself that her sister wife was ever so much younger than herself; otherwise, she might have been rightfully cross at the sight of a mother treating her own children so badly.

It was difficult enough just to lay eyes on the woman she had once regarded as competition for her husband's affection. *Eyo*—truly, now that Cripple was heavy with child, the fire of envy that had once burned within her belly with so much intensity was now squelched. And with the child growing within her, it would be nice to have help with the work after the baby was born. However, the past two months without a sister wife and five children underfoot had ranked among the happiest in Cripple's life. Cripple would have liked few things more than to order Second Wife and her pushy brood back into the rain, and back to their uncle's village where they ultimately belonged. The only thing she wanted more than that was Their Death's happiness.

Their Death, as usual, could sense when she was thinking about her competition. "Brings Much Happiness," he said, naming his oldest daughter, "have you noticed your Elder Mother's *difu*?" He meant, of course, her stomach.

The girl, whose hair was a tight sponge still streaming water, leaned around a younger brother to get a better look at Cripple. The already wet boy got even wetter, whereupon he slapped his sister. Although Brings Much Happiness was only nine years old, the child had passed across the threshold that separates little girls from big girls, and big girls, she knew, could not slap their brothers. Brothers were male, and one did not hit a male. Those who must ask why were either stupid and with broken jaws, or they were dead.

"*Kah!*" the girl cried when at last she could discern the bump that had grown in Cripple's belly during her absence. "Is my Elder Mother with child?"

"She is with a large fish," Cripple said.

The children all snickered, even Brings Much Happiness.

"Do not joke about this," Their Death said sternly. "In my practice I once put a curse on a woman, telling her that the child would be born without limbs like a snake, and it would have scales and a forked tongue."

"*Aiyee*," Second Wife said. "Their Death, dare you tell us if the child did indeed emerge as a snake?"

Their Death poked the fire, prolonging the drama. "*E*, I will tell you."

The children shivered, and it was not from the cold. Sometimes Their Death went too far in his storytelling. Scaring little ones was not the purpose of his job.

"Enough," Cripple said. "You," she said to Second Wife, "help take off their clothes and hang them on the smoking rack. And you," she said to Their Death, her tone softening—both out of deference and devotion—"try to find some dry firewood from the stack up under the south eave."

Second Wife's dark eyes seemed to lock on Cripple's for just long enough to make the smaller woman uncomfortable. Although Cripple hated confrontations, she knew that it was vital for her unborn child that she maintained her position as Number One Wife.

"What is it?" she said.

"Only that it is good to be home."

"*E*," Cripple grunted. Yes.

"You have been a most generous friend, Cripple. We laugh and we cry."

"There is no need to express gratitude, for we are sisters, are we not?"

Their Death smiled happily when he heard this. It was too bad then that he obediently went out to search for dry firewood and did not hear Second Wife speak what was really on her mind.

"There is a new saying written on the walls of Luluabourg," she said, sounding conspiratorial—like a true sister might sound.

"Tell me!" Cripple said eagerly.

"They say that a woman who works outside the family compound should not eat food prepared in her absence, lest it be poisoned."

"*Baba!*" cried Brings Much Happiness. *Mother!* But it was Cripple whom her thin arms embraced, not Second Wife.

"It is also written," Second Wife said, "that she who relies on another woman to wash her clothes might die from the bite of a snake that has been tucked deep inside a sleeve or a pant leg."

"*Yala*," shouted Oldest Boy, whose fear of snakes was unmatched by anyone in all of the Belle Vue workers' village.

One would not mock the lad if only they knew that at the age of four he had been bitten by a mildly poisonous variety of tree snake that had caused him a great deal of discomfort by blocking his airways, and that he had nearly died. At any rate, despite the fact that Cripple's arms were quite full, and Oldest Boy was ten years old and thus very nearly a man, he still managed to wedge himself into his Elder Mother's embrace.

Everyone knows that little children are like baby monkeys and will imitate whatever they see. Still, it must have been difficult for Second Wife to watch Baby Amanda and the other two children try to follow their older siblings' example. One must give credit to Second Wife for holding her tongue as much as she did, and of course Their Death cannot be blamed for laughing as hard as he did when he returned to find his entire family—but for Second Wife—clumped together like a swarm of bees around his beloved.

"What is it?" Their Death asked before throwing down the wood.

"The children thought they heard a leopard," Cripple said.

"Is that so?"

"*Eyo, Tatu*," they chorused.

Their Death laughed.

"But, *Tatu*," Brings Much Happiness said, "one does not hear a leopard; it hears us. Also, leopards hate the rain even more than we do."

"*E*, you are a clever girl," Their Death said, and he laughed again.

"Too clever," Second Wife said.

"How is that?" Their Death asked.

Second Wife would not answer his question easily; nor would Cripple. It worried Cripple that their eldest daughter might be made to pay for the fact that she had been born with a pleasing nature and utterly without guile. Perhaps such people did indeed make good

Christians, but they did not make good heathens, and in the dangerous world of today, one needed every advantage just to survive.

Madame Cabochon despised interruptions of any kind. It wasn't because she possessed an impatient personality; au contraire, Madame Cabochon was really quite agreeable. It was simply the fact that people who interrupted were by and large rude, and circumstances that necessitated interruption were invariably unpleasant. Case in point, no sooner had the drunken headman stumbled out into the rainy night than the entire house shook.

"Bombs!" cried Hélène Fabergé as she slipped out of sight under the table.

"Get up," her husband, Monsieur OP, said. "Don't be such an ass. This isn't Brussels; it's the Congo. And this isn't 1944; it's 1958—the age of Sputnik!"

"No, no!" The poor woman was hysterical.

There, you *see* what a war can do to someone? If only Monsieur Cabochon has been home to witness that, instead of being at the company club getting drunk yet again. That's all anyone ever did in Belle Vue when they weren't working, and some did it when they were working—this is to say, tip back a bottle of Johnnie Walker Red, or Black. Anyway, Monsieur Cabochon might have been be just half German, but he had a full-blooded Nazi heart, and Colette Cabochon hated him as much as she hated interruptions.

And since Madame Cabochon despised bullies even more than she despised interruptions, she kicked Monsieur OP on the shins as best she could. Too bad she was wearing sandals.

"It felt like an earthquake to me," the American girl said.

Handsome Pierre Jardin wasted one of his perfect smiles on her. "Do you have many earthquakes in Stone Hill?"

"I am from *Rock* Hill—Rock Hill, South Carolina. The earthquake I felt was in California."

"I too have experienced earthquakes," the monsignor said, dabbing at the corners of his moist, full lips with a heavily starched and crisply ironed serviette. He rose to his full magnificent height and then casually tossed the serviette on the table. "*Mesdames et messieurs,*" he said, "it is unsafe to stay indoors during an earthquake. Come, we must go outside."

"Don't be ridiculous," the OP snarled.

You see? He was an impossible little man. It was no wonder that all his employees hated him. It was too bad that Marcel Fabergé was hiding some exotic ethnic secret behind his hard-bitten features, because Colette Cabochon didn't harbor a racially biased bone in her body. In fact, she'd given up her virginity at age fifteen to a light-skinned mulatto in Coquilhatville in a short-lived and ill-advised love affair that might well have cost the married father of three his life. If only the OP could be . . .

"*Mamu! Mamu!*"

It was her cook. The poor fellow was so terrified he'd forgotten to speak French. Lucky for him she knew Tshiluba.

"I am already gone, *Mamu,*" he said. *Nakuya.*

I am already gone. It was a construct that never failed to amuse anyone who had not been born to the language. Its meaning, however, was deceptively simple: *I've already stepped outside—if only in my head—so don't try to call me back in, if even just for one more task.*

"Wait!" she yelled through cupped hands. "Stop!"

Both time and guests seemed to freeze in place until at last the cook stepped into the room. Whereas normally Colette would have expected to see the man scowling from ear to ear, so frightened did he look now that she instantly felt as if she were abusing her authority.

"*S'il vous plaît,*" she said, "tell me why it is that you wish to leave so suddenly."

"*Mamu,* it is the Island of Seven Ghost Sisters."

"What about the island?" Colette said.

The cook glanced wretchedly at the monsignor before answering in perfect, although heavily accented French. "It was predicted that the spirits of the seven women would rise together and begin to dance in unison, and when that happened, a piece of the island would break away and that they—the seven women—would ride it back to their village landing."

"Yes, I am familiar with this heathen legend," snapped the monsignor. "Get on with it, boy! And speak French, so that the new OP and his wife may also understand."

Boy? Although her parents had called their servants "boy," Colette did not. It wasn't because she was a bleeding-heart liberal, either, as the Americans would say. By and large Congolese servants were grown men, or at least older teenagers, often married, who had achieved the rank of manhood in their tribes and, as such, deserved respect.

Cook's name was Tshiabo, which means Born-After-Much-Groaning. The look he gave the monsignor signified that he knew his place. Colette, however, who was familiar with her employee's (and dare she believe, friend's?) features, and the way he held his mouth, could see that he was going to great lengths to mask a simmering rage.

"Master," said Born-After-Much-Groaning, "a large piece of the Island of Seven Ghost Sisters has broken away in this storm. Even now it floats downstream to the bridge. If you step out onto the magnificent verandah of my mistress's house, then you might yet see some of it sail by. It is said that when it reaches the great waterfalls of Belle Vue—known to us simply as Mai Manene—it will take the bridge over the falls with it."

"This is outrageous," the OP roared. He reminded Colette of the American cartoon character Steamboat Willie that she had seen many times as a cinema short—well, he would be Willie, if you gave the mouse a lion's voice. The Consortium better face it: sooner rather than later, this little man was not going to work out at all.

"That bridge was built by American engineers," Captain

Jardin said. "It can withstand anything. Dancing maidens are not going to tear it down, I assure you."

The house shook again. Perhaps the maidens were trying to prove Pierre wrong—or perhaps it was an earthquake. What difference did it make? Madame Cabochon was not going to spend another second listening to silly suppositions. She fumbled about for her golden sandals, and not finding them instantly available, ran barefoot from the dining room and out onto the wraparound verandah.

She was just in time to see a tree the size of a freighter bob past on the boiling red current. It was no longer raining, and already the cloud cover was rolling back to reveal a sky illuminated by a blaze of celestial lights. Without the competition supplied by electricity, the starlight would have been bright enough to give Colette a rare, unimpeded nighttime view of the Island of Seven Ghost Sisters, except that the island was no longer there!

"*C'est vrai, c'est vrai!*" she shouted.

"What is true?" The monsignor was the first to reach her. She felt his strong arm around her shoulder and wished that she could crumble in his arms, like she had seen women do in the cinema.

Instead, Colette shrugged off the caring arm of her childhood friend before anyone else could see them and pointed due south. She would play the part of the strong heroine in her own film.

"There! In the middle of the river, we should be seeing a line of inky blackness that is the forest on the Island of Seven Ghost Sisters. You can always see it when the stars are out, or when the moon is full, but tonight—tonight, look! Nothing! Just water and more water. It's like the whole island has been washed away."

"This is incredible," the monsignor said.

By then they had been joined by everyone in the dinner party, which of course meant that the swarthy little OP was there with his ill-formed opinions. "I'll wager that it wasn't even a proper island," he said, "but one of those floating hyacinth rafts that I read about in the papers. Apparently they can be dense enough to support vegetation."

"Let us not speak of dense things," the American girl said in her clumsy French. "Anyone can see that the Island of Seven Spirits is real."

A thrill ran up Madame Cabochon's spine. *Oui*, the girl was not exactly ugly, and therefore she *was* competition, but she was also interesting. There were so few things of interest at Belle Vue these days that didn't involve politics and the pending implosion of the colonial world into which she'd been born. The arrival of an American rabble-rouser—what did they call them in the South—Rebels? Well, at least one good thing had come out of her dinner party.

"The word is *ghosts*, mademoiselle," the OP's wife said. "Not *spirits*."

"Thank you for your correction, madame," the American said. "I did not know the word. However, I do know that the island is real. My housekeeper has been there."

"*What?*" The question was voiced by many, for it was common knowledge that the island was the domain of large Nile crocodiles and angry mother hippos.

The American was not shy when called upon; Madame Cabochon would give her that.

"Cripple—that's the assistant housekeeper I was telling you about—well, she is a heathen," the American said.

"A heathen," Madame Cabochon said, relishing the word. If only one had the choice to be a heathen! Ah, think of the fun!

"You should fire the woman," the monsignor said. "Her beliefs could contaminate the rest of your staff."

Madame Cabochon tried not to smile. "*Contaminate?* Do you mean like an infection?"

"*Oui.*"

"Go on with your story, Amanda," Pierre said softly.

"Uh—when my housekeeper was a girl, just about to become a woman, she was taken to this island in a boat along with many other girls. There they were kept for many months and taught dances that were sure to drive men into madness."

"This is madness," Monsieur OP said.

"Amanda," said Pierre gently, "do you mean 'insane with desire'?"

"Yes, that is it! Thank you."

"*Alors,*" snorted the OP, "perhaps she should say so!"

"We used to hunt hippos out there during the dry season," the monsignor said, sounding wistful. "It became a rite of passage for every white boy growing up here at Belle Vue."

"Why?" Madame OP asked. "Do hippos make good eating?"

"They do, actually. But we didn't eat them. We shot them because they were there, and shooting them was fun. Did we need another reason?"

"No, of course not," Amanda said.

"Imbeciles!" cried Madame Cabochon.

"Look here," Monsieur OP said angrily, "you have no right to judge—"

But Madame Cabochon was not about to be lectured by the latest runt to be sent out from the Consortium's main office in Brussels. She gathered up some of the excessive material of her hot pink palazzo pants in each hand and agilely jumped up onto the low brick wall that ran along the edge of the sweeping verandah.

"My friends," she said without further ado, "let us not remain here and discuss the morality of shooting animals for sport. Just minutes ago I saw a tree the size of this house floating downriver and headed for the bridge. We all felt the shocks, we heard about the legend, and we can all see for ourselves what appears to be open water where an island once stood. That said, I am leaving at once for the bridge to see for myself what is happening. Is there anyone who would like to come with me?"

There was a unanimous show of hands; even the tiny brown Madame OP's hand shot into the air.

"I'll drive," Monsieur OP said officiously. What a pompous so-and-so.

"Don't be stupid—er, precipitous," Pierre said. "I will drive. The road could be just a series of undercut gullies, and it would be very easy to tip over. It is best that all of you ride in the truck now that it has stopped raining."

The OP snorted, his pigeon chest still ridiculously extended. "Will we have to ride in the back—like animals? Like *Africans*?"

Madame Cabochon wished to push the OP off her verandah. With luck he would land on a slippery patch of lawn and slide all the way down into the rain-swollen Kasai River as it tore through the moonlight landscape like a giant python.

The Belgian Congo, 1935–1942

The boy was sold as a slave to a rich fat man of the Bajembe tribe. As there were very few fat or rich men in the Belgian Congo at this time, except for Europeans and Arabs, this Mujembe was quite famous. It was the boy's job to attend to the man's personal needs—a most unpleasant and unhygienic job—and as a result the boy was often ill. Whenever he could not perform his duties satisfactorily, the chief's son was beaten within an inch of his life with the hippo hide (which was also the white man's favorite means of dispensing punishment),

One day, six or seven years after the boy's abduction, two soldiers—one tall, the other short—from the Bula Matadi paid a visit to the fat man's village. Upon spotting the boy, the tall soldier called out to him.

"Boy! Why are you not working for the state?"

"I must work for my master," replied the boy.

"Leave him alone," growled the fat man. "Can you not see that he is just a small boy? Besides, he is my son—the son of my third wife."

"This boy is no Mujembe," said the short soldier, "and he is no small boy either. Raise your arms," he said to the boy.

"Do not do as he says," the fat man commanded.

"If you do not raise your arms," the tall soldier said, "I will shoot this fat man through the belly and then he will die an agonizing death."

"I am a slave," the boy said, "and this fat man is my master. Shoot him first, and then I will raise my arms."

Bulelela. *Truly. This is what the soldiers did, for they were of the Bakongo tribe and they had no use for Bajembe people, and besides, they had taken a liking to the boy. Then after they shot the fat man, the boy raised his arms, and it was plain for all to see that he had hair and was indeed old enough to work for the state; they took him with them and he was taken to a place called Belle Vue.*

The Belgian Congo, 1958

All the living that dwelled in the workers' village had gathered
on the hill in front of the mango grove where the whites buried
their dead. It was a place forbidden to them unless they were there
to dig the graves or to fill them in again, or sweep away the ever-
falling leaves.

When the first Belgians came to take from the streams "the
stones that sparkled"—which was about seventy years ago—
nearly half of them died from a disease called malaria. It was a
disease that also struck Africans, but for them it was mostly a
children's disease. If one managed to survive childhood—and the
odds were slim—one might be able to build up enough immunity
to survive to adulthood.

The first Belgians who arrived in the vicinity of the present town of Belle Vue were for the most part men: prospectors,
miners, overseers, and a few priests. They lived down by the river,
close to the pits from which they extracted their precious stones.
When it rained, these same pits filled with water, becoming the
breeding ground of malaria-carrying mosquitoes.

One by one, as the white men died, they were carried by black men to the top of the highest hill around and buried. There they enjoyed, for all eternity, one of the best views in all of Kasai Province. Up there the breeze kept mosquitoes away and made it a very healthy place for the living to sit and visit these same dead. Since it was such a pleasant, scenic spot, the living ordered the black man to plant mango trees so that they might be shaded from the fierce tropical sun. Ah, what a fine place to spread a blanket and picnic—even to spend an entire day.

But not once during all those seventy years did the living ever consider claiming that healthy location as their own. Except for a small privy shack, no houses were ever built on the crest of that tall, majestic hill. All the while the white men continued to live down by the gravel pits where the mosquitoes bred because they would not be parted from their treasure, and one out of four of them would never leave Belle Vue alive. Meanwhile the Africans, who were forced to live across the river in the hills behind the cemetery, fared much better than the Europeans.

Later, when their womenfolk joined them, the white men acquired some *meshi*—sense—and moved across the river to hilltops opposite their dead. These hills were not as high, and not quite as healthy, but by then the white witch doctors had created potions that protected one against malaria, so that a greater percentage of the whites survived—enough of them, anyway, to form the village known as Belle Vue. Nonetheless, the whites continued to bury their dead on the highest hill around, even though now it was forbidden by law for any white to live there, except for missionaries.

The irony of the situation had not been lost on the young Kibanguist, nor on the headman from Léopoldville. Cripple, who was surely the most reasonable of all women, could not stand either of these two men. Therefore she watched with disdain and horror as the two of them made much fanfare for themselves by beating on a small drum and then leaping onto a flat rock that extended far out into the Kasai River. Before the rain, this rock had stood at the edge of the river and held its head high above the water. Now it lay so low that to some, depending on where they stood, it gave the appearance that the men were standing on the surface of the river. However, the scene gave only the *appearance* that such was the case; unfortunately, there were plenty of ignorant people who were willing to believe that indeed the two men could walk on water.

The two men had abandoned the drum, but the young Kibanguist was quite skilled at whistling through his fingers. Then he shouted through cupped hands, although still one had to strain to hear his words above the rumbling voice of the angry Kasai River.

"People of Belle Vue! Did I not predict a great storm that would wash away this bridge?"

"*Eyo*," many people responded, "you predicted the storm, and it came; in that your word has proven to be true. But the bridge is still here!"

"People of Belle Vue, behold—*tangila*—this bridge is but an illusion. Already the real bridge has been washed away. When Independence Day comes we will have a new bridge, one that will not have been built over the falls just for the white man's pleasure. The new bridge will be built upstream, where the water is quiet. It will be built in a peaceful location where the *baba*s and children can cross and not be afraid."

At that point many people clapped and cheered, for walking across the plunging torrent was a frightening experience for many of them, but something they had to do on a daily basis if they wanted to stay employed. Cripple hated using the bridge, but she resisted expressing her sentiments, because she knew that the Kibanguist was playing on their collective fear. Truly, that hate-filled man did not really care two bananas' worth about how they really felt.

The headman was wiser and older than the Kibanguist, and he was not fooled. "*Bulelela*," he said, "truly, what this man speaks shall come to pass, because when Independence Day comes, I shall remain your headman, and it will be me who sees to it that this new bridge is constructed." He quickly held up his hands as if to silence the applause, although there was none that Cripple could hear. "*My* people," said this man of the Bakongo tribe, and thus a foreigner to the region, "who do you suppose will build *our* bridge? Yes! Your thoughts are correct! It will be the white man. I personally will sit on the neck of the local Bula Matadi and give him a taste of his hippo hide whip!"

"*Aiyeeeee!*" the people cried in one voice, for there was not a man, woman, or child who bore in his heart animosity for Captain Pierre Jardin. Many were the Belgians who deserved to be flogged with the dreaded hippo hide, perhaps some until they could no longer even cling to life, but most assuredly this white man was not one of them. This time Cripple did join her voice with those of her people.

The headman's words were so outrageous that they angered even the spirits in the Original World, which is a heathen belief only. At any rate, these spirits sent a great crocodile to ensure that the good whites, like Captain Pierre Jardin and Madame Cabochon—and of course Mamu Ugly Eyes, even though she was not Belgian—were not harmed after Independence Day. So even as the people were still expressing their dismay, the huge beast leaped out of the water and caught up both of the outside trouble-makers in its jaws. The men emitted the most satisfying screams before disappearing into the dark waters of the Kasai River, and neither the reptile, nor the men, were ever seen, or heard from, again. Privately, Cripple felt quite satisfied; this was indeed a fitting way for these two men to rejoin their ancestors.

"We must be careful," a wizened old man rasped. "It was these dead white people on the hill behind us who sent this *ngandu*—crocodile—to eat the headman and the Kibanguist."

An equally old woman with a faded blue-and-orange turban elbowed her way to his side. Cripple recognized her as the man's wife, although she knew neither of them by name.

"You are but a crazy old man. There are only corpses to be found in the *Bula Matadi* cemetery, for no ghosts reside there. The whites are all Roman Catholic or Protestant, and when they die, their spirits leave the cemetery and journey to a place even farther away than *Mputu*. This place, which they call heaven, is so distant that the spirits cannot return. Thus the spirits of the whites cannot create mischief after death, as can the spirits of our dead. Is not this heaven a clever idea?"

There were many exclamations of wonder, which vexed Cripple sorely. "Do not believe this foolishness," she snorted, unable to control her temper, although she had tried mightily. "If no one has returned from heaven, then how can we be certain that this place exists? As for the white corpses that are rotting in those graves, do you not think it strange that only their dead may join us on this side of the river, but not their living?"

Their Death grabbed Cripple's elbow. "Cripple," he growled through clenched teeth, "you are only a woman. You must not express such strong ideas."

Their Death's wife would not be tamed like a wild pigeon. "But consider this," she said, speaking even louder than before, "at least the dead white men on the hill above us can no longer order any of us around—be it man or woman."

There followed a ripple of laughter, but mostly gasps and some cheers, for a tree the size of a white man's house was just meters away from crashing into the indestructible bridge. It was the bridge that both divided and united the two sides: the black and the white, the rich and poor, the past from the present.

"*Baba, kuata tshianza tshianyi,*" Brings Happiness cried out in a loud voice. *Mama, hold my hand!* It was Cripple to whom the child called, and to Cripple the child clung, not to Second Wife, whose belly had borne the child to a state of ripeness, and whose *bisuna*—vagina—had been torn practically asunder during her delivery.

Such is the ingratitude of a child, but truly, the gratitude of a Second Mother knows no bounds under such circumstances. The feel of Brings Happiness's small arms around her own swollen belly gave her strength, and she did not fear as she stood and observed those things the eyes had never seen, and therefore the mind could not understand.

The giant tree, the one as large as a white man's house, was now turned sideways at an angle, wedged between two of the massive pillars that held up the bridge. Half the tree's broad canopy projected above the water, and in the very uppermost of those branches sat a family of colobus monkeys. Rather than appearing afraid, the monkeys stared glum-faced at the villagers. After all, the colobus monkeys had been every bit as inconvenienced as the people; no, make that a great deal more.

"*Mona buhote buebe,*" Cripple said. *Look at your impudence!* For she was deeply offended by the monkeys' arrogance. Under normal circumstances the monkeys would be shrieking as they attempted to flee from arrows or bullets, because colobus monkeys were highly desirable prey animals. Not only was the flesh of these creatures delectable—when stewed in palm oil with a few chilies—but their beautiful long black-and-white fur was prized by tribal chiefs and kings, who used it to adorn their royal headgear. (But to speak of impudence: Mamu Ugly Eyes actually believed that monkeys bore a resemblance to human beings! Well, perhaps to the whites! But then, only *maybe*.)

"*Kah!*" Their Death said. "Cripple, you should not use such foul language in front of the children."

"*Tch,*" Cripple said. "But Their Death, did you not see how these animals insulted us? One large male even kept his back turned the entire time."

"Cripple," said Dikumbu, who was their neighbor, and a member of the Zappo Zapps tribe, "I did not see any monkeys; I saw only whites sitting in that tree."

Those who heard the Zappo Zapp—and there were many— roared with laughter.

But there was a white face among the crowd that stood on the hill in front of the place where the whites buried their dead. Cripple saw this man and recognized him as the priest of Saint Mary's Catholic Church. He was fluent in Tshiluba, but with a heavy accent, and his French was accented as well. Cripple was not familiar with the various nuances that distinguished the Belgian tribes (how could she be, since even the individuals within a tribe looked so much alike?), but there was something about the *mon père* that caused Cripple to think that he belonged to some minor tribe, perhaps something akin to the Zappo Zapps.

Now, it is one thing to laugh at the expense of many, when you yourself are few in number, but a good heathen is never unkind to the helpless. The *mon père* was alone and helpless—even if he did not know it.

Cripple pressed closer to strange man from *Mputu* (over there), whereas Brings Happiness shrank back in terror. The child of two heathen parents, and just one Protestant parent, Brings Happiness had had little occasion to interact with whites, and she had certainly never had any prior dealings with a white man in a dress.

"*Kah*," said Cripple, "he will not hurt you. He is a man like any other—and an old one at that. If need be, I will push him down and you can jump on his *mihesa*." His testicles.

When Brings Happiness did not so much as giggle, Cripple let the child go and approached the man alone. *Aiyee!* Everything she'd heard about him was true: his eyes bulged, his breath smelled of drinking, and his women's clothes stank of body odor so foul that Cripple thought she might throw up the evening's cassava mush.

"Life to you," Cripple said. She had to say it twice to be noticed, telling herself that it was not so much that the man was hard of hearing (he was that as well); it was that he did not expect a crippled little woman to speak to him in a way that did not portend begging.

"*E, muoyo webe,*" he finally said.

"Master," Cripple said, "you should not be disturbed by what these ignorant people say. You are not all monkeys; I know a white who is almost like a real woman."

The old man smiled, although Cripple had said nothing humorous. "Who are you?"

"My name is Cripple. I am a Muluba, master. I am also the wife of the Baluba witch doctor."

His smile disappeared. "So you are heathens?"

"Yes, master. I am a very proud heathen. Do you wish to try your hand at converting me?"

"Do you mock me, Cripple?"

"No, master."

"Then I do not understand this game that you play."

"It is not a game, master. Many people have tried to convert me to the Jesus way, but all of them have failed."

"Why is that?" he shouted, for it was necessary to communicate at that volume because of the noise of the crowd.

Cripple tried to shrug nonchalantly; as usual, it was wasted effort. Cripple had often thought about the matter in great depth. If she could have a normal body, like that of every other adult in the village, it would not be activities like running, jumping, or lying on the mat with her husband that she would try first; it would be strutting about and gesticulating like a truly angry woman.

"Some say that I am stubborn, master. Yet there are others who say that I am capable of thinking for myself."

"*Thinking?* You are not supposed to think, *Baba*. All you need to do is believe."

"Master, yet you do not believe the legends of our people."

Cripple had sometimes observed that her employer, Mamu Ugly Eyes, turned the color of ripe guava flesh when she was angry. Now in the moonlight she watched the priest's face turn dark with anger.

"*Baba*, you are possessed with demons."

"*Nasha*. I came to comfort you, a lonely and smelly foreigner in a woman's dress, and you repay me with insults! Is it no wonder—"

They were interrupted by a loud groan and a shaking of the ground so intense that it threw Cripple into the arms of the odiferous European. Surely such a deep and eerie noise was the sound of the earth giving up her dead as if in childbirth, and movement beneath her feet was that of a thousand hills shuddering in pain. Then the dead commenced to scream, and the hills began to writhe and shake violently. Such signs could only mean one thing.

"Behold, it is *you* who are possessed!" cried Cripple.

The priest pushed Cripple away, practically knocking her over backward. "*Me*? How dare you, a heathen, accuse me, a priest of the Holy Roman Church of being possessed? In the olden days I could have had you flogged."

Cripple was justifiably outraged. Their Death had often repeated comments such as this that had been said to him. But a woman of no account like herself—one who lived her life exclusively in the village—was not privy to these harsh pronouncements. And although Cripple had lately begun working for the young American *mamu*, the missionary was an unusually kind woman. Thus it was that Cripple's small body surged with adrenaline.

Cripple reared back as much as her twisted body would allow, so that she might lock eyes on the taller man. Her fingers were twisted as well, but that didn't stop her from wagging one in the white man's jowly face.

"You are a most ungrateful man," she said. "Yes, I am a heathen, but did I not send to you a man by the name of Jonathan Pimple so that you might convert him to your strange beliefs? Tell me, white man—for I will no longer call you master now that I know it is your wish to beat me—why it is that Christians, whether Catholic or Protestant, must pay money after they convert?"

Cripple saw that the priest's face registered intense emotion, and since she was not a spiteful woman, she felt compelled to offer soft words as well. "It cost not one centime to be a heathen," she said, "unless, of course, one needs the services of a good witch doctor."

But the priest did even smile. "You are the one who sent the Mupende man, Jonathan Pimple, to me?"

"*Eyo*. But let it be known that I do not approve of his taste in meat."

Again, the man from *Mputu*—the great afar—remained as impassive as stone. "Did he tell you *who* he ate?" he said, his voice barely louder than a whisper.

There was now much noise from the crowd standing on the hill in front of the place where the whites buried their dead. The gods of creation had denied Cripple a well-proportioned body, but one of the many ways in which they had compensated her for that act of cruelty was by giving Cripple an extraordinarily keen sense of hearing.

"He did not give me a name, *mua—na*," she said. She had caught herself just in time, and skillfully managed to change the word *master* into *child*. Surely the priest heard her, for she spoke loudly, knowing that he was old and that under the best of circumstances, one must speak Tshiluba slowly and loudly to the foreigners if one wishes to be understood.

But *if* the priest had taken offense, he showed no reaction. "Did this man, Jonathan Pimple, give you any details concerning the man he—*tch*—ate? Any details at all?"

Cripple could no longer look this white man in the eyes. Besides, his was a very unattractive face, as were his neck and hands, which were the only other parts of him not covered by coarse black cloth. This did not include the rest of his gray sweaty head, with the strange fine hair that resembled the down feathers of a mangy chicken, and which smelled just as bad. Based on what she could see, as hard as she tried, Cripple could not imagine eating any part of the Catholic priest, no matter how tasty the gravy in which he might be cooked.

"He was a white man," she said.

The impassive face of the priest, which had earlier been dark with the blood of anger, now gleamed in the moonlight. He was like a ghost—a *mukishi*—come from the burial place behind him to haunt her.

"Was he a Catholic priest?" He said this without moving his lips.

"*E,* he was a Catholic priest."

She watched, transfixed, as his thick hands, with fingers bent from age, clutched at his black dress. "How could he be sure? He was just a little boy!"

"I do not know, master. I only relate the words of Jonathan Pimple."

A soft moan escaped from his lipless mouth, but almost immediately the sound was drowned out by the sound of a thousand drums; it was the deep sound of hollow logs, the thumping of a thousand elephants, although Cripple had only ever seen one. The sound, the vibration—Cripple imagined that the heavens were being ripped from the earth, and that she was in danger of falling into the great nothingness in between. Such is what she imagined; what she did not imagine was the great roar of approval from the three thousand throats gathered on the hill in front of the place where the whites buried their dead.

Neither did she imagine seeing the last pillar of the bridge crumple and slowly give way. More important than that even, she quite clearly beheld Captain Jardin's truck, which had been racing across the bridge, take to the air like a francolin and fly across a gap that was at least twice its length. Upon landing, two of the tires exploded, but the truck did not come to a full stop until it was completely off the approach of the once mighty structure. By then there was both smoke and steam billowing from the engine, and the police captain was trying to get everyone as far away from the vehicle as quickly as possible.

When Cripple realized that one of the occupants of the blue

pickup was her employer, the American missionary Amanda Brown, she shrieked in protest to the gods.

"*Aiyee!* This young woman has done nothing to deserve your anger. She is kind and gentle. At the most she is simpleminded. Can you not take a cruel Belgian instead?"

Madame Cabochon sat on a wooden bench in the back of Pierre's pickup truck next to the monsignor. The young American sat opposite them, beside the OP and his wife. Pierre was indeed correct: the road was treacherous. The pretentiously named Boulevard de Roi, which was normally a wide dirt road with a flower-filled median, was now a brown river of mud crisscrossed by deep-cut channels. Despite Pierre's expertise as a bush driver, the rear passengers found themselves constantly thrown against each other.

So in the end, did it really matter who initiated what? Madame Cabochon could not help but gasp when the truck lurched, and Monsignor Clemente—half Italian that he was—could not help being gallant and placing a steadying arm around her shoulder, and perhaps giving her a reassuring squeeze from time to time. Besides, they were childhood friends, were they not? Not to the mention the fact that they were in a public place and in full sight of two very sour and disapproving faces, so there was absolutely not the slightest chance of an impropriety. And who should know better than a monsignor, who lived in Rome and was practically the pope?

When the truck lurched past the Club Mediterranean—where Monsieur Cabochon no doubt sat in a drunken stupor—Madame Cabochon, clenching the monsignor's hand so that she wouldn't fall, gave freedom to her voice. First she addressed her drunken excuse for a husband.

"You bastard," she raged. "When the revolution comes and our cook poisons us, you won't even get sick, much less die. You no longer have any blood in your veins; they bleed only Johnnie Walker Red."

She paused a minute, taking in the smell of an earth washed clean in the way that only the tropics can deliver; and the sound of a hundred *muntuntu*—the giant white crickets that were so tasty when cook sautéed them in palm oil; and the sight of a moon bigger than all of Belgium.

She swayed wildly before waving her free arm about, not unlike an American rodeo contestant. "And you Africans—you Congolese—just who do you think you are, telling *me* that I don't belong in the country in which *I* was born? This is where *I* grew in my mother's womb, this is where *I* took my first steps, this is where I was weaned from my mother's milk—these sounds, these smells, this night, these are all *mine,* just as much as they are yours! Yes, you will have to kill me, because you will not be able to drive me from this land on your own accord."

Then she made a fist. "And this is for you, Monsieur Communist Headman from Léopoldville! Come and get me; I dare you to! I will be waiting for you with my own machete; chop, chop, chop!"

Make no mistake, Madame Cabochon had a great deal more to say to the headman, but the steadying hand of the monsignor was also a restraining hand, and it yanked her down into the bed of truck. There, with her nose pressed so close to the floorboard (and in spite of the clean air rushing past), poor Colette Cabochon was privy to the lingering stench of decaying elephant meat. That too, make no mistake, was Africa.

"Don't be a fool," the monsignor growled. "Defiance is one thing; stupidity, quite another."

"My thoughts exactly," the OP said.

"Shut up," Madame Cabochon said, and popped back to her feet like a punching bag.

"My thought has always been to stay alive," the OP said. "My grandmother was an American—one of their red Indians. On account of that—my racial impurity, I mean—I had to keep a very low profile during the German occupation. But that accounts for my dark complexion." He sounded eerily calm, meek even, totally unlike the wicked little slave driver Madame Cabochon believed him to be.

Surprised, Madame Cabochon looked at Madame Fabergé, the OP's wife, for some kind of confirmation. When it finally registered with Madame Cabochon that the OP's wife was gazing at her with something akin to adoration—perhaps even lust—she glanced away too quickly and sat down heavily, one cheek sliding off the side of the monsignor's lap.

"*Excusez mois,*" she gasped as she rolled over onto the other cheek.

"Why, Madame Cabochon," the monsignor said, "how lovely to see you again."

No one laughed. No one dared to laugh; he was the monsignor, after all. Still, he *shouldn't* have said such an inappropriate thing. But it was Africa, late at night, and they had just been threatened by a crazy headman; chop, chop, chop.

The truck braked suddenly; if Madame Cabochon had still been standing, she might well have been sent through the window into the cab—after all, there was no longer any glass separating these two parts of the vehicle.

"What is it?" the OP's wife, Madame Fabergé, demanded in her irritating voice, which somehow managed to be simultaneously a whisper and a shout.

"How am I supposed to know?" her husband said. "I'm not God." He pointed with his chin at the monsignor. "*He's* certainly not God. And she—she's nothing more than a whore."

Madame Cabochon was not surprised by the OP's words, but she was stunned by his vehemence. There were always men who disapproved of her flirtatious ways, but nonetheless they couldn't help but find her charming. What had she done to the OP to deserve such contempt, except to quietly despise him? It was not like she'd waged a campaign against the man aimed at getting him fired—although, speaking of God, he alone knew why such an incompetent imbecile had been put in charge of one of the

Congo's most valuable assets in these, the waning days of colonial rule.

"Shut up!" Amanda Brown said. Although she was sitting in the cab, apparently her young, healthy American ears had heard the OP sink to his lowest level yet.

Perhaps it was true, as Madame Cabochon had often heard said of late, that Americans—particularly their young people—had a strong sense of fairness. *Bon!* If she and the girl were to become friends, she would have to become very clever about the way she went about seducing that handsome young police captain of hers. Very clever indeed! But every woman needed a girlfriend, especially in a backwater town like Belle Vue. Now, Coquilhatville, where there were several hundred whites to choose from—that was a bit different.

But Madame Cabochon had very little time to plan her social life, for the very next second the young captain stuck his head through the opening.

"Hang on to the side of the truck as tightly as you can with one hand, and the person next to you with the other. No matter what, don't let go of that person. I will count to three. When I get to three, you will close your eyes and pray. You too, Monsieur Fabergé!"

"*Oui, mon capitaine.*"

"*Un, deux, trois!*"

The Belgian Congo, 1935

What is your name?" *the tall soldier asked the boy before he was taken from the fat man's village.*

"I have no name," the boy said. "Only 'boy.'" Indeed, he did have a name, which he would never divulge, for it was the only thing that truly belonged to him.

The soldiers laughed.

"You are no longer a boy or a slave," said the short soldier. "You have need of a new name. We shall have to think of something that befits you."

"He is covered with pimples," said the tall soldier. "Let us call him Pimples."

The boy squirmed, but he did not protest. Everything happened in its own time, and eventually everything would sort itself out the way it was meant to be. Just look how far he had come already! He had survived an attack on his village, and the man whose buttocks he'd been forced to wipe had been killed at his suggestion. In the meantime, he'd witnessed other slaves being starved, raped, or beaten to death. He had even heard about a place called Arabia, which was many days travel beyond the sunrise, where many Congolese boys were taken to be sold, and from where none ever returned. An unpleasant name, therefore, meant nothing to him.

The Belgian Congo, 1958

It was with great interest that Jonathan Pimple beheld the wise woman, Cripple, speaking in earnest to the Catholic priest. This was a most unexpected development, for it was well known that the witch doctor's wife was a staunch heathen who had no use for the white man's religion; likewise, the Catholic priest openly disdained what he called "wicked heathen practices."

Then the first of two great wonders happened: the hand of God reached down from the sky and plucked the white man's bridge from its moorings. Yes, Jonathan had seen the hand of God; he was sure of it. It wasn't a white hand either, as in the pictures he'd seen; it was black—like his own hand. God was a black man!

The second great wonder was that the blue truck belonging to the chief of police, Captain Jardin, had flown across the gap formed by the missing portion of the bridge. This was a miracle; there was no denying it, for he had seen it with his own eyes. It was not the same as reading about it in the dank, yellowed pages of a book printed in *Mputu*—"the faraway land."

What was the meaning of all this? Surely the wise woman named Cripple would know. No doubt it was not by chance that it was while she stood talking to the Catholic priest, a white man, that the black hand of God reached down from heaven and destroyed that structure which best symbolized Belgium's vanity: the Belle Vue Bridge. "The Pride of the Kasai," they named it, but it was the white man who took pride in it, and on the backs of the black men who did the actual labor.

So it was that after the heavens closed, and the blue truck landed, spilling out its passengers, and Cripple and the Catholic priest disappeared into the mango grove where the whites bury their dead, Jonathan Pimple beseeched his ancestors. And it came to pass that Jonathan Pimple's ancestors heard his prayers, and he was given just enough courage to follow the mysterious pair into the haunt of European ghosts. For it is a well-known fact that Europeans—that is, anyone whose skin is not black—are not happy being buried so far from the lands of their birth. Indeed, many are heard roaming through this copse at night, their moans and cries disturbing the villagers whose misfortune it is to live closest to this, the healthiest spot for hundreds of kilometers in any direction. Even more unpleasant is the fact that a few—as many as three, and all said to be men—have been seen in the streets of the village and have attacked and beaten those villagers who were unable to quickly find shelter.

One old man, Mulumiana (which is what one calls a man whose name you have forgotten or cannot be bothered to mention), observed a pair of men's shoes emerge from the trees at the cemetery's edge one moonlit night when he had gone out from his hut to relieve himself. The shoes—empty of feet—walked directly up to Mulumiana and then something, perhaps unseen fists, began to beat him about the head and then pummel his abdomen. The next morning Mulumiana was found unconscious, his body draped across the concrete pad that protected one of the white gravesites. It was the grave of Monsieur Toussaint, who had, coincidentally, once employed Mulumiana.

Of course Jonathan Pimple was no man's foolish younger brother. Before entering the haunted grove of mango trees, he prayed to the white man's Jesus Christ and to the spirits of his ancestors, asking all of them to protect him from the vicious ghosts that surely roamed this place where the whites buried their dead. Then he crept as close as he dared to the old priest and the witch doctor's wife. When at last he had gone as far he could go without being discovered, he realized that he was standing next to the grave of Madame Heilewid, the wife of the former OP. It was then that Jonathan Pimple truly felt his blood begin to thicken with fear.

Although Madame Heilewid had burned to death in a savannah fire, and all that had been buried was a charred stump, it was said that on certain nights her stump would roll out of the grave and into the village, seeking the men who had set the fire. The next day the entire village would smell of charred flesh; this part of the story was incontrovertible, as dozens of people would complain of the odor.

As Jonathan Pimple's blood turned to the thickness of sap, and while at the same time he felt no strength in his legs, still he could hear quite clearly the words exchanged between the two people he had followed there. But it was upon hearing these—both in his mind and in his heart—that the sap in his veins hardened into something clear and brittle, akin to glass.

"Behold," said Cripple, "I hold nothing against this man Jonathan Pimple. He is pleasant enough—for a Mupende. For truly, the ugliness of his mouth, with all his teeth filed into points, is just that: ugly. It is not hideous. It is not like the face of a white."

"You truly find us that hideous?" the priest asked.

"Truly, truly," Cripple said.

"For your information, *Baba*, I find that extremely insulting. I do not think that I will ever figure you Africans out."

"*E*, nor will we ever understand you."

"*Touché, madame*—but please forgive me. Do you speak French, *Baba*?"

"*Oui, monsieur*. I am an uneducated heathen woman, but I am not an ignorant woman. Au contraire, I can both understand and speak that most unpleasant tongue of yours."

"I beg your pardon! French is considered by many to rank among the most beautiful-sounding languages in the world."

"*E*, I suppose that is so, if one enjoys the sound of old men clearing their throats in the morning."

A squeal of laughter escaped Jonathan Pimple's lips, startling him to be sure; but judging by their response, the pair that he was spying on was even more surprised.

"Who is it?" the priest called. "Who is there?"

"He is behind that tall stone," Cripple cried. "I saw something move."

"Perhaps it is just a bird stirred up by all the commotion out there."

"As one stirs the birds, one can also stir up the dead. I am telling you, priest, this was no bird."

"Listen, I do not have time for superstitions, for there are no ghosts. Tell me more about the man, Jonathan Pimple. He who once was a cannibal."

"*Aiyee!* How you could know such a thing?"

"Because he told me; that is why! The man felt a compulsion to confess—but that comes as no real surprise to me. The Bible says, 'Be sure your sins shall find you out.'"

"You are like the Protestant missionaries, priest. You speak always in riddles."

"Woman," the Catholic priest said, "you have offended me." To Jonathan Pimple's ears the priest had sounded just like a lion, although Jonathan had never heard an actual lion—just the imitation of one.

"I speak only the truth," Cripple said, "and I do not pass a basket around to those who wish to hear it."

Such was far from the truth, of course, for Jonathan Pimple knew that in her capacity as a wise woman, and interpreter of dreams, the witch doctor's wife always extracted payment of some kind, be it francs, poultry, or perhaps brightly colored fabric from the Portuguese-owned shops on the road to Luebo.

"I will let that comment pass," said the priest, "because my holy book tells me to turn the other cheek. Of course, this is something you savages cannot possibly understand. Nevertheless, I must know the following: was Jonathan Pimple able to identify the white man who was eaten? By his name, I mean? And if Jonathan Pimple was such a small boy as he claims, how can he be sure that the man was a Roman Catholic priest?"

Despite the fact that he was shivering with fear, Jonathan Pimple began to burn with rage. This priest is too clever, Jonathan Pimple told himself. Had this white man been a small Mupende boy and forced to have lived through such an experience, he might not be asking this question. A memory such as this: first, the events that led up to the abduction of the priests, and then second, the killing and eating of the one—these were not the sort of memories that faded.

"*Kah!*" said Cripple, sounding greatly annoyed. "What manner of conversation do you suppose I had? I did not ask him if he enjoyed eating hot chilies with his priest stew."

"What?" the Catholic priest said, not at all comprehending. "I made no mention of chili peppers."

"Priest, you said that if I answered a few questions about this man, you would give me a ride to the Missionary Rest House. Surely my employer waits there for me now, like a wounded gazelle. I am, after all, just a helpless crippled woman."

"What," said the priest, "*you*? *Baba*, you are no more helpless than a young man with six strong legs, for behold, you have the tongue of Satan, and you would be quite capable of charming any one of these dead men to rise from his grave and carry you on his back to the house of that Protestant whore."

It was then for the first time that the Catholic priest performed the simple miracle of igniting the battery torch, such as is also sold in the Portuguese shops to those who have a month's salary with which to part. He shone the bright circle of light on the ground before his feet, and then without even saying *shala bimpe* (stay well), as is the custom, he passed on through to the other side of grove where the whites buried their dead.

By now Jonathan Pimple's fear had grown worse, if that can be believed. With one of their own color no longer present, now the spirits of the dead would doubtless turn their attention to him. The witch doctor's wife, he reasoned, was protected by the strength of her husband's *buanga*—his ritual charms. So powerful, so all consuming was Jonathan Pimple's fear, that he could not control his voice. His throat opened on its own account and out poured the loud shrill scream of a girl not yet old enough to start her menses. At the same time it was very much akin to the scream of the female wildcat when she has been mated, the very second that the male dismounts.

Afterward, when it was too late to save face, Jonathan Pimple realized that the answering scream came from the little crippled woman, she by the same name: Cripple—she who was the witch doctor's wife. The sound of her high-pitched screams propelled Jonathan Pimple forward and into action. His legs remembered their purpose and he began to run, and he did not stop until he was home. There he collapsed in his chair by the hearth.

The following morning Their Death discovered the cold, lifeless body of Jonathan Pimple. He was still sprawled across his chair. How tragic, everyone said, that poor Jonathan Pimple had died quite alone. This could be said with certainty because it was known that the entire village had been gathered on the side of the hill, below the place where the whites were buried.

Because Jonathan Pimple had yet to be baptized into the Roman Catholic Church, his eternal soul stood no chance of ascending into the real heaven. But one must be a pragmatist, *nasha?* So the next afternoon, Jonathan Pimple, wrapped in a palm fiber mat, was buried by a Protestant lay minister, a man with a sixth-grade education, having studied at the Mennonite mission at *Mutena* near the Angola border.

This, then, is the truth that Jonathan Pimple would have others believe. Why should it not be so? Did it not serve the best interests of many people—*his* people? For too long the black man had been told that his ancient traditions, the ones handed down by his mother's brother and his mother's uncle, these were all of no value. Instead, the Bapende were supposed to accept the beliefs of the white man, a truly arrogant race who came from a place where no Mupende had been, and which was supposed to lie across a lake so large that one could not see to the other side. When the black man asked whether a lake this size could exist, he was told he must believe this simply because the white man *said* it was true.

Yet when the Bapende tried to share their beliefs with the whites, the Europeans and Americans both laughed. These foreigners called the tribal traditions superstitions, and they laughed at the Bapende view of the spirit world. They preached at the people, telling them that if they did not ask the white man's idol to forgive their wrongdoings, then they, the Bapende, would be burned alive in a great torture pit. Meanwhile the white man would be permitted the opportunity to gaze down upon this suffering from a place of comfort and luxury. This wonderful place was called *diulu. Heaven.* New missionaries often mispronounced this word, so that it sounded like *dulu,* which means nose, and thus is not quite the same.

It had always puzzled Jonathan Pimple how it could be that

the Christian God, who was supposed to be a spirit, was desirous of a large compound with many houses in it. Furthermore, it was said of this God that he did not have sexual relations with women, nor did he use the bush, or even eat in the conventional manner. *Yala!* Such claims repel, rather than attract, converts!

E, Jonathan Pimple had had no real intention of becoming a Roman Catholic; there had just been a couple of things he had need of clarifying. When he died, the night of that great storm, his mind was very much clearer than it had been in a very long time.

The Belgian Congo, 1935

Jonathan Pimple was taken, along with men from many tribes, to a place that even the imagination could not go without the head as its companion. It was called a city, and the name of this one was Belle Vue. Since no words can properly describe this place, no further description shall be given here, other than to say that there was a Belgian side and a Congolese side, and the great Kasai River divided the two.

In those days it was possible to get back and forth between the two sides via a ferry, a wooden platform lashed atop four large dugout canoes. However, there was, at the time of Pimple's arrival, a war being fought in the faraway lands of the white men, and it was rumored that a bridge connecting the two sides of the river would be critical in providing necessary materials for that war. So it was that Pimple was put to work helping to build what was surely the most impressive bridge in all of Kasai Province, and quite possibly it was the most impressive bridge in all the Belgian Congo, maybe even in the entire world—for who could possibly know how far the world extended?

One day Jonathan Pimple overheard two other men speaking

Kipende and hurried over to them as soon as he was able, which was as soon as the gong had sounded signaling the end of the workday.

"Brothers," he said, "I too am a Mupende."

At first the men looked surprised, and then their looks grew angry. "Do you joke at our expense?" one asked.

"No, I would not do so, for we are brothers."

Then one man pulled a knife from the waistband of his shorts and held it up to Jonathan Pimple's chin. "Listen to me, stranger; there are large crocodiles that lie in wait at the bottom of these waterfalls. It would be my pleasure to feed you to these beasts."

Jonathan Pimple did not flinch. "Truly, brothers, I do not understand your hostile reaction," he said.

The knife blade was lowered the distance of a thumbnail. "A Mupende's teeth are filed, as are yours, but he does not speak with a Bajembe accent," the knife wielder said.

"E," Jonathan Pimple said, "you have spoken the truth; my Kipende accent is atrocious. You see, I was captured as a small boy by a raiding party, and then sold to a very fat Mujembe. My master was a cruel man who forbade me to speak anything but his language. He threatened to cut out my tongue if I so much as uttered one word in my native Kipende."

"I once heard of a very fat Mujembe," said the man with the knife. "This fat man was said to possess many slaves because he could barely manage to walk. It was said that even to use the bush, this man had to be carried. Tell me, where does he live?"

"He does not live, brother, for the soldier who brought me here shot this man in the stomach. It was my pleasure to watch him die."

"Yala!" cried the other man.

"Tell me," said the knife wielder, "how is it that you persuaded a proper Mushilele to perform the teeth-filing ceremony on you, one with the accent of a Mujembe?"

"Because, brother, I was able to persuade this man that I was the son of the great Bapende chief—Chief Nyanga-Yanga."

The two men stared at Jonathan Pimple, their eyes bulging like those of a great carp, one that has been dead two days in a stagnant pool of water.

"Surely he did not believe you!" The man with the knife had puffed his chest out in order to appear larger, and he was breathing hard. He smelled of hate and anger.

"Eyo, it was not hard to convince him, for indeed I was telling the truth. After all, no ordinary boy would confess to being born one of twins."

Upon hearing these words the other man appeared extremely agitated. "What was the name given you as an infant?"

"I was given the name Tshishi." Torment. "For I was the boy who stole the leopard's spots."

The Belgian Congo, 1958

Amanda Brown now knew what it was like to be in love. Despite the devastating destruction of the bridge that stood as the symbol of his country's sovereignty over the local peoples, Pierre's only thought seemed to be for her. The powerful OP and his mousy wife, the voluptuous and seductive Madame Cabochon, the maddeningly influential Roman Catholic cleric—all these people seemed to take a backseat in Pierre's eyes as soon as the battered blue truck jerked to a full stop.

Although they were still many hundreds of yards away from the Missionary Rest House, that rather significant fact did not affect Amanda's progress one whit. Captain Pierre Jardin simply scooped her up in his strong arms and, with the agility of a goat, scrambled over rocks the size of washing machines. In no time at all, he had her at the front door. There, much to Amanda's surprise, they were met by the head houseboy, Protruding Navel.

No, that's not exactly what happened: Mama would scarcely believe the truth when she wrote her, and Papa would certainly disapprove. The front door to the Missionary Rest House was unlocked, as no missionary ever locked his or her doors (there not even being locks on the doors), so Pierre merely pushed his way in. The electric was still not on, of course, and no lanterns had been lit, but by then the moonlight was strong enough that one could literally have read in bed.

One certainly didn't need nearly that much light to see that Protruding Navel was dressed in one of Amanda's very best frocks. The servant was slight in build, only half a head taller than she was, so that her bright yellow, "just in case" party dress with the full-circle taffeta skirt fit him remarkably well. The cheeky fellow had even gone so far as to stuff something in the bosom area because, truth be told, he had a remarkably feminine shape. The funny thing was that, had he been wearing a wig or head covering of some sort, Protruding Navel could have passed for a woman—but an African woman in the latest Rock Hill fashion.

"*W-wewe!*" Amanda said. You! It wasn't even an accusation.

"*Mamu,*" Protruding Navel said, "you must take this dress to the woman in the village who sews for the whites. The middle portion here"—he patted his midriff—"will not fit my wife for she has given birth to four children and the fifth has now taken up residence inside her."

Amanda felt her feet touch the floor, and she was gently pushed into a living room chair. It was a useless gesture of concern on Pierre's part, because Amanda bounded back up like a weighted punching bag.

"Protruding Navel," she shouted. "What are you doing in my *diyeke*?"

The head housekeeper smiled indolently. Yes, even indoors, because of the moonlight she could see him smirk.

"It is not yours, *Mamu.*" This he said with a toss of his small, round Bena Lulua head; indeed, was that not their chief racial characteristic?

"What do you mean by it is not mine? Of course it is! Everything in this house is mine!" She had to stop herself from adding that even he, Protruding Navel, was hers—in a manner of speaking, of course.

"Because, mistress, when the great day of independence comes, all that belongs to the oppressor shall be ours."

"That is a lie! Where did you hear such rubbish?"

The man in the yellow frock stiffened, transfigured into a bizarre mannequin, like one she had chanced to see in a Charlotte shop window when her parents had gotten lost driving back from the circus, and they'd found themselves in the colored part of town.

Amanda had been in the Belgian Congo only a few months and already there was talk of expelling all the whites. That wasn't fair! More important, surely that couldn't be God's plan for her. How did the Lord expect her to atone for the deaths of the innocent people whose lives had been stolen, all because she and some fellow Winthrop College classmates had recklessly decided to drive to Gaffney, South Carolina, while drunk one night?

"There is a great prophet in the village now," Protruding Navel said. "Have you not heard, *Mamu*? *E*, but I am sure that you have. This prophet is none other than our new headman. He knows these things because he is both a Kibanguist and a Communist who has studied in Russia. Unlike other Communists, he preaches that it is not necessary to give up one's beliefs, especially if they are traditional."

Amanda could not deny that she'd inherited a bit of a temper from the Brown side of her family, and she could feel the ire in her rising now from the tips of her toes like floodwaters. Soon she would choke and drown on her rage if she didn't open a sluice gate. At the same time she felt the firm, yet somehow gentle, restraining hand of Captain Pierre Jardin, the young Belgian who had been born and raised in the Congo, and who understood the locals far better than she ever would—even if independence for the Congo never came to pass, and she were to die an eighty-year-old virgin, still on the mission field.

How was it that Pierre, who was not a Christian but a Roman Catholic, was at the same time a far better Christian than she was? This was one of the first questions she would pose to the Lord when she got to heaven. And why was it, anyway, that Catholics were excluded from heaven when they also believed in the saving blood of Jesus? Was it just because they prayed to Mary on the side? If that was the only reason, then did that mean that all the so-called Christians who lived prior to the Reformation were also doomed to spend eternity in hell? Of course this was just cracking open the theological door, because then what about all the people who lived before the time of Jesus?

"Good girl," Pierre whispered. "Just allow me to handle this."

The handsome man of her dreams—her real dreams—crossed the room, spoke a few low words to the houseboy, and the two of them disappeared in the direction of the kitchen. It was then that Amanda realized that she hadn't garnered Pierre's approval through any action on her part, but through her slowness to respond. Well, perhaps that wasn't all bad; after all, the Bible does urge its readers to be slow to anger. For Amanda, this was progress.

The monsignor was at a loss. He'd tried but failed to climb the steep road that led up to the workers' village and Saint Mary's Catholic Church. What had once been a smooth expanse of red brown dirt was now a series of ruts so deep that one slip could easily result in a broken leg, and here in the tropics a broken leg with a protruding femur can quickly become septic, resulting in death. No, any attempt to scale the hill would have to wait until the morrow, even though he knew that Reutner would be frantic. Unfortunately, that geriatric Swiss priest had a very active imagination and might well indulge in some carnal supposition, thereby indirectly involving the monsignor in his sin. After all, anyone with two eyes in his head could see how Little Colette Underpants threw herself at him.

Yes, of course, tomorrow he would try his best again to get up that awful hill—perhaps through that snake-infested *tshisuku*. Then again, who was he, Alberto Clemente, just because he was now a big-shot monsignor—who was he to desert the little lambs of the flock? What about the pitiful, dark-eyed Madame OP? She with the perpetually haunted look? Didn't Christ commend his disciple to especially care for those such as she? *But screw the OP,* the monsignor thought, and then made the sign of the cross to undo this small sin.

Quickly he filled his mind with something else, this time a spiritually borderline thought—if there could be such a thing. To put it succinctly—as he would pose it to his seminary students—he should be billeted in a Protestant home; most especially the home of a young beautiful single Protestant American missionary. Every one of those adjectives just added to the gravity of the sin. *However,* at the same time, the word *missionary* had a very strong pull; if he could manage to convert her to the *true* church, think of what a victory that would be for Mother Rome!

So when the vivacious young American (made somewhat less so by the appearance of her housekeeper in a woman's yellow dress) invited him, for a second time, to spend the night, the monsignor politely accepted. He was careful, however, not to sound too eager.

"*Bon!*" cried Madame Cabochon, "for I too have decided to spend the night. Isn't this exciting?"

"*Exciting?*" said the OP. "We are cut off from our town, and I am separated from my diamond mine—let's face it. We are virtual prisoners here on the black side of the river. Who knows what could happen, *here* or there?"

"What do you mean?" his wife said. She was a very plain, timid little thing who seemed, at least on the surface, better suited to life in a Brussels convent than in the Congo as a diamond mine operator's wife.

"I mean," he said, "that those savages could come running

down that hill anytime they want to and start hacking at us with their machetes."

The OP, Monsieur Fabergé, laughed insanely as he cut the air with his hands. "Chop, chop, chop." When no one even cracked a smile, he repeated his tasteless performance, and then said, "One must have a sense of humor here to survive, yes?"

"Yes," said the monsignor, "but you, monsieur, are not humorous; you are a monstrous fool. And as I have absolutely no doubt that you will *not* apologize to the lovely ladies here, I shall do so on your behalf. *Mesdames et mademoiselle,* our Heavenly Father created men, and he created asses. The creation known as Monsieur Fabergé is not a man. Therefore kindly disregard the remarks he just made. Rest assured that the natives in the village are by and large Christians, and far less dangerous than is he."

The swarthy little Belgian advanced on him, chest out, fists balled. He looked far more pathetic than he did dangerous. Clearly the man had no idea that Monsignor Clemente worked out regularly in the archbishop's private gym.

"*Fermez la bouche,*" the runt said softly. "Or else."

The monsignor smiled, looking past him. "Mademoiselle Brown," he said, "if you will be so kind as to show me to my quarters, I will take my leave for the evening."

At first Amanda thought that the previous night's happenings had all been a bad dream. The nightmare was almost as bad as one of many she'd experienced following the accident—that defining moment back in the Unites States when her entire universe had irrevocably turned on a dime. But unlike those mornings, when she'd awaken to find her sheets soaked with perspiration, and then gradually realize that she'd been dreaming, this morning her bedding was dry, and she knew at once that the horrifying sound of steel girders shearing apart was no dream.

Amanda sprang to her window. From here she normally enjoyed a breathtaking view of the falls, and the bridge that spanned it. A visiting missionary had once remarked that when Belgians chose to site the bridge over the most spectacular waterfall in the province—if not the colony—they were tugging playfully on God's beard. When the Belgians went ahead and actually built the bridge, they gave the beard a hard yank, laughed, and then sat back to wait and see what would happen next. Well, now they had their answer; the Good Lord didn't like his facial hair abused.

In the daylight, the first thing Amanda noticed was the color of the water. For much of its length the Kasai River runs through red clay hills and the runoff reflects this. Today, however, the water was gunmetal gray. The next thing puzzled her; the bridge appeared to be intact.

It was only after removing the screen and leaning out the window a good deal that Amanda was able to get a visual of the entire length of the bridge. The closest end, the one nearest the Missionary Rest House, remained fastened securely to its concrete pad. However, shortly beyond that, a gap of over three meters existed where once there had been metal girders covered by wood planks. Beneath that, crammed between the cliff face and next concrete piling, was a tree, the likes of which Amanda had never seen before.

The tree was one of a species that grew buttresses—wooden wings, Amanda liked to refer to them. These natural supports for the tree extended a dozen feet in every direction at head height, so that the trunk, which by itself had a radius of ten feet, seemed even more massive than that of the ancient live oaks Amanda had often observed growing along the Carolina coasts. In addition, the height of the trunk rose untapered and limb-free for at least sixty feet, whereupon it exploded, virtually forming its own little forest. Even from this great distance the young missionary from Rock Hill, South Carolina, thought she beheld a troop of black-and-white monkeys leaping about in its still leafy boughs.

It was a mesmerizing scene, and the avoidance aspect of her personality (which was quite considerable, actually) was willing to pull up a chair and watch, when movement to her right caught her eye. Oh my gosh! There, on the back patio, was Monsignor Clemente, all decked out in his spotless black robes. He appeared to be serving coffee to the OP and his wife. Seated next to them on the back patio was Pierre, one brawny tanned leg crossed over the other at the knee. For some reason he'd already been served and was looking down at his cup. Then suddenly he looked up and waved at her, just as calmly as could be.

Amanda ducked back behind a curtain. What was going on in the world? Had everyone gone mad, including herself? Or were these people truly so adaptable, so used to calamity, that they could sit and enjoy a cup of coffee outdoors while surveying so much damage to the infrastructure that shored up their lives?

"*Bonjour*, Mademoiselle Brown!"

Amanda whirled. Madame Cabochon stood in the doorway, swathed in a diaphanous peach robe that covered a matching baby doll pajama set. The pajama set belonged to Amanda and was something that she regarded as intensely personal. It was part of her trousseau, but now, as she felt her cheeks burning, she could not remember why she had decided to bring it to Africa.

Her extra pair of cotton pajamas had gone to Madame Fabergé, who had nonetheless complained that she had never worn sleepwear with "legs." Then it was either lend Madame Cabochon the baby doll pajama set or allow her to sleep in the nude. For the record, Madame Cabochon had been all for the latter.

"Why aren't you dressed?" Amanda said.

"But I am," Madame Cabochon responded cheerily. "Come, there is something you must see."

The younger woman took a deep breath and then exhaled slowly. "Perhaps you should come see this instead."

Madame Cabochon strode to the window, trailing her chiffon robe and a heady scent behind her. A cursory glance in either direction elicited merely a Gallic shrug.

"What fools they are, *non*? One would think that they are

English, and that they are drinking tea, instead of coffee. Tell me, do you find their calmness admirable?"

"I most certainly do not! Why, in America we would be—"

"You would be screwing around like ants, yes?"

"The word is *scurrying*."

"And the bridge would be half rebuilt, am I correct?"

"Well—"

"You must remember, Mademoiselle Brown, that in America you have access to better technology and better means of communication. Here we live much like you did fifty—maybe one hundred—years ago. This means that there are many times when one must be happy to wait in the present."

Frankly, Amanda did not cotton to taking spiritual advice from a floozy, especially one wearing the baby doll set she'd bought and put aside for her wedding night—should that ever happen!

"Madame Cabochon," she began through clenched teeth, "I hardly think that—"

"*Non, non!* Now is not the time to think; you must come with me now." Madame Cabochon grabbed Amanda's hand and literally pulled her from her bedroom, through the living room, and out into the dazzling sunlight that invaded the front porch at that hour of the morning.

"*Voilà!*" she said, pointing to the dirt parking area in front of the Missionary Rest House. Overnight the muddy red space had erupted into a carpet of tiny yellow daisies that were quivering in a gentle morning breeze. It was a sight so beautiful that Amanda felt tears in her eyes, and her throat began to tighten. It was a miracle; it was truly a gift from heaven.

"Oh, thank you," she cried. "Thank you for insisting that I see this first thing—although I can't imagine how flowers can grow and bloom so fast. I mean, yesterday, it was a sea of mud. I must go get my box Brownie camera and photograph this sight. Someday, Madame Cabochon—mark my words—someday they will invent an affordable camera that photographs in color. If only

I had such a thing, I could capture the true essence of these gorgeous flowers."

"But mademoiselle, those are *not* flowers! Those are—how do you say in English? 'Butter that flies'? Yes, I am sure of it, butter that flies!"

"*What?* Do you mean *butterflies?*"

"*Alors*, is that not what I just said?"

"Yes, but—"

Madame Cabochon, still clutching Amanda's hand, pulled the girl down the front steps. "Come, mademoiselle. We must dance with these butterflies! It is good luck, *non?*"

"*Excuse* me?"

"Ah, this is a game that my sister and I played when we were little girls. Always we pretended that we were like Tinker Bell, *non?*"

"Like fairies?"

"*Oui*, that is the word! Come, you will enjoy; it is a harmless game."

As much as Amanda wished to dance among the yellow butterflies, in the golden sunlight with Madame Cabochon in her borrowed swirling chiffon, there was one rather major problem; Southern Baptists of Amanda Brown's ilk did not dance. Dancing was of the devil, for it brought on sexual thoughts. Dancing with the extravagantly endowed Colette Cabochon—well, God only knew to what abomination that might lead.

"Madame Cabochon," Amanda said, pulling her hand away from Colette's. "Dancing would not set a good example for the natives. They might confuse it with their heathen practices."

The Belgian woman laughed. It wasn't that she seemed to be mocking Amanda, so much as she appeared to be thoroughly amused. It was as if Amanda had told her a good joke.

"I am serious," Amanda said as she stamped back up the steps.

"But truly not!"

"Madame Cabochon, I am going back inside now."

"Ah, so it is also true that you Protestants are forbidden to have any pleasure in life!"

Amanda turned and glared. "Who said this?"

"Father Reutner. He is the priest—"

"I know who he is! But how dare he say that? What else did he say?"

Madame Cabochon shrugged, causing her large breasts to bobble in a way that was practically seductive. "He said that this philosophy is what makes you Protestants always look so angry. Like angry mother hens, *oui*?"

The nerve of that woman to use Amanda's own thoughts against her! How dare she compare her to a hen! Amanda would show her!

"*Non!*" Amanda said. "We are not all like angry mother hens!" She grabbed Madame Cabochon's hands and pulled her down the steps and into a sea of quivering yellow butterflies. "Let's dance!" she said.

Madame Cabochon smiled. "*Oui, chérie.*"

The Belgian Congo, 1935

*C*higger Mite felt such extreme pressure clamping his head from all directions that his vision was blurred. Therefore, when he addressed the man he knew by the name Jonathan Pimple yet another time, he was actually facing his friend.

"Torment?" he said. "And you a twin. This is a very strange story, the likes of which I have never heard. Tell me, Torment, son of the great chief Nyanga-Yanga, does your brother yet live?"

The new worker's eyes seemed to take him to a faraway place. His jaw muscles twitched.

"Of that I cannot be certain; I can only hope. When I was yet the slave of the fat Mujembe, I heard that the Mushilele who captured me was but a scout for a large raiding party that shortly afterward descended on the men's camp, slaughtering many and taking the rest as slaves. The women and children in the village were said to have suffered the same fate.

"I know for certain only that my father, the great chief, Nyanga-Yanga, was sold as a slave to work in the house of another great chief *in the land of* Alabia [*Arabia*]. *A chief turned into a slave! Can you imagine that, my brothers?* Yala! *Such a thing has never happened since the beginning of our tribe, since the days that the gods pushed us out of the spirit world and into this dream world of hardship and suffering.*"

"*Enough of this sentimentality,*" snapped the man with the knife. "*What do you know of your mother?*"

Jonathan Pimple returned from his memory place. "*Kah? What business is this of yours?*"

"*Do you recall a timid boy by the name of* Tshibia?" said Chigger Mite.

Jonathan Pimple stared openmouthed at the man whose name meant "*burden.*" "Eyo," he said, after a long pause. "*Tshibia was the name of my brother. Tell me, please, do you have word of him? Is he alive?*"

Chigger Mite smiled, revealing every one of his pointed teeth. "E, *your twin brother is very much alive; for* I *am your brother!*"

"Bulelela?" *Really?*

"E!"

The men embraced. So great was their joy that they fell to the ground, still locked in their embrace, and rolled on the ground, like schoolboys in a schoolyard tussle. Then Chigger Mite prevailed upon his friend not to reveal that they were twins, lest those villagers who were superstitious (sadly, there were many) react to the men in a negative way, such as making bad medicine against them with a witch doctor.

In the end, it was agreed that nothing should be said of their past—even that they were brothers, because the people in the Belle Vue workers' village were not of the sort to mind their own business. To the contrary, many among their number delighted in stirring up trouble. Would not these troublemakers feed like a pack of hungry hyenas on the knowledge that the brothers had once partaken of the flesh of a white man? Not only a Mutoka—*a white*—*but a* Roman Catholic *priest?*

As for news of their mother, Chigger Mite was unable to tell his brother anything except that he had heard that all the women in the village over a certain age had been butchered by the raiding party. Was their mother of such an age at the time? Neither man could remember, for neither of them could draw forth her face.

The Belgian Congo, 1958

Alberto Clemente was of the opinion that much in this world was accomplished by people sitting back and doing nothing. Unfortunately, the net result of this was also often nothing. Others were given to wringing their hands, still others to barking out orders. One could expect only wrinkled hands from the former, and no more from the latter than a sore throat—unless one had the manpower to back up those commands.

At the Missionary Rest House there were only hand wringers and barkers, and, of course, the ever-alluring Colette Cabochon—formerly known to him as Little Colette Underpants. Although some Belgians had been brave enough to venture out onto the bridge on the other side, none had dared get close enough to the massive tree to do battle with it by using a machete or some other sharp tool. And while Belgians are usually quite good at screaming their houseboys into submission, none had succeeded in convincing their servants (those unlucky few marooned on the white side of the river) that it was safe to hack into a tree from the sacred Island of Seven Ghost Sisters. As for that handsome, strong young police captain with the bulging muscles, all it took was for him to discover the beautiful American virgin frolicking in a field of golden butterflies with Little Colette Underpants, and he was rendered utterly useless.

Si, but these were not the thoughts that a priest should be having. These sorts of bitter thoughts were for altar boys or young men who had still to take their vows. It was a good thing that today, two days after the great storm, the weather was sunny and hotter than ever. In his black cassock the monsignor would surely be punished by the heat as he tried to forge a new path up the hill to the workers' village. So be it. It was the least he deserved, for he was a wicked, wicked man with base, carnal thoughts. He was hardly worthy of elevation to the position of bishop in the one true church—yet, isn't that the one thing that he desired most? At the same time, wasn't it his desire, his hubris, the very thing that—if he were to be entirely honest with his confessor—would hold him back from advancement?

Too bad the order to which Alberto Clemente belonged did not wear hair shirts. If so, then Alberto would own the hairiest chemise known to man; that was the running joke back at the seminary where he taught advanced New Testament Greek on Tuesdays and Thursdays, and biblical Hebrew on Mondays and Fridays. Well, at least that hair shirt might help to keep the black material of the cassock from sticking to his back, the monsignor thought as he began to hack his way through the thick *tshisuku* that clung stubbornly to the almost vertical side of the hill.

With the dirt road now nothing more than a series of parallel ridges interspersed by gullies, some of them more than twenty feet deep, it was only logical to consider a new route to the top. Normally one would send a work crew with machetes and hoes up to clear out the head-high elephant grass and scrubby acacia trees. Invariably one would hear the cry of *"Nyoka, nyoka!"* Snake, snake! Quite possibly someone would be bitten; most likely by a mamba, but possibly by an adder or a cobra. The mamba patients usually died—there just wasn't time to do anything for them, *except* give them last rites, and at least that was *something*. That's why Alberto Clemente, when he was a mission priest, always preferred to hire good Catholic boys whose baptisms he could verify.

Today the risk was all his. A long black skirt had its advantages as well as disadvantages. He was wearing trousers under it, of course, so the garment offered him a fraction of additional protection. But it also made him a larger target, and it certainly hampered his ability to run. *If* the monsignor temporarily removed his cassock while forging a new path up to the village, it was not to avoid the discomfort caused by the sun, but the possibility of not being able to outrun an aggressive snake like the mamba. That was only because Alberto Clemente was sure that God intended to go through with his promotion back in Rome, and, for that, God needed a *corpus animus*—a living body. Then again, there really was no point in pushing it. Heatstroke could be just as deadly as a snake bite.

A grove of mango trees with high, rounded crowns of thick dark leaves stood between the Missionary Rest House and the base of the hill. Only God and the circling hawks were privy to the sight of Monsignor Clemente undressing; first the hot black cassock came off, then he stripped completely to the waist. Still, a half-naked priest out and about in broad daylight—ah, but almost immediately, the Lord sent a cool breeze up from the river that ruffled his chest hair. For the first time in years—yes, years— Alberto Clemente felt like a *man*, not just like a priest in service of the Lord.

Wait: there was even one more thing that he could do that would add to this sensation. It was a very natural thing that even the Lord himself must have done hundreds of times while he roamed about in Galilee with his little band of disciples. It was something, however, that Alberto Clemente had never had the opportunity to enjoy surrounded by nature—not since leaving the Congo so very many years ago. Without further ado, Alberto unbuttoned his trousers, extricated his very impressive member, and started to piss.

"*Tangila! Lubola wa muambi udi mutoke-to!*" Look! The master's penis is whiter than white!

Monsignor Clemente shivered with fear. He'd been seen—and by a woman no less. He fumbled for his cassock first, cutting himself on the coarse blades of *tshisuku* grass upon which it lay. His sweat-soaked shirt be damned for now.

"*Nganyi we?*" he called out. Who are you? There is an age-old protocol one must follow when approaching members of the opposite sex who might be engaged in private acts—such as bathing in streams, using the bush as a toilet, or, God forbid, sexual relations not approved by the church. If one even *suspects* this might be the case, one is obliged to call out the word *basope* in a loud clear voice. Reserved just for these occasions, it allows the invaded participants to restore their modesty.

Immediately a short hunchbacked woman stepped out from between two dense clumps of elephant grass. Wherever she had come from must have been as cool as a gelato, because she wasn't sweating a drop. Her traditional "Christian" outfit—ruffled blouse and wrap skirt—were sewn from the usual cheap cotton one sees in the native stores, this one from bright yellow, sporting orange and black scenes of leopards and parrots. Her head was bare, but her hair had been expertly combed into precise squares, and then twisted into giant cloves. She was, of course, barefoot; very few, if any, village women wore their plastic sandals unless it was to church.

"*Tch,*" the woman clucked. "Do not be afraid, master. It is only a woman of no account. I am a cripple by the same name, and my husband is a witch doctor. In your eyes we are like the maggots that riddle the carcasses of the jackals that Belgians delight in leaving by the side of the road, in order that we black monkeys must walk through their stench on our way to the market."

"*Kah!* I do not run down jackals," the monsignor said indignantly, "and I call no one 'monkey.' *Mamu* Cripple, now please avert your eyes in order that I might dress properly."

"*E,*" she mumbled, but rather than ducking back into the grass whence she had come, she waddled farther out into the path he had cleared, and there she plopped herself down as if entitled to the space. As she turned her back on him, it became quite apparent that the witch doctor's wife was soon to bear him a child.

When he was satisfied that his dignity had been restored, Monsignor Clemente cleared his throat. "*Baba,*" he said— Mother—"come, let us go down to the shade of the mango grove and get better acquainted."

The woman called Cripple rose slowly. Twice she almost fell over backward, thanks to the steep incline, and had she been a white woman, the monsignor would have reached out and grabbed her hand—or her arm. If in the process of doing so, he had accidentally brushed any other part of her body, he would have been sure to bring the matter up to his confessor. But this was the Congo, and although the monsignor really did not view the natives as monkeys, neither did he see them quite the same way that he saw whites.

For one thing, they had a higher pain tolerance. One was always hearing tales of native women giving birth in the fields, and then walking home with the babies strapped to their backs, a basket of manioc roots balanced on their heads, at the end of the day. No white woman could do that. It was akin to the cur dogs back in Europe that could stay outdoors all winter, no matter how brutal the weather, while some fancy purebreds had been known to die indoors just from catching drafts near windows. Besides, any attempt to grab her could be interpreted as sexual imposition on his part. The country was already a tinderbox of emotions; one had to be ever so vigilant.

"Master," Cripple said, having stabilized herself, "what is it that you wish to discuss? Let us hope it is not religion, for you will be bested in any argument entered into fairly."

He laughed with surprise. "*What* did you say?"

"Only that you cannot hope to outwit me on the matter of religion; I am a proud heathen and will not be swayed by the primitive superstitions of the white man. Behold, not three months ago, the other priest tried to make a Christian out of me while I stood high upon the gallows, waiting to join the spirits of my ancestors in the other world. I was not swayed by your myths then; therefore, if you are of sound judgment, you can only conclude that there is nothing that you can say now to advance your cause."

Alberto Clemente forgot being embarrassed and, throwing back his head, laughed with sheer delight. This woman was truly a treasure. What did the Americans say? Yes, the same thing: priceless! Rarely had he encountered an African as straightforward as this tiny, misshapen Muluba woman.

"I am Monsignor Clemente," he said, extending his hand. In that moment he felt real joy at being back in the Africa of his birth.

She took his hand without hesitation—as if they were equals. *Equals!*

"Tell me," she said, "why were you, a white man, fighting your way up the hill through the *tshisuku* to the village in the heat of the sun? Was that not an exceedingly foolish thing to do? I have heard of more than one white who has fallen over dead from such behavior."

"*E*, you have heard correctly—there have been quite a few of us to die this way. But were you not also fighting your own way though the *tshisuku* at this hour? True, you have the advantage of owning a skin that is better suited to the sun than the ugly one that I inhabit; however, you are heavy with child. Surely the burden of that adds to your exertion."

"*Kah!*" She laughed so hard that she had to support the child in question with both hands while she rocked forward and back. "Does it not amaze you, master, how a tribe as ignorant as yours was able to subjugate a tribe as clever as the Baluba? Surely you must shake your head in wonder every time you give the matter consideration."

Alberto Clemente quickly discovered that his expansive mood was not boundless. Back in Europe he had heard and read a great deal about how cheeky the Africans were becoming now that independence was glimmering on their political horizon, but this was a bit much to take when one didn't have to—especially since it was coming from a woman.

"Madame," he said coldly, switching to French, "this stupid white is no longer interested in making conversation."

"A thousand apologies," said Cripple, switching to near perfect *Latin*, "for while it was indeed my intention to offend, at the same time I believed that the citizen of Rome was not so easily offended as all this."

The priest from Rome couldn't help but stare openmouthed at the strange little creature standing before him, like a broken bird, in the shade of a large mango tree. It was hot even there, and since in every direction heat waves danced, it was easy for him to imagine that he might be having delusions.

"What did you just say?" he finally managed to croak.

"In which language, master, do you wish for me to repeat my words?"

He shook his head. "How is it that a Congolese *woman* knows *Latin*? Where could you possibly have learned it?"

"I learned it from the old priest who is yet here, and from another who is now gone. I was not allowed to attend school myself, as I am but a lowly, and crippled, female whose worth is barely that of three goats, two pigs, and a one-eyed duck—and it was a milky eye, at that. But I could not be stopped from following my older brother to the Roman Catholic school, where I sat outside on the grass all day and absorbed everything that his teachers had to say. My brother failed the sixth-form exams and became an auto mechanic like my father, but I, writing in the pages of a discarded third-form *cahier*, made a perfect score. However, the fact that I was already somewhat fluent in Portuguese—which, as you know, is derived from Latin—was of a great help to me."

"*Aiyee!*" said Monsignor Clemente, but not in a bad way. "Your story is most incredible."

"*Eyo,*" Cripple said. "I am of the same opinion. *Kadi*"—but— "even more incredible is that you did not consider the fact that you were a large man fighting your way through the clumps of *tshisuku up* a steep hill, whereas I am but a small woman despite my belly and that I managed to slip *between* the clumps as I worked my way *down* the hill. Behold, *muambi*, there is a saying: even very dull water knows that it is easier to run down a hill than up it."

This time Monsignor Alberto Clemente virtually roared with laughter. Damn it, if this little woman didn't tickle his funny bone, as the Americans called it. Being a demonstrative person, quick to express himself, he unconsciously slapped the tiny Muluba on her back, which knocked her off her feet. Fortunately his large hands caught her before she hit the ground and he was able to set her down gently, almost as if nothing had happened.

"*Aiyee,*" she cried in a loud and tormented voice. "Master, why do you beat me?"

"*Beat* you? I do not beat you, little one. What sort of game is it that you play?"

She glanced around deviously. Weren't they all devious— women, that is? Alberto's mother had spent her life seducing men for their fortunes, and when she had bled their bank accounts dry, she discarded them like silk stockings that had accumulated too many runs. Even the nuns that he'd run into at the Vatican were devious by their supposed absence. Oh, they were there all right, but only as part of the machinery that kept the great establishment going, so it appeared to Alberto that they went out of their way to make themselves inconspicuous. Yet there they were, always on the fringes, always ducking out of sight around some corner, always on one's mind. Talk about deviousness!

"I do not play games, *muambi;* games are for children. I only wish to offer you silly whites my help."

What cheek! Delightful cheek, yes, but it was beginning to look like this bite-size woman might not know where to draw the line.

"You dare to call your superiors silly?" he said.

"I would not dare to call my superiors silly," she said, holding his gaze, "for I myself am not a silly person. But listen, *muambi,* can you not hear the bleating of sheep above the noise of the waterfall?"

Alberto mopped futilely at his brow with a monogrammed handkerchief. It had begun the journey from Italy as starched white Egyptian cotton, whereas now it was various shades of gray and decidedly limp. It was like wiping one's face with a dead codfish.

"Those are not sheep!" he cried. "Those are white people: Belgians. They are on the bridge, but a stone's throw from this end, but because there is a missing section, they cannot get across."

She cocked her head almost like a red-tailed parrot would. "What is it that they clamor for so loudly?"

"Their houseboys, of course! Are you not aware that the power plant is still not functioning? This means that one must chop firewood to boil drinking water. And someone must cook and do the washing up afterward. And who is there to sweep the floors and mind the children?"

The little woman had the temerity to laugh right in his face. This reaction was so unbelievable that Alberto didn't even have a chance to get angry.

"Is it true, *muambi,* that your God created white women without bones?" she immediately asked.

"What? That is a stupid question!"

"I thought perhaps that they were incapable of holding a broom—or an infant. Perhaps, even, they lack breasts with which to feed an infant, *muambi.* I say this because I have never seen the breasts of a white woman."

"They have breasts!" the monsignor shouted. "And yes, they have bones, and they are quite capable of holding their own brooms; it is just that they are—uh—"

"They are lazy," Cripple said.

"Look here," the monsignor said, his voice rising in fury, "if every white woman pushed her own broom and cooked her own supper, there would be many families in the village without a source of income."

"*Aiyee*," Cripple said and clapped the sides of her head. "Sometimes the mouth on the woman named Cripple does not know when to stop. It is not my intention to bring bad luck upon the working men of my village."

The monsignor grunted.

"Well then, because we did not meet under the best of circumstances, and because I have already induced in you great rage, no doubt causing you to sin—"

There is only so much that a man can take, even a man for whom spiritual warfare is a vocation. "You have not caused me to sin, little woman!"

"*E*, but all the same, I have a gift for you."

"I do not want your gift, *Baba*."

"It is the remembrance of an old ferry crossing upriver from the Island of Seven Ghost Sisters."

In that moment the monsignor wished to grab the twisted little Muluba woman and hold on to her so that she could not escape, lest she be an illusion. "What?"

"In the days before the bridge, there existed a ferry. It was constructed from dugout canoes—as many as four or five—that were lashed together. This ferry was attached by a pulley to a thick metal cable that was strung from one bank of our mighty Kasai River to the other. Somehow the current pulled the ferry across—it was like magic to my eyes, but I was just a girl then.

"When the bridge was built, the cable was dismantled and

used for other things. The ferrymen were given the canoes so that they might fish—although Two-Fists Goiter was swept over the falls the very first week and was never seen again. As for the ferry landings themselves, perhaps they are now washed away or overgrown with jungle and *tshisuku*, but the important thing is that the land there is flat. If *muambi* were to use his authority— perhaps resort again to torture with the hippopotamus hide whips—a new landing could be speedily constructed. Assuredly for the right price—along with some beating—"

"*Mon Dieu!*" The monsignor turned and ran.

The Belgian Congo, 1958

Cripple," Amanda said as she positioned a kitchen stool beneath the ripe yet twisted body of her former employee, "you are a hero."

"*E, mene, mene,*" Madame Cabochon said.

"*Parlez-vous français, s'il vous plaît,*" Madame Fabergé, the OP's wife said. Her lips were a thin brown line in a slightly paler brown face.

"*Bien,*" Cripple said. "Although my French is not the finest, given that I learned it sitting on the grass outside my brother's classroom. Would you prefer to converse in Flemish instead? Or perhaps Latin? Now Latin—there is much about Latin that reminds me of my own remarkable tongue—"

"Cripple!" Amanda was forced to say sharply. "Quit showing off."

"*Eyo,*" said Cripple. "Too quickly I forget my number five status in Congo Belgique."

"Number five?" said Madame Cabochon, sounding greatly amused.

"*Oui, madame.* Number one is the white woman who is called *Flemand* Belgian—but there is no example here. Number two is the white woman who is *Walloon* Belgian like yourself. Number three are the Americans. Then come the Portuguese and their mulatto children—oh yes, madame, is it not true that the Portuguese are less apt to look down on us, and therefore are more willing to shake the bushes with a black woman like me?"

The sex-crazed, and altogether crass, Madame Cabochon howled with laughter. No matter which way you sliced the red velvet cake, that woman was, as Mama would say, from the other side of the tracks—well, except that she was born right here in the Congo. Obviously then, it had to be her papist upbringing that made her who she was.

Amanda flushed, remembering their shared dance among the yellow butterflies. Before coming to Africa, she had agreed to act as a beacon of light, not only to the natives, but to the godless Belgians as well. Oh, how she'd failed! Instead, since arriving, just three short months ago she had drunk alcohol again, kissed a man, skipped church (even on Sunday mornings), and danced with a woman!

"*Mamu*," Cripple said, slipping back into her own tongue. "You have turned *mukunze*." Red. "Are you ill?"

"No!" She had not meant to respond so sharply this time.

"She feels shame," Madame Cabochon said, for the word *embarrassment* did not translate directly into Tshiluba.

"Shame?" said Cripple. "For what?"

"You spoke of shaking the bushes," said Madame Cabochon. "I am afraid that when these American missionaries go into the bushes, the bushes do not shake. They say that the only way to tell if a missionary is in the bushes is to toss a snake in with them." Madame Cabochon commenced howling again.

Of course Cripple joined in and was quite pleased with herself too. Poor Madame OP; one could hardly blame her for wandering off by herself.

"Stop it," said Amanda and, grabbing a saucepan, she brought it down on the stove with a resounding *whack*. Too late did she remember that in her Congo orientation class, this was exactly the sort of behavior one was not supposed to exhibit if one was to retain the respect of one's employees—especially if they belonged to the dignified Baluba tribe. Well, dignified my foot; Cripple was practically down on the floor rolling around.

"Stop it," Cripple croaked. "Stop it, stop, stop it!"

"*Nyoka*," Amanda cried. Snake! If Cripple was willing to use the dreaded snake word, then so was she.

Cripple's sad little body snapped to attention. "Snake? Where, *Mamu*?"

"There is no snake, Cripple; I wished only to frighten you."

"Why, *Mamu*? Do you not want the child within me to stay his allotted time?"

Geez o' Pete! Now look what Amanda Brown's big old Rock Hill mouth had gone and done? She would never, ever have forgiven herself had she caused Cripple to miscarry. Oh Lordy, was there still a chance of that? How would she know, since there wasn't a doctor on this side of the river?

"No, Cripple, no! I would never wish for you to miscarry!"

"Shhh, *Mamu*, you must not speak so loud, lest the spirits hear you and get ideas."

"Yes, never speak aloud your true thoughts," Madame Cabochon said. With that she extended her hand and, in the most brazen manner imaginable, cupped Cripple's belly in the palm of her hand. It was rude, it was paternalistic, it was contemptible; and worst of all, Cripple appeared to be fine with this behavior. At least she made no discernible attempt to pull away.

Tears welled in Amanda's eyes. They were tears of frustration for having failed in her vision of being a shining light for others; by no means did they spring from self-pity—not that the other women would come to the correct conclusion. Therefore, under no circumstances must she allow those tears to fall. If in the future she hoped to save either one of their souls, Amanda must come across now as nonchalant.

"My true thoughts are," she said, "that Captain Pierre is a most unattractive man and I wish never to see him again."

"*Aiyee!*" Cripple said and slapped her thighs with merriment. Clearly all thoughts of miscarriage had been abandoned.

Madame Cabochon swept over to Amanda's side and laid a Rubenesque arm around the American girl's slim shoulders. The Belgian woman smelled of sin: cigarettes, alcohol, and a cloying perfume that didn't even come close to masking her body odor. Why was it that Europeans bathed so infrequently and eschewed deodorant, and the women were comfortable with having shaggy armpits?

"We will make a proper African out of you yet," Madame Cabochon said to Amanda.

That got Cripple going again. "*Mamu?*" she gasped. "You will turn Mamu Ugly Eyes into an African woman like me?"

It was time for Amanda to step up to the plate. "Cripple! Now we talk seriously."

"*Eyo, Mamu.*" But yet she giggled.

"Since you have made the difficult journey down the hill through the *tshisuku,* and you are heavy with child, do you wish to rest in that little room next to the woodshed?"

"*Aiyee, Mamu,* but that cement floor is very hard."

"And so it is. Permit me to set up a *cot*—a folding *bulala* that does not touch the floor. You will find that even more comfortable than the slipping mat in your own hut."

Cripple clapped her hands with glee. "*Mamu,* indeed you are very kind for a white woman. Perhaps what this *mamu* with the big breasts says is true; you are turning into an African."

Amanda smiled broadly. She felt like clapping as well. Actually, she felt like hugging the outspoken Muluba woman and the worldly Belgian. After all, they came closer to being her friends than any other women at Belle Vue. And to think that neither of them were Christians! At least Colette Cabochon, being a Roman Catholic, stood a small chance of going to heaven—perhaps a small house on the outskirts of the Protestant mansions—but poor Cripple, who was an outright heathen, was going to writhe in agony for all eternity in the literal flames of hell. Oh well, those thoughts had to be put on a back burner for now.

Anyway, in the end, wasn't the question of who got saved really up to God, even if the Bible already did spell everything out clearly? If only Amanda had another Southern Baptist her age whom she could talk to—*really* talk to about such troubling matters. Funny, but since coming to Africa to share her faith, she found that her faith had been shaken like never before.

"Cripple," Amanda said, "it will make my heart very happy to do this. If you so desire, you may even stay in that room until you have birthed your child."

"We laugh and we cry, *Mamu,*" Cripple said, by way of expressing thanks. "Will you also serve my meals to me in my little room next to the woodshed?"

"*Nakuya,*" said Madame Cabochon. *I have gone.* But she stayed, her feet firmly planted to the kitchen floor.

"*E,* I will bring you meals," Amanda said, "but only in the event that you are no longer able to come to the kitchen."

"The meals must not be European," Cripple elaborated, "because European food is not real food."

Madame Cabochon clamped both hands over her mouth to stifle a laugh that still managed to escape as a loud snort. For that she received withering glares from both Amanda and Cripple.

"It is agreed, however, you must bring me only *bidia bia Bena Baluba.* I cannot eat the cassava mush that the Bena Lulua make, for it is not as smooth and silky as ours. As for the stuff that the Bapende people call cassava mush—bah, I have tasted better mush made by a goat."

"Cripple, I do not know how to make mush of any sort; besides, for now I have neither cassava flour, nor palm oil."

"*Aiyee,*" Cripple wailed, "then how will my family join me?

They have never tasted this European food—except for Their Death, my husband. They will not like it; that I can assure you."

"Cripple, how can this be? Many times I have sent you home with leftover food to share with your family. What did you do with it?"

"I ate it, *Mamu*," Cripple said without blinking an eyelash. "On the way home I sat in the *tshisuku* and ate it."

"But so much food?"

"I was hungry. Besides, if I took it home, then Their Death would eat it all, and then I would have none. Was that your intention, *Mamu*? That I should not have any of it?"

"No, of course not! It is just that I find it very hard to believe— I mean, I have met Their Death, and he seems like a very nice—"

"She is telling the truth," said Madame Cabochon in rapid-fire, if not quite perfect, English. "In her culture, the men, they eat separately, and they get to choose first if there is protein."

"Even if a pregnant woman is involved? Or growing children?"

"*Oui*, my little innocent American cabbage; this is the real world. This is not Stone Hill."

"It is *Rock* Hill, madame, *not* Stone Hill," Amanda said, her eyes narrowing. At the moment she didn't feel very much like a missionary—at least not like a good missionary. Of that much Amanda was certain.

"*Tch*," said Cripple. "I find this gibberish you speak most annoying. Do you not see how I wait patiently for you to supply a solution?"

"A *solution*? For what?"

"*Aiyee, Mamu,* is it not a most fortunate thing that it is the Belgians who are our oppressors, and not you Americans? At least the Belgians, cruel as they are, are not without ideas. For instance, how will you satisfy the appetite of Their Death, Second Wife, myself, and our seven children?"

"There are *seven* children now?"

"*Tangila* [behold], this is not a ball of cassava mush that protrudes from beneath my blouse."

"Indeed it is not," Amanda said, feeling only slightly relieved. Six children, seven children, all of them running around half naked and screaming in the cramped courtyard between the outbuilding and the main house; this would not do at all—not if this was to continue on as a missionary rest home.

Of course, a missionary rest home, for all the Protestant missionaries of the right persuasion; that is what this establishment was intended to be; that is why folks back in the States sacrificed and put an extra dollar or two in the offering plate each Sunday. They certainly didn't do it so that one misshapen Muluba woman with an attitude the size of Texas could use it as her personal convalescence home.

"*Wewe tangila* [you behold]," Amanda said. "My offer was to you, Cripple, but only to you. I am sorry if this offends you or your family, but the people in America, to whom this Missionary Rest House belongs, do not wish me to allow anyone—Belgian or African—to live here. Only American missionaries are permitted to stay here, and even they must leave after two weeks. That is their rule."

Amanda had no doubt that the woman was insulted and possibly even very angry, but the Mission Board had tied her hands. What could she be expected to do? Besides, it wasn't realistic to expect just Cripple and her family to occupy the small courtyard. Amanda might be a newcomer to the Congo, but already her knowledge of local ways gave her a pretty good idea that along with any extended family came chickens, ducks, and the ubiquitous goats. Even the constant roar of the falls would be unable to drown out that cacophony of cackles, quacks, and bleats.

"*Nakuya kashide, mene mene,*" Cripple said, and hobbled straight outdoors.

Her parting words—"Now I have truly gone *forever*"—stung Amanda like a face full of pea gravel flung up by a stock car on a dirt road. She stood there helplessly, wanting to chase after her, but not knowing what to say. She wouldn't—she *couldn't*—give into Cripple's unreasonable demands. It was so terribly unfair! And even if she decided to chase after that irritating little woman—well, Cripple had already turned and been swallowed up by a bougainvillea hedge.

Madame Cabochon touched Amanda's elbow gently, although it still made her jump.

"It is hopeless, *non*?" Madame Cabochon said.

"What is?"

"This Congolese friendship circle. You are familiar with this custom, *oui*?"

Amanda quickly sifted through the mountain of facts she'd packed into her brain during language school. Ah, yes! The custom of friendship reciprocity. First the African presented you with a gift, often with a great show of friendship—but it wasn't a *free* gift, you see. You were expected to give one in return. And that new friend presented you with a second gift, after which you presented her with another, and so on and on it went. Of course since you were the unimaginably rich white, your gifts were expected to get bigger and bigger (think larger and larger gifts of cash). Presumably this went on forever, or, until you, the white, turned into a bad friend and stopped the cycle.

"I think it is a horrible custom," Amanda said. She could feel her nostrils flaring with anger at just the thought of being used that way.

"*Oui,* some understand it as such. However, it is really quite different from a sociological point of view."

"Huh?" It was one three-letter word that Pierre had told Amanda he wished he could remove from the American vocabulary. On that account, he and Amanda's mother would certainly have seen eye to eye.

"Mademoiselle, it will undoubtedly amuse you to learn that I possess an undergraduate degree in sociology from the Sorbonne in Paris. It was purely an affectation on my part, since it was my intent to marry rich men, never to work—instead, I have done neither!" She laughed heartily and did not seem the least bit embarrassed by her confession. "At any rate, it is my belief that this custom of giving gifts is a way of making strong bonds between individuals. There are cultures in the world where men allow visitors to sleep with their wives as an act of hospitality. The customs of others are sometimes hard to understand, *non*?"

"*Non*—I mean *oui*. Do you think that I was too hard on Cripple? There really wasn't anything that I could do! It wasn't just the rules, you see." Amanda lowered her voice, although to the best of her knowledge there wasn't anyone else around to hear her. "I'm not above breaking a few stupid rules. Don't get me wrong; I'm still a good missionary and all that. It's just that friends count for something with me."

"Mademoiselle, one cannot be friends with servants, and one cannot be friends with the natives. Therefore, most especially, one cannot be friends with native servants."

"I think you are a snob, Madame Cabochon. And what I was about to say is that if I thought I could get away with it, I would have made an exception for Cripple. However, some of the other missionaries are real sticklers for the rules, and I have no doubt that they would report me if they saw native children staring in their windows. Then I'd lose my job and get sent packing back to the States. And I mean pronto." She took a deep breath, knowing that she shouldn't go further, but like a semitrailer truck headed down a steep incline, she was quite unable to stop herself. "That would suit you just fine, wouldn't it?"

The belle of Belle Vue, the woman to whom every man gravitated like ants to a picnic, turned as pale as the October moon. "What do you mean by that, *chérie*?"

"I know all about you trying to seduce my Pierre," Amanda said. "Don't you try to deny it, because there are witnesses who saw—who saw—well, it was just shameful what they saw. And I know it was all your fault, because Pierre is not that kind of man."

The color flooded back into Madame Cabochon's perfect complexion. "Oh, that! *Oui,* you are quite correct; indeed, I did attempt to seduce your young handsome Pierre, for he is a most attractive man. He is like a fine dessert—perhaps a *pot de crème au chocolat;* I could eat him with a spoon. But you see, Mademoiselle Brown, there is a problem, and it is that he is *your* Pierre." Colette Cabochon jiggled her considerable assets. "He is interested in only you."

The Belgian Congo, 1958

The men were overjoyed to learn that there had once been a ferry crossing. They tried to communicate this information to the people on the other half of the bridge, but to no avail. Finally, in desperation, Pierre commandeered one of the Missionary Rest House's oldest sheets and painted the message on it. Unfortunately, the moving water generated its own breeze, and since the oil-based paint did not dry as fast as Pierre wanted, some of the words on the sheet became illegible. Still, without a doubt the bulk of the message was understood.

Of course, that didn't mean that the men on the other end of the bridge turned around and made a beeline for the jungle at the edge of town in search of the old ferry landing. How preposterous that would have been. Supposing one of them would have discovered something useful, then what? Which of them was actually going to perform manual labor in the withering heat of the suicide month?

"They don't look like they're in very much of a hurry," Amanda shouted into Pierre's ear as they moved away from the roar of the falls. She'd watched in utter amazement as the crowd of Belgians disbanded; surely she'd seen sunburns fade away faster than that.

"There is not much they can do," the young Belgian police captain said.

"You mean, there isn't much they are *willing* to do—not without some African to do it for them."

Despite the heat, she had brazenly linked arms with him, hoping that he would see it as a playful gesture. However, he pulled away.

"Amanda, I think maybe Colette is right when she said that Americans feel obligated to judge everyone else."

"*What*? I can't believe you said that."

By now they were far enough from the falls that they no longer needed to shout in order to be heard. "How long have you been here? Four months?"

"Three."

And two days, she might have added, if she hadn't felt quite as miffed. Instead she reminded herself that she was a responsible adult now, a missionary, not a rebellious teenager, and although it was a struggle, she put her best foot forward.

"Well, if *they* can't do anything, then what can *we* do?"

"*We* will wait until tomorrow. That will give the mud on the hill more time to dry. It needs to be more—uh—staple, yes?"

"Stable."

They continued to walk back to the Missionary Rest House in silence. Halfway there Amanda stopped abruptly, and quite on purpose, causing Pierre to execute some fancy footwork in order to avoid bumping into her. It was definitely not the mature—not to mention Christian—thing to do—and she instantly felt guilty. What a boob she had been. She'd berated the local white populace, been properly upbraided for it, and now she'd just thrown a tantrum.

"I'm sorry," she blurted.

"*Mais non*, it was my fault. I should not have been following so close."

"Not that. I'm sorry for being such an all-around jerk."

"*Jerk?* What does this mean?"

"It means that I've been a fool."

He took her in his arms, right there in the open—in broad daylight! "You are not this round jerk, Amanda; you are under very much pressure. But soon everything will be back to normal. I promise. Life is always like this in the Congo; we move from one crisis to the next."

"They have been this bad before?"

"Believe me, much worse. Ask any of the older people, like Father Reutner, perhaps. He will tell you stories that you will not believe."

Amanda wrinkled her nose; she'd been told that it was not her most endearing habit. "Hmm. You know, I've only seen him once. I was taking a walk through the village and I passed the Catholic mission. Father Reutner—at least I think that was him—was crossing the lawn from one building to the next. He was talking to an African, but he looked over and saw me. Then he looked away quickly and never looked back again. Don't you think that's odd?"

The sun was now high in the sky, and the heat searing. Perhaps that is why Pierre released her so suddenly. Or perhaps once again she'd come across as self-centered and vain.

"Ah, well, Father Reutner is very shy—among us whites, that is; among the Africans he is just the opposite. In fact, there have been complaints that he—well—it is best that I do not go into details. I have heard it said—by a certain sociologist—that the reason for this is because he thinks of the Africans as children, and therefore certainly not his social equals."

"Oh my," Amanda said. She had heard similar comments from some of the older members of her church back home. In fact, even her father once cited this very reason for why the Negroes in the American South had yet to achieve social and economic parity with the whites. That conversation—at the Sunday dinner table—had ended in an explosive argument, following which Amanda drove all the way into Charlotte with some students, all girls, from Winthrop College, searching for some real-life Negroes to whom they could express their solidarity.

It was a cold, blustery day, with few people out and about, and those that were wouldn't even glance their way. At last they spotted a cluster of tightly huddled youth in West Charlotte, but as Amanda and her friends approached and slowed their car, the Negro youth eyed them suspiciously. Then one of them, a girl, flipped them the bird.

"What you white folks doin' here?" she said. "Beat it before we whip y'all's skinny white asses!"

Amanda related this story to Pierre on the remainder of their return walk. She left no detail out, and he listened intently.

"This race matter is *très difficile, n'est-ce pas*? There is what we have in our head, then what lives in our hearts, and then what lives under our skin."

"But you mean skin *color*, not under our skin. Am I correct?"

"Exactly not. I mean under the skin—just under the skin. These are the things that make us react without thinking. Your head knew better, and so did your heart, but under your skin it was necessary to prove that you were not a racist. And for this girl you describe; she too reacted to what was under her skin. She is poor, she is cold, and then you come with your white face, in your warm car, and you look at her as if she is an animal in a zoo."

"I most certainly did not! You take that back." *Talk about an "under your skin" reaction,* Amanda thought. Jeepers, but Pierre had a way of getting under her skin like nobody's business!

Pierre had the audacity to remain calm. "Speaking of priests," he said, although the idiom didn't sound natural coming from his lips, "the monsignor asked me to inform you that he will not be at dinner tonight."

Amanda was grateful for the change of subject. "Oh? Why not? Is he not feeling well? It must be all that sun earlier."

"If that was a problem, then perhaps he feels even worse. He will not be attending dinner because he has already gone up the hill."

"*What?* How?"

"The same way that Cripple came down, through the *tshisuku*."

Amanda felt tears of frustration well up. "But if *he* can do it, then why can't *you*—why can't *we*?"

"Tomorrow we will climb up the road—I promise. We will not be surprised by snakes on the road. Trust me; you will be glad that you waited."

"Maybe," she said, and she forced a small smile, although on the inside she felt like she was going to explode with frustration.

Early on the morning of the third day, three miracles occurred. The first was that the generator was repaired and electric power was restored. This miracle was witnessed by all the whites and those few Africans who were wealthy enough to afford such a luxury.

The second miracle was the birth of a two-headed goat to Mbushi Mutu, the cranky old woman who sold kindling wood in the marketplace. Two-headed kids were not unknown to the villagers, but these freaks of nature generally died at birth or shortly after; they certainly were not viable. However, Mbushi Mutu's kid was born with heads of equal size and development and centered on the neck. The youngster stood right on schedule, and both heads were able to locate its mother's teats and took equal turns nursing. When the mother walked, the kid walked with it without any difficulty, the outer eyes on the two heads apparently cooperating with each other.

This most astonishing sight attracted a huge crowd of people; unfortunately, it also meant that the morning mass at Saint Mary's Catholic Church was sparsely attended. When even the altar boys did not show up, the monsignor lost his temper. He had managed to struggle up the hill the day before, covered in mud and cuts from the sharp blades of *tshisuku*, only to find that the old priest, Father Reutner, had suffered a mild stroke—well, at least his speech was slurred and the left side of his face seemed to be sagging. And yes, the monsignor had checked the septuagenarian's breath, and although it reeked, he couldn't detect alcohol.

What irritated the monsignor so much that morning was that he'd wanted to be on the road as soon as possible. With the bridge out, he needed to take the long way around to get back to Luluabourg, and it was critical that he make his flight back to Rome. This meeting with the cardinals—well, the monsignor didn't have to have it spelled out for him in Latin beforehand to know that he was about to be made bishop. Now, unexpectedly, he'd been called upon to lead Mass. But for so *few*, and all of them infirm, or else elderly. *Si, si*, these were just the sort of people Our Lord would have ministered to, but the monsignor was not the Prince of Peace. He was not even yet a prince in the church. Unless he got his butt back to Rome in time, he might not even be made a bishop.

But just because the monsignor was human, with a man's emotions, that did not mean that he was any less punctilious in his religious observance. Mass began at the appointed hour and continued in the usual way until it was time for the handful of attendees to file down to the front to receive the host. Just as the first of them stepped into the aisle and was genuflecting on arthritic knee, the doors to the church were flung open and brilliant rays of sunlight flooded the dim sanctuary.

"He is risen!" With the sun to her back, the woman who cried out was in silhouette, helping her cut a dramatic, almost biblical figure.

"*Eyo*," the congregants responded in unison. "Jesus Christ *wakubika bulelele!*"

"*Nasha!* It is the man Jonathan Pimple who has risen from the dead!"

"Blasphemer!" shouted the monsignor. "Get out of my church!"

"No, you must come and see for yourselves. The night before last, my kinsman Jonathan Pimple was found dead in his chair. It was the heart-stopping disease. Yesterday morning we buried him in front of half the village. This morning when I was taking some food and drink to him at the grave, I saw him standing there."

"Food and drink?" cried the monsignor even louder. "If you were taking him food and drink, then he was not dead!"

It was a curious and most irritating habit—one which the monsignor never understood—that when Africans got nervous, they laughed. Well, at least he understood that much. Some whites thought that the blacks were laughing *at* them, which was usually not the case. Still, the laughter in the church did nothing to improve his mood.

He felt a gentle tug on his sleeve. "Monsignor," Father Reutner said, "this woman is a heathen. The food and drink were not meant for a living person; it was a symbolic meal to feed the dead. When the dead person eats this tiny portion of cassava mush—about the size of a walnut—it will turn into a full-size ball of mush, the size of a soccer ball."

"But that's ridiculous! How can they possibly believe such non-sense? Something real like a bite of mush turning into something they can't see?" In that moment he remembered one of his many frustrations with the Congo, one of the reasons he had chosen to pursue his spiritual path in Rome.

"It's because they're heathens, Monsignor."

"I am not a heathen," the woman said. Her eyes were blazing with defiance, right there in the house of God. This very attitude did little to support her assertion.

"*Tangila mukashi*" (look, woman), the monsignor said. "Dead people do not rise from the grave in these days. Truly, this has not been the situation since the days of Jesus Christ, which was before your ancestors' ancestors."

"*Muambi*, I do not call you a liar; I only ask that you come and look."

"This is preposterous," Father Reutner mumbled in Latin. It was the secret language of the priests.

"Go! Leave my church at once, for you bring the devil with you along with your lies."

Still the fire would not leave the woman's eyes. She was a Mupende woman—he could tell by her pointed teeth—which helped add to her devilish appearance in his mind. And since Monsignor Clemente had a very keen mind, and an even more active imagination, he thought he could actually smell something satanic about her. A faint odor of sulfur perhaps?

"*Mukelenge wanyi*," she said—my lord—"it is not just that my kinsman lives; there is more that may interest you. Even now as I speak Jonathan Pimple is preaching to the people of this village in the marketplace."

"Preaching?" rasped the old man, Father Reutner.

"Explain this, sister," said the monsignor, but he was already walking toward the large twin doors at the front of the church.

The wild-eyed woman began to explain but was not given a fair chance. The monsignor would not have denied that this was so, because the courtesy of fairness is not something one extends to the Prince of Darkness.

It had been many years since Monsignor Clemente had visited the marketplace in the Belle Vue workers' village. In fact, he had never been to this exact location, for the old place had become disease-ridden during a smallpox epidemic, so the stalls were demolished and houses built in their place for the new wave of workers brought in to replace those who had died. There was no need, however, for the monsignor to ask directions to the site of Jonathan Pimple's preaching, for the earth practically shook with periodic roars of approval from what sounded like a vast and enthusiastic throng.

And that is exactly what the monsignor beheld: it was a scene straight out of one of the Gospels, except that all the participants were black. Whereas John the Baptist had preached repentance, and Jesus the Christ had preached atonement, this Jonathan Pimple was clearly preaching blasphemy. After all, he had not been ordained into Holy Orders; he was not even ordained as a lay deacon. He was a Protestant. More to the point, and more dangerously, the people liked what he had to say!

Forgetting his Italian manners, plus the benefits of maintaining goodwill, Monsignor Clemente shouldered his way through the wall of unwashed and somewhat odiferous humanity. Initially, not knowing who he was, the people pushed back. Then one by one, realizing that they had dared to elbow their master, they would cry out in panic or abject apology and yield their place to a man who assumed too much to be grateful. At last, his best "dress" stained with mud and mucus, Monsignor Clemente was given a front-row seat on a rickety homemade wooden chair.

"Ah," Jonathan Pimple said, wasting no time to point out his presence, "our benefactor has arrived."

The Belgian Congo, 1958

Amanda made sure that everyone got an early start. She set her alarm for an hour before the sky turned pink so that she could fire up the Primus stove and boil coffee. But then when the electricity returned before she was through with her morning ablutions, she literally cried with relief and thanksgiving.

By the time the rest of her guests were dressed, coffee was ready and so was a pile of toast and a freshly opened tin of Blue Band margarine, as well as the jar of Crosse & Blackwell marmalade. Thank goodness for the fact that these continental Belgians didn't go in for a proper breakfast like the English did.

"I have enough *mikasu* that we can each have our own."

"*Pardonnez-moi*," said Madame OP apprehensively. "What is the meaning of this word? My English is just so-so."

"Your English is excellent, Madame Fabergé," said Pierre, with utmost sincerity, although he winked at Amanda. "*Lukasu* is the Tshiluba word for a hoe—the sort one uses in the garden." He turned to Amanda. "Tell me, mademoiselle, why will Madame OP be in need of a *lukasu* today?"

"Because, Captain Jardin," Amanda said archly, "you promised that today we would do our best to carve a path up the hill so that we can get to the workers' village. Once we get there, we can direct our workers to begin repairing the former ferry line. And since we all have servants who live in the village, then it seems to follow that we all pitch in equally to achieve our objective. There, now I'm sure it all makes sense." Amanda stood and, using a clean bread knife, began scraping crumbs from the red-and-white gingham tablecloth into her hand.

Pierre and the OP stood as well. "Ah," Pierre said, "your objective meshed perfectly with mine, and your means of execution is really quite admirable. However, you have forgotten one small detail."

Amanda's lips formed a perfect circle. "Oh?"

"Yes!" roared the OP. "You forget that my wife is not a common laborer!"

"You Americans," Madame Cabochon said, and laughed gaily—or perhaps it was with forced gaiety, in order to diffuse the OP's wrath—"you have no sense of class."

"Colette!" Pierre barked. "There is no need for insults."

"Oh no, it was not an insult," Amanda said quickly. "She was quite correct on that score. We did, after all, fire our last king on the grounds that he performed poorly at his job."

"Touché," she said, "what cheeks!" Then she laughed even harder.

Perhaps it was going too far to say that the OP and his wife, Madame Fabergé, were amused as well, but at least they dropped the subject and suddenly became intensely interested in their coffee. They did not, however, pick up a *lukasu* and set forth to toil under the broiling sun as did the rest of them.

Although to be perfectly honest, that morning the work that everyone else did was minimal. Pierre was in the prime of his life and as fit as they come. His baggy khaki shorts offered him complete freedom of movement (and for Amanda a far more personal view of the captain than she felt was appropriate just then). Pierre was able to leap from clay ledge to clay ledge, and he hauled the women up after him, so that almost no hoeing was required. He assured the women that he would get "boys" in the village to do the work later.

By then Amanda understood that the term "boys" in this context referred to house servants of any age and/or field workers, usually in their late teens or early twenties. At first she had bristled at hearing the word, thinking to be at last cut free from a world of racial prejudice, but now just three months into her term of missionary service, the word *boy* was part of her everyday lexicon, and it no longer troubled her. Amanda's house*boy* was Protruding Navel. When the Missionary Rest House was booked solid during the cool months, he had a helper whose position was table *boy*. Then of course, one must take into account the wash *boy* and the yard *boy*.

At any rate, the trio scaled the high hill much quicker than any of them had envisioned. In fact, they managed to enter the narrow, canopy-covered lanes of the village before the cruel sun was high enough to bake them senseless, but it was a village strangely devoid of life. Clucking hens scratching among fallen mango leaves along with their peeping chicks, and swarms of flies that rose from piles of dog turds, were the only signs of life.

Then an old crone, who must have been fresh from the bush, stepped shakily from a hut. Her naked breasts hung down to her belly like a pair of ripe avocados at the end of twisted black socks. When she saw three white people coming directly at her, she bleated pitifully and staggered backward out of sight. But as she was the only person they had encountered thus far, Pierre had them stop so that he might question her.

"*Baba*," he said without looking at her, "do you know where everyone is?"

"*Aiyee*," she said. "Truly, I know nothing."

"Surely you must know something, mother."

She cackled nervously. "I know that I am very old, master. Very, very old."

"How old is that, *Baba*?" Pierre asked. It was not an insulting question; to the contrary. If one was old, one was blessed. To be old meant having survived tribal wars, famine, a host of tropical diseases, and the most dangerous thing of all: the capricious white animal known as the *Bula Matadi*—the Belgian.

"My name is Locust Swatter," she said, "for I was born in the year of the great locust plague. Therefore, I can be certain of my age."

"This woman is fifty-eight years old," said Pierre after some quick mental arithmetic.

"Surely you are mistaken," Amanda said. "No one can look like that and be just fifty-eight! Besides, she claims to be ancient."

"But she *is* ancient!" Madame Cabochon said. "In the Congo, if you make it to forty years of age, you are old. Beyond fifty, you are ancient, believe me."

"She is right," Pierre said. "Sixty is almost unheard of in the rural areas."

Locust Swatter cackled again to get their attention. "How old is the one with the ugly eyes?" she asked.

Pierre laughed. "Guess."

"We didn't come to play guessing games," Amanda snapped in English. While it was true that she didn't need to be so touchy about her pale eye color, they really were wasting time, weren't they? Because somewhere, perhaps in the direction of the market, she could hear what sounded like the roar of a crowd cheering. Then silence. Followed by more cheering.

"*Baba*," Pierre said, *his* ugly blue eyes sparkling with barely disguised amusement, "we recognize your status as an ancient woman, and we can see that you are a woman greatly to be respected. In the light of this new knowledge, I must humbly ask you again: where is everyone?"

"*E*, that, master. Why did you not ask this sooner? They have all gone to the marketplace, to hear this new preacher by the name of Jonathan Pimple."

"Jonathan Pimple?" Amanda cried. "That man is no preacher!"

The crone recoiled at the force of the young missionary's reaction and stumbled back into the darkness of her hut. Amanda lunged after her, but she was stopped abruptly by one of Pierre's strong tanned arms.

"Mademoiselle," he said curtly, "that is not wise."

"I won't hurt her," Amanda said. "I just want to know what's going on."

"As do I. But she is *musenji*—an uncivilized one from the bush—and she might hurt you. She may appear to be frail, yes? But she has many years of experience that you do not have."

They headed straight for the marketplace after that, and with every step they took, the old hag's words were confirmed. Sure enough, the entire village had turned out to listen to the ranting of one man. He stood on a homemade wooden table at the north end of the square. It was there that the Belgian flag was raised every morning at dawn, and then lowered again at dusk, but as no Belgians had been there to enforce the rule as of late, the pole remained empty.

Jonathan Pimple held a megaphone to his mouth. It was the sort used by cheerleaders back in Rock Hill. At first he seemed oblivious to the new arrivals, as were his rapt listeners, so Amanda was forced to resort to colonial protocol.

Congo culture was one of jostling, not of silly "excuse me's" and "*Pardonnez-moi's*." Of course whites were above all that. They simply had to make their presence known by speaking a word or two in their clumsy accents (assuming their presence wasn't already known), and any crowd was guaranteed to part like the Red Sea. In the villages, older women unaccustomed to white faces would emit little shrieks of terror, babies would scream, and although some youths would laugh to showcase their bravery, not a soul dared stand his or her ground.

The citizens of the Belle Vue workers' village were more sophisticated, so that when Amanda and her entourage (for Pierre now followed *her*) worked their way through the throng, they initially went unnoticed by Jonathan Pimple.

"After three days—just like Jesus Christ—I too rose from the dead."

A great cry went up, a hundred voices woven into one. "*E, bulelela!*"

Amanda was dumbfounded. Just a few weeks ago she might have given Jonathan Pimple the benefit of the doubt and supposed that he was trying to be ironic—in the most inappropriate, sacrilegious way imaginable—or else that he was playing some sick joke. But these were not the words one would hear from the mouth of an African, not unless he actually meant them. That left only one other possibility: Jonathan Pimple was possessed by the devil.

"In the name of Jesus Christ I command you to leave the body of Jonathan Pimple," Amanda shouted. She held one hand high above her head and the other over her heart. Back home, at the tent revivals, the preachers had held a Bible over their hearts. They had also spoken with a great deal more confidence than Amanda. Then again, none of them had felt brave enough to come to the Congo and preach, had they?

"*Mamu!*" said Jonathan Pimple. "Please take a seat by the Roman Catholic priest, for I have saved you this chair. And yet another for the madame. Regrettably, there is none for the *Bula Matadi*." Jonathan Pimple no longer sounded the least bit possessed, nor did he sound angry.

Amanda looked to where he pointed and spotted Monsignor Clemente, then made haste to join him. When Madame Cabochon was also seated, and with Pierre squatting between them, Jonathan Pimple resumed his sermon. Or was it a political speech? Amanda wasn't sure at first.

"The followers of the Apostle preach that on Independence Day you will receive everything that is in your heart. Everything that belongs to the white man—if you desire it—it will be yours: his house, his car, even his woman and children. But I, Jonathan Pimple, who have likewise risen from the dead, am here to tell that this is not true. And it is all for our own good that these stories are not true."

"Speak for yourself, Mupende," an elderly man of the Bena Lulua tribe said. There was a drift of gray in his hair, which was rare to see, as few men lived to such a ripe old age. "I wish to have this white woman, the young one with the small breasts who is seated before you. She appears to have strong arms and would be of help in pounding the cassava flour in our mortar. My wife of many years has the 'weakening of arms' disease."

Amanda was dumbfounded. Gobsmacked, as her British friends would say. She had come to Africa to gather in lost souls for Christ, and instead, in front of the entire village on a Sunday morning, she was being spoken of as a commodity. As if she was a workhorse about to be auctioned at a farm sale. Or perhaps even a slave.

"*Kah!*" A bearded young man with a comb stuck into the back of his hair—a distinctly modern, urban style, to be sure—had pushed his way to the forefront of the assembly. "This *white* is indeed young, and thus she will need a nice hard tree to keep her happy." He thrust his hips a couple of times in Amanda's direction to underscore his point, and the crowd roared with laughter. Small children—of both genders—who had witnessed this shameful act immediately began to imitate what they had just witnessed, thrusting their tiny hips suggestively as the crowd grew ever more boisterous.

There is only so much humiliation one can take. Even missionaries have their limits.

"*Stop tormenting me!*" Amanda cried out in a loud voice as she jumped to her feet. The crowd convulsed with hysterics. Even

adults began to mimic Amanda's outburst. The really embarrassing thing was that some of the men were doing a darn good job
with their falsetto voices. Why didn't Pierre *do* something? After
all, he was the chief of police. Undoubtedly some of the men there
had to be in his employ. At the least he could have blown that
stupid whistle he insisted on wearing around his neck everywhere
he went—even to dinner parties. But oh no, he just sat there,
like a blond sphinx, with the slightest of smiles spread across his
too-handsome face. It was a face that she suddenly wished to slap,
because she now saw it as arrogant.

Pierre Jardin had warned her not to respond on a personal
level to provocations of this nature. He had made it very clear to
her that Africans did not laugh for the same reasons that Europeans and Americans laughed. He had urged her not to judge them
on that account.

Yes, she had heard all that he had to say on the matter, but that
didn't mean that Pierre's conclusions were the morally right ones.
What if the Lord had called her to Africa to teach the natives how
to behave as responsible citizens of the world? Face it, if no one
corrected their rude behavior, how on earth would they someday
be able to conduct themselves on the world stage? All this talk of
independence—in the light of how they were behaving now, that
was just so much silliness, wasn't it?

Amanda raised a clenched fist, more determined than ever to
educate these poor lost souls. *"Nuenu,"* she said, *"nudi bana—"*

At the same time that Pierre jerked Amanda's hand down, the
monsignor, struggling with his skirts, got to his feet. He raised
both arms, with his palms turned to the sky, and faced the people.
A calm smile lit his handsome Mediterranean face. Some might
have thought that it was by magic, or witchcraft, that the laughter ceased abruptly. For Amanda, who remained steadfast in her
faith, the scene she observed was a reenactment of Jesus stilling
the stormy waters on the Sea of Galilee.

Jonathan Pimple clapped delightedly. "It is good that the

people listen to you, priest. That means that they still subscribe to superstitions. All the more then will they believe the great truth that I will reveal for them."

The monsignor was a master manipulator. He bowed ever so lightly; it was a dip of his head, really—just enough to be ambiguous.

"Please begin your revelation, Monsieur Pimple. For those of us who arrived late"—he seemed to look at Madame Cabochon specifically—"please start at the beginning. How did you die? Who found you dead?"

After asking his questions, the monsignor took his time arranging his skirts and resuming his seat. Jonathan Pimple waited patiently.

"It was the heart-stopping disease," he said at last. "As I watched the great tree filled with monkeys sailing by, I began to feel pains in my chest and thought only to sit in my own chair again. The desire became strong, and so foolishly I ran, but when I reached my own compound I found that I could not breathe. Not even one breath—not the breath of a newborn infant. With great difficulty I struggled to sit in my chair, but then my memory on this earth stops."

"You passed out," Father Reutner said. "You were drunk."

Jonathan Pimple remained unflappable. "I do not drink, old man; I am a Protestant."

"The dead *stay* dead," Father Reutner said.

"How about Lazarus?" Amanda said, and then clapped her hands over her mouth.

One of these days her big mouth was going to get her into serious trouble. Pierre, the consummate pessimist, once said that it might even get her killed.

The Belgian Congo, 1958

Virtually everyone in the marketplace that morning, even the non-Christians, had heard the story of Lazarus rising from the dead. It was the sort of tale that was easy to translate and was well suited to being told around the hearth fires at night. To the hardworking inhabitants of the Belle Vue workers' village, almost nothing could have been funnier than hearing the young white girl besting the old white man at his own game—and not just any old white man either, but one who had brought a switch down across many a black buttocks just because it had not sat still during church, or perhaps it had squirmed a little during class.

The people cheered and clapped. They danced and stomped their feet.

"*Mamu, Mamu,*" they chanted.

Amanda gave serious thought to bolting. At the same time, her heart was pumped with evil, undeserved pride. She had bested an old man at his game, a man about to retire after decades of service to the Congolese people. The fact that he had nothing to bring them concerning a true understanding of Christ did not negate the work he had done in running a first-rate primary and secondary school; sadly, the Belgian government left the education of its subjects totally up to the missionaries.

So it was that while Amanda's soul struggled, balancing pride with shame, Jonathan Pimple raised his arms high above his head the way the monsignor had. However, Jonathan Pimple's hands gripped a thick pole or a staff—depending on how you chose to look at it. Amanda preferred to see it as a staff, for Jonathan Pimple emitted an aura. She saw in him elements of a modern-day Moses. After all, as soon as the noisy throng beheld the staff held high, they fell silent; the babies stopped crying and the old men ceased coughing. Obviously, this was not to say that Amanda bought into any of the nonsense that Jonathan was preaching.

"*Muoyo wenu,*" he boomed. Life to you.

"*E, muoyo webe,*" the crowd roared in one voice.

"Listen, good people," Jonathan said. "The followers of the Apostle believe that on Independence Day an automobile will magically appear in the sheds of anyone who has the faith to build such a thing. As you know, it must be built in the cemetery of one's ancestors. But in order to have the knowledge needed to drive this automobile, one must first mix the brains of a white man with palm oil and then smear it on one's own head. Good people, have you heard this prophecy before?"

"*Eyo!*" cried the people as if in one voice. "We have heard this."

"Friends," said Jonathan Pimple, "I have risen from the dead to tell you that this prophecy is all nonsense!"

"*Kah?*" Hundreds of people all said the same thing.

Jonathan Pimple grinned. "Think about it, friends; what if the brains came from a very *stupid* white man? Believe me, I have met many such men."

The people laughed. Amanda laughed with them, pretending to be oblivious to the glares from both Pierre and Father Reutner.

"These *B'Apostela* have already begun their quest for knowledge by digging up a white grave up in Port Francqui and removed from it a dead white man's brains. Now I ask you, my friends, what will you learn from a dead white man's brains? For it is their belief that after death the white man's spirit travels far to this place called heaven and the body rots, is eaten by worms, until all that remains is dust. Do these *B'Apostela* up in Port Francqui territory now know how to communicate with worms?"

It was plumb amazing to watch the way Jonathan Pimple worked the crowd, causing the people to explode into laughter and then silencing them just as quickly with his upraised staff. Of what did he remind her? Oh yes, a concert conductor. A black Moses concert conductor—what a spellbinding man! And to think that he had sought out Cripple for advice.

"It is far better," Jonathan Pimple said, now jabbing the staff in a multitude of directions, "that each one of you who so desires to drive an automobile learn how to operate the machine in a special school that I will establish just for this very purpose. I will find and recruit men who have served as chauffeurs to the white masters, and they will teach you everything that they know. I assure you, friends, that the citizens of the Belle Vue workers' village will drive far better than worms."

On and on Jonathan Pimple preached; nothing he said was seditious, and nothing was really sacrilegious barring his first statement that he had risen from the dead. When he finished forty-five minutes later, the natives had been whipped into a joyous frenzy and the whites, with the exception of Madame Cabochon, were foaming at the mouth.

"Truly, after rising from the dead, I am very hungry," Jonathan Pimple said. "Who among you has sufficient meat in his pot such that he might share with one who has peered into the future? Let it be known, however, that I am a Mupende and prefer the taste of cassava mush that uses millet as its base, and not corn."

"What a cheeky bastard," Pierre said.

"Our Risen Lord did not eat," Father Reutner said. "This man piles blasphemy upon blasphemy."

"What did you think of this performance, Amanda?" Madame Cabochon asked.

"The man performed very well," Amanda said curtly. "As a manipulator of human emotion, that is. But as to whether or not Jonathan Pimple is a cheeky so-and-so, well, I have no idea if his parents are married or not."

"Touché," the monsignor said. His hand rested lightly on Amanda's right shoulder as they pressed through the crowd. Then it slipped, accidentally to be sure, before glancing off her elbow, and grazing her hip. For a split second it was even pressed against her right buttock; but this was to be expected when you were worming your way through such densely packed humanity!

Humanity. *Bantu.* Whites are people too, Cripple reminded herself. It was a concept she struggled with every day. She had become very fond of the young *mamu* from America, the young woman she called Ugly Eyes, but from the time she could first remember, Cripple's ears had been subjected to the stories of the atrocities perpetrated on the black man in the Congo by the white man, things that only creatures lacking empathy could possibly have committed.

It has been said that even a leopardess will sometimes spare a newborn antelope fawn in favor of the doe, and is not the leopard the animal most lacking in empathy of all the beasts that roam the earth? How is it then that a white man, King Leopold of Belgique, had commanded that the right hand of each black man should be chopped off with a machete if he did not supply the king a certain quota of wild rubber tree sap? Chop, chop, chop; thousands of black hands severed by machetes—not to lie rotting on the forest floor—but to be collected by overseers and stacked in piles. And photographed! Millions more black backs bent under forced labor building roads and bridges and structures that were said to brush the clouds, so great were their height. All the while those accused of intransigence, or crimes, against the crown were beaten with strips of hippo hide, which dries to the thickness of two men's thumbs pressed together. When this hide is kept supple, there is nothing that can equal the pain that it delivers.

The American *mamu* shared the same white skin as the oppressors, the same pale eyes, and she said that she came from a place that was equally as incomprehensible as Belgique. Yet despite the fact that she screamed when she once saw a centipede in the room where she bathed, she did not permit anyone to kill it. Instead, she insisted that it be swept up and released outside so that there it might be free to bite someone else. But even if Mamu Ugly Eyes had the reasoning of a simple child, there could be no doubt that her intentions were good.

In many respects she was like Mushinga, the simple woman who lived in a lean-to by herself at the village edge. She had been born with her cord wrapped around her neck—as had others before her and since—but in the case of Mushinga the breath of life had been slow to fill her lungs. Hers was the mind of a child in an adult's body, and it was understood and accepted by all that no man should mount her for that very reason, just as no man would take her for his wife. As she was without parents or brothers and came from a no-account clan, Mushinga relied on the kindness of others for her survival, and in this she was most fortunate. Never a day went by that a hunk of *bidia ne matamba* wrapped in banana leaves—sometimes with a taste of meat—wasn't left on a stump in front of her hut. Occasionally the befuddled girl, who was now a woman bending with age, would discover a slightly used head wrap, or even a serviceable waist wrap, draped over the coffee bush at the edge of her clearing.

Likewise, as the people of the workers' village pulled together to care for the village idiot, so would Cripple do her best to care for the helpless white creature that fate had thrown into *her* path. But just as no village was capable of protecting its idiot from every danger—snakes and evil spirits to name just two—neither could Cripple guarantee that the bumbling young missionary would come to no harm. Fortunately, Cripple was now in possession of some knowledge that might be useful to the younger woman, she whose mind was used to thinking in untraditional ways.

"*Mamu Mesu Mabi!*" Mistress Ugly Eyes! When Cripple spotted Amanda Brown, she called to her in a voice that was rounded and soft, like that of a dove. She did this knowing that the white woman would hear her own name, yet at the same time the soothing sound would fall soft, perhaps even unnoticed, upon the ears of others.

The missionary turned. "Cripple! I thought you were angry with me!"

"Step into the next alleyway, *Mamu*. Go but a short distance to where a Flemish mulatto sells scrawny chickens in cages. Pretend you are interested in buying one of these pathetic creatures."

After speaking those words, Cripple fell back into the dispersing crowd, until she had observed all those who had been milling around them disappear in various directions. Then she too set out for the mulatto's shop and, being a no-nonsense sort of woman, arrived almost on the heels of young Amanda Brown.

"Cripple," Mamu Ugly Eyes said immediately, "I do not understand this at all. Why do we play games?"

"*Mamu*, it is not a game that I play. To the contrary, it may be a matter of great importance, but as yet I do not know how. You see, Jonathan Pimple has—*aiyee!* Behold, is this not the sickest chicken to ever stand upon one leg? I tell you, not even a starving jackal with eight pups would come near this creature."

"Blackie," growled the Flemish mulatto angrily. He had wandered too close and had heard his birds being disparaged. Now he was retaliating.

"*Katuka,*" Mamu Ugly Eyes said to him.

It is a very rude way of saying go away; nonetheless, it delighted Cripple to hear it come from the mouth of her former employer. Mamu Ugly Eyes insisted on kindness *too* much, the result being that she reminded Cripple of gravy without salt.

The Flemish mulatto reared back as if he had been struck by an open hand. "Protestant," he hissed.

"*Eyo*," Mamu Ugly Eyes said. "I feel no shame in being Protestant. Now go and leave us be, so that we might examine these fortunate birds in peace."

The Flemish mulatto cocked his head. "*Mamu*, how is it that you think my chickens are fortunate, whereas your slave believes that they are unfit even to be jackal meat?"

"I am no one's slave," Cripple growled.

"They are fortunate chickens," the white *mamu* said quickly, "because they are safe from all predators. Not only will the jackals ignore these chickens, but so will the hawks." She pointed to the sky, where at any hour of the day one could see these birds circling directly overhead, because there was always some small creature below that lay dead or dying. "Behold," she said. *Tangila.* "Above your chicken pen there is only the sky."

Cripple slapped her thighs with laughter as the Flemish mulatto slunk away muttering. Then abruptly Cripple stopped her merriment and pulled Mamu Ugly Eyes into the blazing sun of the open alley.

"Cripple! *Biwaswa, umusha bianza biebe!*" Please remove your hands.

Lordy, if Grandma Brown could see how the two of them were acting this morning, she'd send them straight to that finishing school in Charleston that she'd always threatened to do. No, most likely Cripple would never even have been allowed inside the Brown family home, no matter how well she spoke English, not unless she happened to look like the Flemish mulatto.

"*Mamu,* you must listen to me; these are words of great weight."

That's when Amanda first felt a goose walk over her grave. "*E,* I will hear your words."

"This Jesus, whom you hold in much esteem, do you truly believe that he died and was buried beneath the earth?"

Amanda's heart skipped. Perhaps it wasn't a goose after all. Could it really be that Cripple had finally been moved by the Holy Spirit and was searching for the truth? If that were true, oh how exciting!

"Yes, Cripple! *Mena, mena.* Except that he was not buried beneath the earth, but in a small"—she paused to search her memory in vain for the word *cave*—"room carved out of rock. On the morning of the third day, he came back to life and walked out of that room."

"So he was not dead for three full days?"

"Cripple, what matters is that he died for our sins—"

"*Mamu,* did someone push hot chilies up his nose to see if he was dead?"

"No! But someone did something else equally as awful; a soldier cut him, here, on the side."

"*Aiyee! Mamu,* is it possible that a witch doctor gave your Jesus a potion to drink that made him appear as if he was dead, when indeed he was not?"

Amanda had thought she'd heard it all from skeptics, but this question truly took the cake. Then again, it was a distinctly African question, and it certainly made sense within the local culture. Actually, it was exactly what one might expect to hear from the heathen wife of a down-on-his-luck witch doctor. So, as irked as Amanda was by the question, she decided to do her level best to not let it show.

"No, there was absolutely no witch doctor involved. In fact, I do not think there were any witch doctors in that tribe of *Bena Yuda.*"

"Surely, *Mamu,* you are mistaken; when I was a girl, I sat outside my brother's classroom at the Catholic school and listened to many stories of *mualu mua kukema.*"

Miracles; Amanda had never been satisfied with the Tshiluba translation. First of all, Tshiluba used an expression, not just one word, and that expression had more than one meaning. It could mean remarkable things, extraordinary things, wonderful things, but even strange things. Given that linguistic restriction, the two-headed goat kid and the parting of the Red Sea were both miracles of equal standing.

"Cripple," Amanda said, trying very hard not to come across as irritated as she felt, "let us not argue about words. Instead, if it pleases you, tell me the kernel of your story."

"Yes, Mamu Ugly Eyes. This man, Jonathan Pimple, it is true that he died and was buried, and it is true that he rose again from the dead, but it is also true that he did so with the help of a witch doctor."

Amanda felt the goose step out over her grave for a second time. "What did you say?"

The Belgian Congo, 1958

*M*amu, there is medicine that can be obtained only from a witch doctor, which, if taken under proper supervision, brings on the symptoms of death. It was—"

"Symptoms?" The word in Tshiluba was new for Amanda.

"It appears as death, yet it is not death."

"Ah—like zombies."

"Like God? *Mamu,* are you ill?"

"No, Cripple. But when Africans were taken to my country as slaves, they brought with them knowledge of this medicine. These slaves were of the Bakongo tribe and their word for people who had taken the medicine and appeared to be dead was *nzambi.* But as you know, we whites have very poor hearing; we heard the word as zombie.

"*Mamu,* next time only the kernel, please."

Amanda smiled. "Continue, please."

"This *buanga* can be made to last for up to three days—sometimes even four—but always the person who takes it must be in very good health, and the entire time of death he must breathe through a—a bamboo reed!"

"So he is not really dead!"

"*E, Mamu,* he is really dead."

"*Nasha,* Cripple, he cannot be dead and breathing at the same time."

"*E.*"

"*Nasha.*"

"*Mamu,* you are most frustrating. I am telling you; a man who has taken this *buanga* is truly dead, for he has no movement here." She pressed her wrist with her fingertips. "Or here." She did the same with the artery behind her ear.

"Perhaps it is very slight and you just cannot feel it."

"*Tch,*" Cripple said, pursing her lips. "You offend me. There is more to tell, but clearly you do not wish to know."

"But I do!"

"Very well." Cripple cocked her head this way and that, wasting plenty of valuable time by posturing, before getting down to business. "It was Their Death who sold the *buanga* to Jonathan Pimple. Because it was his *buanga,* Their Death made sure that just the right amount was taken, and that the grave was at the proper depth. It was Their Death's responsibility."

Because Amanda cared so deeply for Cripple, she found herself feeling furious at that second-rate witch doctor. What if Jonathan Pimple had died during this stupid exercise? Then what? And what were those two men really hoping to accomplish? Surely Their Death didn't buy into the legend of a false prophet that he had helped create—wait just one cotton-picking minute! Maybe he did! The human mind was capable of tremendous feats of self-deception, particularly during times of extreme stress. Amanda had learned *something* in Psych 101 her freshman year at Winthrop College for Women.

However, just maturing a bit into adulthood had taught her that yelling at someone like Cripple was not going to achieve anything except to shut down the lines of communication. While frustration may be a difficult thing to swallow, at least it seldom leads to weight gain.

"Please tell me," she said, choosing her words carefully, "did Jonathan Pimple say why it was that he wanted to die and then to rise again on the third day?"

"*Nasha.*"

"*Tch,*" Amanda said, and it felt good to do so. "Do you *know* why it is that he wanted to do these things?"

"*Aiyee,* Mamu Ugly Eyes, it does not become you to make such a rude noise!"

"Cripple, answer my question—please."

"*Mamu,* clearly the man seeks to have a great following."

"I can see that, for I have brains in my head rather than a coconut, do I not?"

The witch doctor's wife smiled. "*Mamu,* there are many kinds of coconuts. Nevertheless, it is possible that I overheard Jonathan Pimple express the wish to avenge the death of his brother, Chigger Mite."

"Brother?" Amanda asked. "In what way were they brothers?" There is no specific word in Tshiluba for brother. Instead one uses a phrase that translates as "a male child of ours." In a polygamous society—especially in a society that is simultaneously polygamous and polyandrous such as that of the Bashilele—there exist many possible sibling combinations.

"They were brothers of the same mother *and* the same father. Their father was a chief of the Bapende tribe."

"Yet they came to you for help in settling a dispute?"

"*Tch, Mamu,* would you rather that they settled it using machetes?"

"*Nasha!* You see, that is why you are a wise woman, and I but one coconut among many! Cripple, how does being a man who has risen from the dead help Jonathan Pimple avenge his brother's death?"

Cripple clutched Amanda's arm tightly, and, while limping more than Amanda could remember, pulled her along until they were quite alone inside a small grove of guava trees on the western edge of the Belle Vue workers' village. Curiously, no one had followed them; to the contrary, the few people who may have noticed them approach the grove seemed to suddenly busy themselves, even if it just meant sweeping an already clean family compound. Amanda liked to think that she wasn't born yesterday (although many were the times her mother would beg to disagree). At any rate, there was a decidedly tawdry feel about the clearing that she found hard to put her finger on. And as for the guavas, they hung ripe on the tree, or rotting on the ground.

"What is this place?" she asked Cripple.

"*Tch.*"

"You know that eventually I will get an answer."

"Do you treat your slaves in America so badly?"

"You are *not* my slave!"

"Perhaps."

"Cripple, this is obviously a very important matter—otherwise you would not have brought me here. You must trust me."

The older woman rolled her eyes. "This place is where the *bena masandi* perform like wives for men who are not their husbands."

Amanda gasped softly. The first word that came to mind was *ick!* She knew about the birds and the bees—what went where—well, sort of. She had watched a bull and cow mate on her grandfather's farm down in Chester County, South Carolina. But heavy petting in the backseat at a drive-in movie—*that* was the scope of her actual experience! To be standing where women of ill repute actually did it was the ickiest thing she could think of. This was something she would definitely *not* write home about to her parents.

"*Mamu,* you must listen to me; I do not want to stay in this place all day."

How foolish she must have looked. "Nor do I; therefore, I am listening!"

When Cripple spoke again, it was in a whisper. "There was one other great prophet besides Kibangu who was said to have died and then risen again, *nasha*? Your Jesus Christ." She did not bother to pause for confirmation. "The claim that Jesus Christ was the first to do so is very important for both Roman Catholic and Protestant—"

"No, Cripple, Jesus Christ was the *only* one to do so."

"Perhaps. But you see, a claim such as this is sure to make Jesus Christ's followers very angry, is it not?"

"*Eyo*. Christians are to live in peace, but what this Jonathan Pimple is doing is very offensive."

"And it is more offensive to some Christians than to others."

"I guess so, but—"

"Mamu Ugly Eyes, do you not think that the priests at Saint Mary's Catholic Church might be the most offended?"

"*Kah!* Why is that?"

"Because, *Mamu*, they are the most Christian."

"*Bulelela* [most certainly] they are not!"

"But, *Mamu*, I respectfully ask that you consider the facts: they have a much larger building than the Protestant pastor who must worship his Jesus Christ at the edge of the village. Besides, they are white, and he is but a black man, and a *Muchoke*." She made a face whereby her upper lip practically touched her nose. "In addition, the Roman Catholic priest honors his Jesus Christ by displaying statues of both him and his *baba*—although the statue of Jesus Christ being tortured is not so nice. However, the priest wears a most attractive white dress on Sunday, burns secret herbs, and says magic incantations. The Protestant does none of this, which is why that church has so few members."

Amanda literally counted to ten before speaking. She did it silently, and she did it in Tshiluba since all the words for those numbers in that language have more than one syllable. Then she smiled before speaking.

"Cripple, the things that you mentioned do *not* make one a

better Christian. But are you suggesting that you think that Jonathan Pimple is trying to get the Roman Catholic priest angry at him because—wait! Do you really think that Father Reutner killed Chigger Mite? We may not worship the same way, but Father Reutner is still a man of God!"

The older woman regarded Amanda beneath lowered eyelids. "*Tch,* and still it is that you wonder why I remain a heathen? Do you not recall reading about the man named Judas Iscariot, who betrayed your Jesus for thirty franc pieces the night before he died? Was he not an even closer follower than this priest? Truly, truly, he was, *Mamu,* for this Judas knew your Jesus personally. Therefore, it is possible that anyone can be capable of murder—even a Roman Catholic priest."

Amanda felt like she'd just had the stuffing knocked out of her, and by a heathen yet! Yes, of course anyone was capable of anything if you put it the right (or was it wrong?) way. Who would guess that sweet, charmin' little ol' Amanda Brown from Rock Hill, South Carolina, had once been a drunk driver and should be banned from the roads?

"Yes," she said. "Cripple, you are absolutely correct. We are all capable of the worst sins. Therefore now, please advise me; what do you think it is that we should do next?"

Madame Cabochon was feeling utterly miserable; and when Colette's gorgeous exterior felt this bad, her somewhat less-than-stellar personality became downright irritable. Crabby—wasn't that the American slang? The heat and humidity of the suicide month had plastered her clothing to her body just as surely as if she'd stood under a rancid shower. As she made her way back through the workers' village, every fly from every dung heap, and its brother from every oozing sore on man or beast, immediately turned its attention to Madame Cabochon. Just when she thought that she couldn't stand any more misery, the salt she secreted attracted the tiny biting insects to her eyes. On top of that, her tear-filled eyes couldn't see well enough to do anything about this invasion.

Was Madame Cabochon the type to whine about her excruciatingly uncomfortable predicament? No! But she was most certainly the type to curse—which she did, and with great aplomb. She excoriated the gods and goddesses of antiquity, she damned the God of Father Reutner, the monsignor, and Amanda Brown, and she made several references to the devil's abode—all without the slightest twinge of guilt, and none of it did her a bit of good.

Both the handsome police chief, Pierre Jardin, and the handsome monsignor seemed to have slipped off somewhere into the crowd, and although it gave Colette a brief thrill to think that they might have slipped off together, she quickly discarded the thought as highly improbable. Pierre was very much the heterosexual. No doubt the monsignor was heterosexual as well—at least he had been before Rome got its hooks into him. The two were most probably off somewhere "putting fires out." That was an expression that the silly American had used the day before, and Madame Cabochon had rather liked it.

At any rate, without the opportunity to practice the harmless art of mature female flirtation, Madame Cabochon no longer had a reason to stay among the diseased and odiferous native population—although she wasn't the least bit prejudiced—so she walked back to the Missionary Rest House at the bottom of the very steep hill.

As is often the case, going down can be more difficult than going up, and Madame Cabochon's ill-fitting white cotton skirt (which she had had to borrow from Amanda) made several firm acquaintances with the red clay soil of the washed-out road. In addition, she broke two of her fingernails, twisted an ankle (just a little), and had a stick jam between her big toe and the next due to the fact that she was wearing sandals. *Mais oui*, Madame Cabochon had every reason to lash out at anyone who crossed her, especially if that someone had been lying around all morning on American-made patio furniture.

"*Sacré-coeur!*" It was the OP's mouselike wife, and she wasn't stretched out relaxing, she was lying for all the world as if she was prostrate with grief.

The small, dark woman didn't even have the courtesy to turn over and present her face so that she could be comforted efficiently. This further confirmed Madame Cabochon's belief that Madame Fabergé was rude and not suited to preside over Belle Vue's white society as its first lady. The woman *was* no lady; she knew *nothing* of manners. She lacked style, she found poise offensive, and she didn't even know how to set a proper table—more specifically, she didn't know how to instruct her table boy in this art.

"Madame Fabergé," Colette said, "if you do not turn over and look at me, then I shall have to turn you over myself."

Still there was no response, save for the heaving of her small thin shoulders and great sobs that sounded loud, even though the roar of the falls was practically deafening.

Madame Cabochon leaned in closer. "Not only will I turn you over myself, but then I will roll you off this ledge and over the cliff. The giant crocodile at the bottom will gobble you up in two bites. Of course he will spit you up a few seconds later because you are bound to be toxic—given your unpleasant nature—but you'll be dead nonetheless."

Although it was beyond belief, that stupid little troll remained just where she was, except that now she'd curled up in a ball like a hedgehog. Understandably, Madame Cabochon grabbed the fool by her disheveled dark hair and dragged her into Amanda Brown's salon, where she propped the woman up in a cane bottom armchair.

"Tell me," she shouted, "what is wrong with you? I have no patience today for the likes of you—but I am trying to be kind, I really am."

Madame Fabergé appeared startled by such honesty. Her swollen eyes blinked rapidly and she nodded.

"I am sorry, madame. It is because—well, Monsieur Fabergé has left me."

"*Qu'avez-vous dit?*"

"He left me. He said that Africa was too crazy for him. He said that because of the war and everything that he has lived through—you know—he just could not take the pressure. It was building up, you see. Now with the bridge destroyed, the mine production will be behind by many months, and it may never catch up before the day set for independence. The Consortium will surely fire him. When that happens, both his career and his reputation will be gone. He said that he may as well quit while he is in control, so that is exactly what he is doing."

"This is very tragic," Madame Cabochon said, trying to sound sympathetic. "I assume that Amanda Brown has a shortwave radio. And now that the electric power—"

"*Non, madame,* my husband came to this decision last night. Shortly after you made it to the top of the hill this morning, he also ascended. His plan was to appropriate a bicycle from one of the blacks, and then to take the old road to Luluabourg."

Appropriate? Blacks? This was not going to go well for Monsieur Fabergé, the soon-to-be-former OP of Belle Vue. His opinions and behavior aside, the old road was all but abandoned because it was almost a hundred kilometers longer than the new, direct one. Only missionaries dared travel it now, and they believed that they had angels sitting on their shoulders. What remained of the road would be rutted. Monsieur OP's tires would surely suffer multiple punctures, making progress so slow that he would run out of drinking water before covering even a tenth of the distance. Also, big fat poisonous pit vipers liked to sun themselves on dirt roads.

To sum it all up, one way or another, Monsieur Fabergé was doomed to further failure. The questions were *how* and *when*, but not *if* it would happen. Of course Madame Cabochon could not share such morbid thoughts with a grieving widow-in-the-making, not even one as unlikable as Madame Fabergé.

"Your husband is a resourceful man," Madame Cabochon forced herself to say. "I am sure that he will be just fine."

"*Oui?* Then I am crying for nothing."

Madame Cabochon perched her shapely rear end on the edge of the dark waif's armchair, given that there was plenty of room. American furniture, even when made in the Congo, was oversize and sturdy just like its owners.

"Indeed, you are crying for nothing. Just think, in a few weeks you will be back in Belgium; then this entire African nightmare will be over for you."

Then Madame Cabochon actually—possibly for the first time—looked into the other woman's eyes and saw the same look she'd seen in the eyes of captured monkeys in the village marketplace. Clearly, the woman dreaded returning to Belgium. But *why*?

"Madame," she said, "excuse me for asking, but are you and Monsieur Fabergé having problems?"

"That is an understatement," the OP's wife said, and she proceeded to laugh bitterly. "Monsieur Fabergé cannot stand me, and he has told me so on many occasions. Once he even sent his goons to rough me up."

"*Goons?*"

"Cousins; contacts from within"—she lowered her voice, which was already annoyingly soft—"the Gypsy community. Madame Cabochon, we are Gypsies."

"*C'est vrai? Fantastique!*"

"Madame, surely you cannot approve. As a true Belgian, you must find us reprehensible."

"A *true* Belgian? Madame Fabergé, do you ever attend Mass?—no, of course you do not, or else I would have seen you at church."

"I go at Christmas and Easter."

"Bah! But never mind. It is just that if you knew anything about our faith, then you would know that all mankind descends from Adam and Eve, who lived in the Garden of Eden. This was somewhere in Mesopotamia. I believe that today it is called Iraq. At any rate, it certainly was nowhere near Belgium. Therefore, our ancestors migrated *to* Belgium—*to* Europe—both your ancestors and my ancestors. While it may be that my ancestors took a more direct path, neither group started out in the area."

Madame Fabergé, pitiful creature that she was, let out a brief laugh despite her misery. "Madame Cabochon, just because the goons that Marcel hired to rough me up remain behind in Belgium, it does not make me any safer now than I was before."

"I am not sure that I understand; does this mean that *he* hits you?"

She twisted her body and pulled up her blouse to expose her back. Then she pulled up a bit of her hem to show Madame Cabochon her right thigh.

"He hits me in places that will not show, although once he accidentally hit me in the face and split my lip. You see this white line. It was during the war, and the only person available to sew it up was a seamstress. Fortunately, we *Belgians*"—she smiled now—"have always been rather good with the needle and thread."

Madame Cabochon nodded and without giving it much thought put her arm around the slim shoulders. "Madame Fabergé, if only I had known why it was that you are your mousy little self, I might have warmed up to you sooner. For you see, we have much in common. My husband also abuses me; oh no, not with his fists—you must put that picture out of your mind—but with his words. Monsieur Cabochon gets drunk every night that the Club Mediterranean is open, which is six nights a week; and when he comes home, his anger knows no bounds. Then I am a whore, a piece of excrement, an African monkey—and always, of course, the most stupid creature ever to walk this earth."

Tears spilled down Madame Fabergé's face. "Is this really true?"

"I would not lie about such things," Madame Cabochon said,

which wasn't strictly true, because she did lie about such things if it served her purposes. But as it happened, she was not lying at the moment.

"Why do you stay with him then?" Madame Fabergé asked.

Madame Cabochon yawned, suddenly feeling the need for a nap. "It is the other way around, really. He stays with me, and the reason is that I am rich. *Very* rich. My parents made their money off a palm oil plantation up near Coquilhatville. They made tons of money, but they are both dead now.

"The important point is that I have decided to invest in the future of this crazy country and start another palm oil plantation here, as close to the workers' village as I can procure land. You see, already the village has drawn too many people for the jobs available in the Consortium mines, and who knows how long the diamond deposits will last. On the other hand, every African in the Congo consumes palm oil at least once a day—usually twice—so that a working farm, with a processing plant and a distribution center, can be a source of employment for many people long after I'm gone."

Madame Fabergé smiled through her tears. "You are a very smart woman, Madame Cabochon. And very brave as well."

"Please, call me Colette."

"Colette," the little Gypsy woman whispered.

"Good. But I have more news to share. You see, I am kicking that drunk out of my life when his current contract with the Consortium expires, which is December thirty-first. At that point, my brother, who is a confirmed bachelor, will be moving down from Coquilhatville to move in with me, and we—well, I will get right to the point. Are you good with numbers, Madame Fabergé?"

"Numbers?"

"Adding, dividing, more adding—maybe a *little* subtraction, but not too much." Madame Cabochon laughed.

"I was number one in my class at maths."

"Excellent! Then the job is yours if you want it."

"Job?"

"Vincent and I are looking to hire a Belgian bookkeeper and secretary. She must be a mature, responsible woman who knows her own head and who has at least some acquaintance with the Congo. We will build you a house—"

"I accept," Madame Fabergé said as the tears resumed flowing.

The Belgian Congo, 1958

The rectory of Saint Mary's Catholic Church contained a small private chapel reserved for whites only. It was used primarily for life-cycle events, such as baptisms and funerals. First Communions, unfortunately, had to be integrated to show that the Body of Christ was one.

Father Reutner shuddered when he recalled the one wedding he'd been forced to perform. A high-ranking Consortium bachelor fell in love with the daughter of a Portuguese merchant from Angola, and since both were Catholics in good standing, he couldn't very well refuse. But the man was of good, blond Flemish stock, and she was the sort of Portuguese who one could tell, by just a quick glance, had Moorish blood coursing through her veins. Say what you will, but it was an interracial marriage.

And then there were the relatives: scores of them. Loud, the women heavily perfumed, everyone crowded in that little cement block room barely larger than a seminarian's cell. Surely that was what hell was like—that and what he'd seen in Europe during the war. Oh, and he'd seen plenty of evil here in the Congo as well.

In fact, Father Reutner had seen enough evil—and so little goodness—that he'd slowly, over a lifetime, come to the conclusion that he'd been fed a myth. God was not good; God just was not. For in Father Reutner's mind there was a scale, and every time he witnessed an act of cruelty, or the result thereof, that was placed on the left side of the scale, and each time he was privy to an act of kindness, or even heard of one, that he placed on the right side of the scale. Sadly, from almost the very beginning of this experiment, the left dish of the scale never left the ground, while the right dish swung high in the air, its contents sometimes so old that he couldn't even remember what they were.

Nonetheless, Father Reutner had remained true to his vows. Yes, of course, there were times when extenuating circumstances intervened—he was only human, after all! But he really had done his best to run a good race, as Saint Paul put it so well. And when he stumbled, he made his contrition and then kept on running. After twenty-plus years of tending to people's souls, their health needs, and their educational needs, along came the monsignor with the news that Father Reutner was to retire.

Retire? In the outside world, was not involuntary retirement the same as being fired? And what did retirement for Father Reutner look like? For one thing, it looked like confinement to a cold, drafty dormitory with a bunch of garrulous old men who have never even set one foot out of Europe, yet who would each have a million opinions about Africa—every one of which would be wrong.

Retirement would mean having to look out from time to time and see a world that he had chosen to opt out of, and it would be a constant reminder that he had made the wrong decision. He might find himself in situations where he would see new faces, meet new women, and be acutely aware of the fact that he, and he alone, was responsible for the fact that he was doomed to live out the remainder of his days alone. How was one supposed to live with consequences that severe? Perhaps there were those who could plod ever onward, taking one day at a time, hoping that each morrow would bring a shred of happiness, but such people were fools. Such people were masochists.

Having come to the conclusion that God did not exist, Father Reutner felt a huge burden lift from him, for only then did he truly stop fearing death. For if there was no God, then there was no eternal damnation; there remained just the hell we created for ourselves here on earth. And as for heaven, any first-year seminarian would be able to tell you that the Book of Revelation contained detailed descriptions of the hierarchies in that mythical place. Since the church here on earth was one immutable hierarchy, with Father Reutner inexplicably stuck on its bottom rung—well, no thanks, even if it was a real place, heaven no longer held any appeal for him.

Father Reutner missed conversing in German, but he often spoke it. German was both his private language of prayer and the language in which he thought *and,* with increasing frequency, spoke to himself. *Aloud.* He had often heard it said that talking to oneself was normal—particularly among clerics living alone. It was only when you answered yourself that one had to worry. Ha-ha. People who said this sort of thing either were not being completely honest or else did not know the first thing there was to know about living alone.

"To hell with those people," Father Reutner said as he finished tying off the rope to the heavy wooden beam that was one of six that supported the galvanized iron roof. Then he laughed at the irony of what he had said.

One of things he had always hated about this small chapel was how closed in it was; there were no windows. The point had been that the whites should be able to celebrate their private moments *privately.* One was forever shooing the natives away from the dining room windows of the rectory, if one desired to eat unobserved. Otherwise, it was like eating in a fishbowl. Rows upon rows of big, dark eyes followed every movement that the strange white man did with his shiny utensils, and the way the white man patted his mouth with his napkin. The blacks marveled vociferously at the amount and sorts of food that the white man ate. Sometimes scuffles would break out as boys—even men—fought for the best vantage place to look at the freak show. Of course the freak show was always Father Reutner.

Besides the door, which opened off his study, the only opening in the chapel walls was a vertical ventilation slit about a meter in height that was positioned just below the peak of the roof. From where he stood atop the stepladder, the bottom ledge of the slit was at eye level with the old priest. About half of the slit was taken up with layers of feathers and grass and whatever else it was that sparrows wove into their nests. However, through the top half of the slit Father Reutner could see the crown of an oil palm tree. *Elaeis guineensis.* It was one that he had planted himself from a nut one day during his very first month at Saint Mary's.

"We will grow old together," he had told the seedling when it germinated.

Now he was old—and scheduled to be shipped back to cold northern pastures where oil palms couldn't grow (although he had seen windmill palms growing along Lakes Lugarno and Como). The oil palm still produced large bunches of palm nuts, but each year it grew taller. Eventually the day would come when its great height would make the palm too intimidating to climb, and for this reason or that, the palm would be declared "inconvenient," and then subsequently it would be chopped down. Chop, chop, chop. In one way or another, that was the fate that awaited everything slated to die in Africa.

"Eventually we are all no longer wanted," Father Reutner said to the palm through the slit in the wall.

He was not mad, of course. He realized that the palm could not hear; he even felt a bit foolish for having spoken to it. But every man deserves a witness to his passing, even if that witness is only a palm that he has planted from a seed.

Then just to cover his bases, for he was truly a rational being, Father Reutner addressed the Almighty: "Have mercy on me, a sinner," he said as he kicked the stepladder out from beneath his feet.

Their Death was not a foolish young man who gave no thought to consequences. When his wife, Cripple, came to him with the problem of the Mupende cannibal, Jonathan Pimple, he gave the matter much thought before offering a solution. When the old Roman Catholic priest approached him, likewise, it was not a situation to be treated lightly.

All witch doctors—even the mediocre ones—descend from men with prodigious memories, and Their Death was no exception. As Their Death recalled it, the priest's visit happened exactly like this:

"Life to you," the old priest said as he entered the family compound unbidden and unannounced.

Of course, such a visit is truly never a surprise, for even a white man who lives among the Congolese in the workers' village, such as this priest, cannot move about beyond the grounds of Saint Mary's Church without children announcing his whereabouts. Some of the noisy children were laughing at him, others were begging, yet others screaming in terror at his advance. Nevertheless, Their Death's heart beat faster when he realized that the man in the black dress had come to see him, and not one of his neighbors.

"*E*, life to you," he said politely.

"May I sit with you and talk?" the priest asked.

Their Death's heart raced even faster. Although some of the children who had followed the priest were his, not all his little ones could be accounted for. Second Wife had yet to return from the spectacle at the marketplace, nor was Cripple anywhere in sight. Had anything happened to his family? Had anyone in his family violated the white man's laws?

"You have nothing to fear," the old priest said. "I wish only to speak with you—man to man."

Their Death nodded and pointed to a hand-carved chair. It was formed of two pieces of wood, one that intersected the other at a forty-five-degree angle. Their Death had carved it himself and then rubbed it with red palm oil and ashes to give it the rich dark color that others so admired.

By the way in which the priest seated himself, for the first time Their Death appreciated just how old the man might be. He had always found it puzzling, this matter of whites and the number of years that they claimed. Once, when he was a schoolboy, he had pulled weeds for a Belgian who claimed to be seventy-plus-three years old—an impossible number of years for any human being. Their Death had never known anyone in the village to live past the age of sixty-three.

It was out of respect, as much as fear, that Their Death waited in silence for the priest to speak. However, the entire time he wished fervently that his family would stay far away from the compound. If he had had the time, he would have made medicine (an incantation) to that effect.

"I understand that you are a witch doctor," the priest said at last.

"*Eyo*. But I am also a Roman Catholic, *muambi*."

"*Kah!* That is blasphemous! You cannot be both a Christian and a witch doctor. Perhaps you are a Protestant and a witch doctor."

"*Nasha, muambi*. I was educated at the Roman Catholic school right here at Saint Mary's Church. Although my father was a witch doctor, I was baptized along with all the other students in my class, and together we made our First Communion."

"That is impossible," the old man said. "There will not be a witch doctor in heaven."

"*Muambi*," Their Death was quick to assure him, "I have no desire to go to this heaven of yours. I have been beaten many times by white men who will also go to heaven. My grandfather had his hand chopped off with a machete because he could not fulfill the rubber quota."

The priest was silent for a long time; too long. Their Death listened for the sounds of his family. He could hear the shrieks of children at play, the rhythmic pounding as women prepared *tshiombe* flour in mortars, and the squabble of weaverbirds overhead. In a moment such as this, and in the absence of bodily pain, it was possible to imagine the world as it was supposed to be— *except* for the foul-smelling white man in the black dress.

Finally the priest spoke. "You are a Muluba, a member of the Baluba tribe. In my opinion this is the greatest tribe. In Europe we also have many tribes. For instance, I am a Swiss; my tribe occupies that part of Europe known as Switzerland. We are *not* Belgians. *I* am not a Belgian. We do not cut off the hands of any sort of man, be he black or white—or any other color for that matter."

Their Death was a self-educated man. His employer at the post office had lent him many books, covering many subjects. To look at the witch doctor in his patched khaki shorts, short-sleeve white cotton shirt with two missing buttons, and necklace of leopard claws, one might not suspect that here was a man with such a broad understanding of the world. How wrong that person would be. Their Death had read of trolls that live among the hot springs in Iceland, he had read of the Battle of Hastings, he had read a very bad French translation of Hiawatha, he had read that if you meet the Buddha on the road, that you should kill him.

These were but some of the books Their Death read, and he read them aloud to Cripple and, when they were present, Second Wife and the children. After reading many and various things written by the white man and the brown man and the yellow man, Their Death had come to the conclusion that all of them were crazy; every tribe on the earth was crazy save one, and that was the Baluba. His tribe. However, the Swiss priest seemed to be making a point; the Swiss tribe did not cut off hands, and therefore the Swiss priest was worthy of an audience.

"Tell me what is truly in your heart," Their Death said to the priest. "Speak as if we are brothers."

"We laugh and we cry," the old man said, for that is the traditional way of saying thank you. He plunged on. "I have heard that great witch doctors such as you have the power to bring on a sleep so deep that it can reunite a man with his ancestors."

Their Death struggled to keep his composure. "If that were so, and were I to engage in such a practice, the *Bula Matadi* would hang me without even asking questions. Such *buanga* is strictly forbidden."

"*E.* Of course. But what if by selling some to a very discreet individual, you could help that person end a miserable life? A worthless life of needless suffering?"

Their Death was nobody's fool. He had not just hatched from the egg; his down was already dry and he could eat and run with the best of the chicks.

"Does this person suffer from elephantiasis of the scrotum like Nzevu, he who must sit at the marketplace all day and beg as he awaits his death? Is this person as miserable as Mutokatoh, the albino, who cannot step outside her hut lest she get burned by the sun and her eyes be blinded, yet she must toil in the fields because her husband is cruel and will not listen to reason? Is this person's life as worthless as that woodcarver from Djoka Punda—"

"Enough," the priest said. "Enough! *Biwaswa.*" Please.

"It is like this," the witch doctor explained, his heart softening, for he too was a man and not a beast. "I cannot risk the lives of those whom I love to ease your pain. And I want you to know in your heart that it is not because of the color of your skin or because you have ruined many simple minds with your perverted teachings.

"You see, even if I were a bachelor, with no family to protect, I do not believe that a man has a right to end his own life. Life is a gift that we are given, and in the end it is taken back; we ourselves do not take it."

"Do not lecture me!" the old man sputtered.

Their Death smiled. "You are afraid, priest. But I tell you, there is nothing to fear. All of life is like a swinging rope bridge over the waterfalls; the secret to crossing is not to be afraid. Do not be afraid at all. Hear my words, priest; there no use to living a life of fear."

The priest did not appreciate these words. He called Their Death a heathen and a son of a heathen. He told the witch doctor that he would be having words with the OP at his earliest convenience, and that soldiers would come and burn down Their Death's family's hut, his medicine hut, and that his children would be taken to the Roman Catholic orphanage in Luluabourg. When Their Death protested, saying that his children had two mothers, the priest said: "Not after the soldiers are through with them."

A wise man must not take angry words at their face value, and so it was that Their Death managed to wear a calm face when Second Wife and the children returned from hearing Jonathan Pimple preach in the marketplace.

"*Tatu*," gushed Brings Happiness, "we heard the most amazing story."

"*E*," Second Wife said as she switched Baby Amanda from her right breast to her left breast, "it was a story of much imagination."

"Tell me all about it," Their Death said, settling back into his favorite chair again. Something powerful was stirring up the currents of his emotions, but he would heed his own words and not be afraid.

The Belgian Congo, 1958

Pierre Jardin was nowhere to be found—at least no longer in the vicinity of the marketplace—which meant that he was probably well on his way to check out the old ferry landing. Amanda realized that she could make far better progress without her lame companion, but she was more concerned with the toll all that brisk walking would take on Cripple, so she urged her to stay behind. In fact, she even *ordered* Cripple to stay back in the workers' village, which turned out to be a huge mistake. Not only did the little Muluba woman refuse, but she was mightily offended and wasted valuable time railing about the indignity she had just suffered at the hand of her oppressor.

"I am not your oppressor," Amanda said, her eyes brimming with tears. "I am your friend who cares very much for you."

"If you are indeed my friend," Cripple said, "then you will respect me as a woman, and not treat me as a child just because I am small and twisted. I am quite capable of making my own decisions, *Mamu*."

"*Eyo*." Amanda nodded, but she kept walking.

"Walk faster," Cripple said. "Or are you an old duck headed to the meat pot?"

"*Kah?*" Amanda said. "I am not an old duck!"

No matter how fast Amanda walked, Cripple kept up. First it was astonishing, then slightly amusing, and then eventually infuriating. Finally, she could no longer contain the question that burned within her like the wick on a Coleman lantern.

"Cripple, if you can keep up so well, why did you make me push you in a wheelbarrow to see the giant snake the other day?"

"*Mamu?*"

"Come on, Cripple, it is a simple question; just answer it. Please."

"*E.*" Cripple shrugged. "*Mamu,* Their Death reads to me many books, and some of these describe a sort of cart—ah, a chariot—that is pulled by a large beast called a horse."

"I know what a horse is," Amanda said crossly.

"*Mamu,* since you are large like a horse—"

Amanda smiled, turning her head as she did so. "You do realize, I'm sure, that the chariot is *pulled* by the horse, and not *pushed.*"

"*Mamu,*" Cripple said, "one cannot know everything. Besides, you are a very clever horse."

"Indeed. And I am a horse much in need of exercising. So then perhaps you will not mind if I run; after all, the *kabalu* is a beast that is made for running." Instantly Amanda regretted saying that, fearing that perhaps she had gone too far in her teasing.

It was so hard to tell where the line was that one shouldn't cross. This was particularly true with Protruding Navel, the head housekeeper. They would be discussing some subject amicably, laughing, seemingly bantering, then suddenly and without warning Protruding Navel would look like he'd been slapped across the face.

"You offended me," he'd accuse her. "You offended me with great strength."

But how? What she had said had been completely innocuous. So it was with tremendous relief that Amanda saw Cripple literally collapse with laughter. The tiny woman rocked back and forth, practically choking on it.

An outside observer might even draw the conclusion that she was ill—because that is exactly what one did. As Amanda stood watching Cripple, feeling both amused and embarrassed, a sleek black sedan with tinted windows barreled up and lurched to a stop. Almost simultaneously from the rear, with his skirts drawn up in one hand, out jumped the very handsome Monsignor Clemente.

"What has happened?" he said. He spoke in French, which seemed to be his default language, given that he had grown up in the Congo.

"She is laughing," Amanda said. "We were making jokes."

"Jokes? With an African? Mademoiselle, is this wise?"

"I may be a devout heathen," Cripple said, struggling to her feet, "but I am not a savage! I speak the language of my oppressors."

"Is that so?" the monsignor said.

He looked quizzically at Amanda, as if he were actually waiting for an introduction. For an African, if you can imagine that! Talk about being a hypocrite. Very well then, what was good for the goose was good for the gander.

"This is Madame Cripple," Amanda said. "Of course, the two of you have already met. She is the woman who reminded you about the old ferry landing. She is my former housekeeper. Together we are looking for Captain Pierre Jardin. Do you know his whereabouts?"

"This time it is truly a pleasure to see you, madame," the monsignor said, with a mysterious twinkle in his eye.

"*E*," Cripple said. She laughed inappropriately. "Now here is a white man like no other," she said in her native Tshiluba.

"Cripple," Amanda warned her, "he grew up in Belle Vue, so he speaks Tshiluba quite well."

"As well as he does Latin?" Cripple said, and then she said something else intended just to show off to the cleric in that very language—at least presumably so, because Amanda spoke nary a word of it, having almost failed Latin at Rock Hill High School. Needless to say, the poor girl was both extremely proud of her former housekeeper, and justifiably most annoyed.

Fortunately, the monsignor was practiced in reading the feelings of others, and he turned the conversation right back to the question she'd asked him a moment earlier. "No, I have not spoken with Captain Pierre Jardin. Is there something that you wish to tell him?"

Amanda thought fast and hard. Yes, she was compulsive by nature, but she also had good instincts—that is, unless she'd been drinking, and she hadn't touched a drop of alcohol since coming to the Congo three months ago. Actually, not since applying for her post at the Missionary Rest House and undertaking her language training in Brussels. Add it all together and she'd been sober longer than a year. She prayed about her decision now and had an immediate sense of peace. The monsignor could be trusted.

"I—I mean, we—are convinced that the old priest at Saint Mary's Church poisoned a man by the name of Chigger Mite."

"*Kah!*" Monsignor Clemente shook his head. "These African names are so amusing," he whispered as an aside in English to Amanda.

"Chigger Mite was a Mupende, *not* a Muluba," Cripple said archly.

"Then I am mistaken," Monsignor Clemente said, for there is no direct way of saying "oops" or "I'm sorry" in Tshiluba.

"Why is it that you are not surprised by our suspicions?" Cripple demanded to know. "Is there yet something else?"

Again Monsignor Clemente shook his head. "Madame, you are not a Roman Catholic, or else you would understand."

"What he means," Amanda said, "is that if a member of the

Roman Catholic Church tells the priest something in confidence, it cannot be repeated. Ever."

"*Kashide, mene, mene?*"

"*E.*"

Cripple placed her hands on her crooked hips, a stance that emphasized her condition. "Mamu Ugly Eyes, although this white man in a woman's dress refuses to talk, in his silence he speaks much about the old priest."

"This is *not* a woman's dress," Monsignor Clemente said through clenched teeth. "It is what Jesus wore."

"*Nasha,*" Cripple said, and wagged a finger at him in a scolding manner. "I have been to Saint Mary's Church to see the idols, and I know for a fact that the idol of Jesus does not wear this blackest of blacks. To the contrary, the dress of your Jesus idol is the whitest of whites."

The monsignor turned to Amanda, his eyes dancing with laughter. "Madame, I tell you, if I were to remain in the Congo, I would surely attempt to hire this woman away from you. Seldom have I encountered an individual who is so—so sure of herself. Your friend Cripple is intelligent, articulate, and extremely perceptive."

Amanda was taken aback. "Y-You mean for a woman," she stammered.

"Mademoiselle, you are not correct; believe me when I say that she is exceptional."

"*E,* believe him," Cripple said, nodding in agreement. She appeared to be taking herself quite seriously too.

Then the unbelievable happened. Monsignor Clemente and Cripple struck up a conversation, chatting about the "old days" in Belle Vue when she was a child and he a young priest—like old chums meeting outside Friedman's Department Store in downtown Rock Hill. They seemed oblivious to the blazing sun, which, coupled with the oppressive humidity of suicide month, felt like a million degrees. Sweat streamed down Amanda's brow, attracting tiny wasps that sucked at the moisture collecting in the corners of her eyes. Even more maddening were the bees, which actually stung, piercing the inside creases of her elbows and behind her knees.

Darn the two of you, she thought, although she would never swear aloud. This farce of an exchange between European man and native woman, between cleric and heathen—surely this was nothing more than a charade. To what purpose? Perhaps to ease guilty consciences on both their parts, consciences made heavy by the hate they harbored for the other's race. In the meantime, the old priest, Father Reutner, was not only getting away with murder, he was—well, he was such a darn hypocrite!

There was practically nothing Amanda hated worse than a hypocrite. Yes, she had known it was wrong to drive while drunk. She and her friends had done that anyway. Not that it excused their behavior, but from whom had they learned this bad behavior? From their parents! Every last one of them had at least one parent who was guilty of guzzling a beer or two at a picnic or backyard barbecue and then driving home. And Amanda knew for a fact that the judge in the courtroom on the day of her sentencing—the judge who had been so lenient with her—he too drove while under the influence. Amanda knew this because he went to her church and attended the same functions.

Finally Amanda had all she could take of other folks' reminiscences and the brutality of the midday sun. "Monsignor," she snapped, "can we not do something *besides* compare our life stories?"

He fixed her with that infamous smile; or was it really just a smirk? "Certainly, mademoiselle. Do you have any idea what the captain's intentions were the last time you saw him?"

"*E.* He was going to search for the old ferry landing. That is why we are on this abandoned road."

"Of course. But as you can see, it is not such an abandoned road after all; Madame Cripple, I see here footpaths that are yet clear enough so that my chauffeur might drive my car. Who uses this so-called abandoned road?"

"*Muambi*, it is only fishermen. Never cars. The fishermen tie their dugouts up somewhere up there"—she waved her arms with more verve than she had ever shaken a rug in Amanda's experience—"but exactly where, I do not know, as I have not had the motivation to drag my tired, misshapen body up this tortuous path in many, many years."

"My eyes have already seen evidence of your bravery, Madame Cripple, so I know it is not fear that has kept you from going farther. I am also quite aware that when the mood strikes you thus, you are quite capable of dragging that tired, misshapen body of yours anywhere it is that you wish to go."

"*Tch*," Cripple said. She turned to Amanda. "Please tell the white man in the black dress that even *you* are better at making compliments than he is. If he had not been so rude, I would have told him that the fishermen take those same dugouts over to the Island of Seven Ghost Sisters to fish for a creature called *capitaine*. Have you ever eaten this *capitaine*, Mamu Ugly Eyes?"

"*Capitaine* is a fish," Amanda said. "It is not a creature. But yes, I have eaten it. It was wonderful."

Monsignor Clemente sighed. "Ah, *capitaine*! It is by far the most delicious fish I have ever tasted. Believe me when I tell you this, Madame Cripple, there is no finer-tasting fish in all of Europe."

"*Bulelela?*"

Amanda sighed as well, but that time not with pleasure. "Please, may we return to speaking of Capitaine Pierre Jardin?"

"*Tch*," Cripple said again.

"*E*, let us do that," the monsignor. He gestured expansively at his sedan. "I am confident that this car can complete its journey on this road, and I would be pleased if the two of you accompanied me. Together we will see if the man *capitaine* is to be found at the end of this road. If he is not there, then we will have spent but a short time looking. Afterward this car and I can transport you back to the village, and we can search those areas where the lanes are wide enough to accommodate an automobile. Is this agreeable?"

"*E!*"

The monsignor started. "Miss Brown," he whispered in English. "Isn't she afraid to ride in a car?"

"My father was a mechanic," Cripple said in French without missing a beat. "I often rode with him on his test drives."

It was hard to say who was the most shocked, Amanda or the monsignor. Amanda finally closed her mouth when she remembered something that her mother used to say—it was something along the lines of: "One day you're going to swallow a fly, dear." There were lots of flies buzzing about her now, as well as sweat-sucking wasps and insidious little bees.

"Do you speak English?" Amanda demanded incredulously.

"*Non, Mamu,* but I understand this simple language of yours. Perhaps someday we can discuss some changes to the pronunciation of various words. Like French, there are many unnecessary sounds, and others that are simply unpleasant to the ear. Do you not agree, *Muambi* Monsignor?"

It was perhaps then that the monsignor closed his mouth; it was, after all, necessary to do so first in order for him to speak. "Madame Cripple, I could not agree with you more. Do you not find the sound of Latin much more pleasing to the ear?"

"*E.* Latin is a beautiful language."

"Then perhaps you should consider becoming a Roman Catholic."

"Absolutely not!" Amanda said. She pounded the dashboard of the sedan with such force that the dust swirled up around them, creating the effect of a snow globe.

"Is it not possible for a heathen to speak Latin?" Cripple asked.

"Let us speak no more of religious matters—or of Latin," the monsignor suggested. "Our only task now should be to find Captain Pierre Jardin."

* * *

Pierre's heart raced. It was a familiar feeling, an enjoyable feeling, one he experienced every time he hunted, no matter his prey—beast or man. And since he was an exceptionally honest man, if he'd been asked just then, he would have answered quite truthfully that he found hunting man the more exciting pastime, if only because most men at least were fair game. Made it a fair game? How did one say it in English? Never mind, the point was that he enjoyed the *hunt* when it came to man. Only the hunt.

You would think that someone so visible one minute, like Jonathan Pimple, could not simply disappear the next minute. But that is exactly what he did. Jonathan Pimple vanished right before his eyes. He just melted into the crowd. True, the natives all had coal black hair, and most men kept theirs cropped short, but by no means did they all look alike. There were tribal differences often relating to skin tone and height, and of course there were always individual differences.

Every person, every animal, indeed every piece of vegetation on this planet is an individual in that it has been shaped by outside forces peculiar to the space it occupies. It is these differences, sometimes virtually invisible to the untrained eye, that both the sophisticated government spy and the illiterate bush tracker learn to pick up on. Although Pierre was neither of the two, he leaned toward tracker, yet with all the people milling about he knew that tracking in the literal sense would be a lost cause.

So would looking for Jonathan Pimple at his hut; Pierre didn't even waste any time considering that. Well, the main thing, now that he couldn't find Jonathan Pimple, was to find Amanda. All Pierre really wanted Jonathan for was to warn him away from harming Amanda. She was new to the Congo, he'd intended to say, and she didn't understand the power that the resurrection cults had on a people who had been oppressed for centuries. Also, this Jonathan Pimple fellow better be sure he knew what he was getting into, if he was going to be concocting similar scenarios between his cult and the Kibanguists. The latter did not respond lightly to mockery.

He was considering his course of action when he heard a cough at his elbow. Coughing to get attention was an African thing to do; thus Pierre was rather surprised to see a tall, thin white man with blue-gray eyes. After a second or two, he realized it was the Flemish mulatto, the poor lad who would be forever trapped between two worlds, yet stuck in one.

"*Excusez-moi, Capitaine,*" the merchant said softly, "if you are wondering where your friends are, I can tell you."

"What? How do you know who my friends are?"

"Monsieur, I am a lonely man; or have you not recognized that it is I, the dancing, singing, happy mulatto resident of Belle Vue workers' village? I am too white to be black, and too black to be white—like a spotted goat, *nasha?* I have no friends—not even a wife. So I content myself with keeping track of everyone else's whereabouts."

"*Ah, très bien!* Do you know where Jonathan Pimple is?"

"*Tch,*" the Flemish mulatto said, sounding just like a native, for indeed he was, no? "Monsieur, is he your priority?"

"Do not tell me my priority!" Pierre roared. Then, aware that his outburst had drawn a great deal of unwanted interest, he lowered his voice. "Please, give me news of my friends."

"Very well. First, Madame Cabochon—she with the large *mabele*—she went back down the hill to the Missionary Rest House. The other two—the pretty young American woman and the Muluba woman named Cripple—they have foolishly set off down the road that the fishermen use when they catch *capitaine* in their dugouts next to the Island of Seven Ghost Sisters."

"*Merci.*" Pierre grabbed the man's slim hand, gave it a quick shake, and then, just before he turned to go, the thought occurred to him. "*Why* is it so foolish for them to go down that road, monsieur?"

The Flemish mulatto beamed. No doubt he was enjoying such a long exchange with a real white man.

"Because Monsignor Clemente is pursuing them, monsieur."

"What nonsense," Pierre said angrily, for he had caught on to the half-caste's game. "Why would the monsignor pursue them?"

"Ah, now you have asked the important question! You see—"

"Out with it, you fool!"

"He intends to kill them."

The Belgian Congo, 1958

There was no sign of Pierre at the river's edge, just a pair of dugout canoes and a bazillion dancing yellow and black butterflies. The water level seemed up, but not like it had been immediately following the storm. Although Amanda had never viewed the Kasai River from this location, she was still very much aware that something was missing from the scenery, that something being most of the Island of Seven Ghost Sisters.

In the island's place was a tangle of immense, upended trees, their circular root systems and flying buttresses denuded of soil. Some of the trees terminated like the tips of ski poles, others like eggbeaters, but all on a giant's scale, of course. Nowhere in that mess was there even a suggestion of dry land.

"There is no need to even stop," Amanda said to the chauffeur.

"Mademoiselle," the monsignor said gently, "he is my chauffeur, *oui?*"

"*Certainement,*" Amanda said. Perhaps she had overstepped her bounds, but there was no need to make her feel like a schoolgirl. Not in front of her former housekeeper.

"We will stop," the monsignor said.

"*Mamu*," said Cripple, just a bit too loudly for normal conversation. "Please tell your friend that I am a woman in the family way and, as such, I must return to the village."

"There will be no returning," the monsignor said. "Now get out, please."

They stumbled once more into the unforgiving sun, but Cripple would not be stilled. "*Mamu*, please tell this man in a dress that a woman in my condition must frequently use the bush."

"Monsignor, uh—what she means," Amanda said, "is that—"

"She should have thought to use the toilet earlier," Monsignor Clemente said. "Now, walk this way down to the canoes."

Clouds of butterflies rose with every step they took. Even with the weight of suicide month pressing down upon them, the lifting bank of yellow and black was an ethereal experience. In her heart Amanda believed that this was a gift from heaven at the hour of her death, something to make the impending suffering more bearable. Because even though no words had been spoken to that effect, the young American knew that she and Cripple had guessed wrong, and that it was the charming Monsignor Clemente, and not the abrasive Father Reutner, who had murdered Chigger Mite.

"Cripple," she said softly in Tshiluba, although she knew the monsignor could still hear and understand her, "I know that you do not share my beliefs, but—"

"Mamu Ugly Eyes, you need not worry about my soul; if I am wrong about my beliefs and you are right, and if your god is truly merciful, then he and I will have a palaver after I am dead."

"But, Cripple, by then it will be too late."

"*Aiyee, Mamu*, then that is most unfortunate for your god, is it not?"

"Cripple, this is no time to joke!"

"I do not joke, *Mamu*. Nor am I afraid. Does this disappoint you?"

"Surely you must be afraid," the monsignor said sharply. "It is impossible to approach death without fear; one does unimaginable things in order to escape death. Everyone does!"

"*Tch.*"

"I was young," the monsignor said. He'd begun to ramble in English, his eyes darting from one woman to the other, like he was looking for sympathy or understanding. "I was barely out of seminary. Yes, I wanted to be a missionary to the Congo—I love this country—but you get teamed up with another priest, you see. That is supposed to keep one out of trouble. But tell me, how is that supposed to work if they team you up with a pedophile?

"Our first assignment was a Bapende village—some of them were still cannibals back then—and Father Eugene's target happened to be one of the chief's twin sons—"

"*Yala,*" Cripple said. "This cannot be true. The Bapende do not permit such abnormalities as twins to exist!"

"All children are gifts from Yehowah Nzambi," Amanda said.

The monsignor waved his arms impatiently. "This chief was strong-willed. The twins were born to his favorite wife who had remained barren up to perhaps her fortieth year. The chief broke all the rules for those two boys. Then we came along, we who were doing God's work, and then one day when I was away from the village—I had gone off to fetch some medicines for a woman with a badly infected leg—Father Eugene undid all that work."

"I do not understand," Cripple whined. "How does one undo something that has not been done?"

"Stop making noise," Amanda said gently.

The monsignor resumed speaking immediately. "Their witch doctor said that the only way that the twin who had been molested could take back that which was stolen from him—his soul, I presume—was for everyone present at this feast to—well, you know what I mean."

"We do not," Amanda said, although she really did.

"So I tasted. That is all they made me do—taste—although

looking back on it now, I should have chosen death. How could I confess such a sin as eating human flesh? To whom could I confess it? Not to another human being. I could not confess to a priest that the man I had eaten was also a priest! I could confess this only to God."

"Isn't that enough?" Amanda said. But therein lay the great divide between their two faiths, and with the monsignor about to kill her, it was hard to dredge up any ecumenical feelings at that moment.

"You don't understand, Amanda Brown. For a Catholic, for a priest, the secret I lived with was an intolerable burden. It ate away at my soul. It turned me into an empty, hollow man. I thought that by returning to the Congo, to the place where I was born and where I grew up, I might find some little bits of my soul that I could begin to piece back together. But then my first day here, I happened to see Chigger Mite, and just the opposite thing happened."

"*E*," said Cripple. "He recognized you from when he was a boy, so you killed him. Now you will kill us."

"*What?*" The monsignor threw his hands in the air and then clamped them to the sides of his head. "Is *that* what you think?"

Amanda stepped forward, unconsciously protecting her friend from the sudden explosion of emotion. "It's a reasonable supposition, isn't it? You drove us here, down this deserted road. Then you made us get out. Now all this talk of death."

"*Mon Dieu*," the monsignor said as he shook his head, still clutching it. "I offered to drive you here to look for Captain Jardin. I had you get out so that I could talk to you in private, away from my chauffeur, who is like a gossipy old woman—no offense intended to Cripple."

Cripple scowled. "It should be obvious even to a man that I am not old; for behold, I am with child."

"But still," Amanda said, pointing an index finger at the monsignor's chest, "you *did* kill Chigger Mite."

The monsignor sank to his knees in the mud, amid a cloud of butterflies. "Yes, of that I am surely guilty. That very day, when I saw him with the snake, I knew that he recognized me—just as Madame Cripple said. I inquired as to where he lived and paid him a visit late that night, when the natives believe that only the spirits walk freely about. I saw the fear in his eyes. Why? I do not know, but I played off it. I told Chigger Mite that I was putting a white man's curse on him—one even more powerful than the curse that had brought the white man to Africa so many centuries ago. I told him that the curse would go into effect only if he told anyone that I was the same priest he had seen at his restoration ceremony those many years ago."

"Was it Jonathan Pimple he told?"

The monsignor raked his hands through the mud and then smeared it into his hair. It wasn't an act Amanda was witnessing; the man was truly distraught. If ever there was a man who regretted what he'd done, this man fit the bill.

"Yes, he must have. You see, mademoiselle—although I'm sure you know by now—the belief in curses can be so strong that some people will actually die when one is placed on them. But as God is my witness, I did not intend to kill Chigger Mite; I meant only to silence him, to keep him from revealing what happened that night."

"You swear to me that you did not touch him?"

"What difference does that make, mademoiselle? I am guilty, all the same!"

Undoubtedly the sun had broiled Amanda's brain beyond the point of functioning properly. What other explanation could there be for what came out of her mouth next?

"Do you swear to me that you did not touch Chigger Mite?"

"I did not touch Chigger Mite."

"Did you poison him?"

"As God is my witness, mademoiselle, I did not poison Chigger Mite."

"Then, Monsignor, you did not kill him. If you are truly a Christian, you cannot believe in superstition."

"Witchcraft is not superstition," Cripple said.

"Tell me then, Cripple, do you think that the monsignor should be arrested and hanged for the murder of the Mupende named Chigger Mite?"

"*Tch*, Mamu Ugly Eyes, must you always jump to conclusions? This white man did not kill Chigger Mite with a curse, for a white man is incapable of speaking such a curse. The white man conquered Africa with guns, not curses! Now, let us return to the village or I shall be forced to urinate in front of this man." She turned at once and commenced hobbling back to the sedan. Midway back she paused and turned again, this time to wag a finger. "*Kah!* You must move, both of you! *Lubilu!*"

Madam Cabochon was determined to enjoy her breakfast out on the terrace *and* get to church early. This morning it was doable, because she'd managed to both get a full night's sleep and get up extra early! This was all thanks to a husband who came home so drunk that he fell asleep just inside the front door, and who didn't even bother to get off the floor at any time during the night to bring his snores into bed.

It had been just six weeks since the storm to end all storms, the one that had washed away the Island of Seven Ghost Sisters, but much had changed since then. For one thing, the bridge that spanned the mighty Kasai River connecting Belle Vue to the workers' village was now repaired. That had taken a little more than three weeks, if one can believe that! The big steel replacement girders had been manufactured in Luluabourg and then driven down to Belle Vue on a caravan of enormous trucks. These monstrous vehicles had to pass right through the heart of Bashilele territory.

The Bashilele had a reputation as headhunters, but they must have been scared out of their wits at this bizarre sight, because they kept shooting out the tires of those trucks with their powerful longbows. Madame Cabochon chuckled over her thick black coffee while dwelling on that image. She'd always found the Bashilele men to be very enticing, in their low-slung loincloths, and one of her favorite jokes—shared by bored Belgian housewives of similar taste—had to do with equating a hunter's bow length with the length of his manhood.

Madame Cabochon shook her head enviously; one Bashilele village now had an actual white girl, a Belgian, as their chief. *Oui*, Madame Cabochon had been given more than her fair share of beauty, but overall, life was still unfair. The enigmatic, devilishly attractive Monsignor Clemente was married to his church. The somewhat plain American missionary and the handsome Belgian police captain had eyes only for each other. There was not even a chance of a ménage à trois, should one be so inclined—*ooh la la, shame on you, Colette, to have such a thought as that, especially on the Sabbath.*

"Madame Cabochon, are you all right?"

Madame Cabochon was so startled that she threw the contents of her bone china cup straight up into the air. The thick black coffee splattered all over her silk fuchsia blouse. Being that Madame Cabochon was scarcely more talented than Jackson Pollock, and her blouse sported a deep scoop neckline, much of the hot liquid landed on bare skin.

"*Sacré-coeur!*" Madame Cabochon said as she jumped to her feet.

"*Pardonnez-moi.* Did I scare you?"

There you see! The person who had so rudely intruded on Madame Cabochon's inner life was that most despicable of all men, Marcel Fabergé. *Oui*, somehow the most incompetent OP in the history of the Consortium had managed to keep his job. The coward hadn't walked to Luluabourg after all; he hadn't even made it out of the village!

Several hours after leaving his mousy wife to dissolve in tears,

the big shot returned. He was shouting then, huffing and puff-
ing, and waving a stick—a "cudgel" he called it in English, even
though Amanda Brown politely informed him that this word
was not often used. At any rate, the pigeon-chested OP claimed
to have been chased by a pack of vicious dogs. "Curs," he called
them. That was another word he must have picked up from a
novel. He wanted Pierre to start shooting these curs on sight.

The really sad thing is that it wasn't dogs that attacked
the little man with the big chip on his shoulder; it was a male
turkey—how do you say this in English? Ah yes, a tomboy. He
was chased by a tomboy with its tail spread wide and its wings
scraping the ground. Madame Cabochon had several times been
chased by territorial tomboys, and she knew just how intimidating
they could be. She couldn't blame the OP for backing down from
the turkey, just as she couldn't blame the fifty-plus natives who
had witnessed the sight for laughing their heads off. But the next
day when the OP's mousy wife, Hélène Fabergé, sported a black
eye and a bruised lip, she knew who to blame for that, and she did.

"Get off my terrace, you toad!" she said.

"*Oui, madame,*" the OP said, but he didn't move a muscle.

"I said to go," she said.

"Should I first bring you some butter?" the OP said.

"*Butter?*" Madame Cabochon said.

"To apply to the burns," the OP said. He leaned forward, as
if inspecting the damage. "Is that not what one does in this situation?"

"I am not a roast, you idiot! You just want to get your hands on
my considerable charms." Madame Cabochon was both flattered
and repulsed, and, yes, she was disgusted with herself for having
been flattered.

"Absolutely not, Madame Cabochon," the OP said. "I am here
because my wife, Hélène, wishes to ask if you will give her a ride
to Mass."

"Why don't you drive her there yourself?" she said.

"I no longer wish to go to church, madame," the OP said.

The coffee drops no longer stung Madame Cabochon's chest, and since she was genuinely curious as to why the OP no longer wished to attend church, she decided to risk a brief conversation.

"You may sit," she said. It was an order; it was not an offer.

The OP sat. "The weather is much more bearable now," he said almost pleasantly. "I am given to understand that it is the daily rains that keep the humidity from building up."

She tried not to smile at his clumsy attempt at deflection. "*Why* do you no longer wish to go to church?"

"It's the hypocrisy, madame. Surely *you* understand that."

She had been standing, but now she pulled a chair up next to his and grabbed his left hand, his dominant one, in both hers. Had she been a dragon, there would have been smoke pouring from her nostrils and her blazing red hair would have been real flames.

"Is that an insult, Marcel?"

"*Mais non!* I am not accusing you of hypocrisy, Madame Cabochon; I am merely suggesting that you have witnessed it firsthand."

She shrugged. "*Oui.* But perhaps you can give me an example."

"*Bien,*" the OP said. "For instance, take the case of a certain priest who ate another priest—I mean literally—and then on top of that, this certain priest scared a poor man to death, but no one seems to care because—well, you tell me." He took a deep breath before jerking his hand away from Madame Cabochon's grip.

Madame Cabochon jumped up again. She could feel the tiny golden hairs on her arms stand on end, like the quills of a porcupine in defense mode. Mostly, however, she felt confused. She'd heard the OP's disgusting words, but she wasn't sure what they meant—not for *sure*. She'd heard similar stories—actually several versions of it—floating around the kitchen and yard.

Her employees always shut up immediately when they noticed her lurking about, but she'd caught enough to get the gist of the story. That was one of the reasons she wanted to get to church early today: to do a little investigative work. To be sure, she'd already tried the direct approach, but neither Pierre, Amanda, nor her sidekick the delightful little Muluba woman, Cripple, would even comment on the matter.

The injustice of it all! He was *her* Alberto Clemente; she was *his* Little Colette Underpants. They had been childhood friends, and now they were nothing? The fact that his return to Belle Vue was completely unrelated to her was the most painful thing she had ever had to face in her entire life. Plus, he didn't even care enough to say good-bye. It was one thing to skip out on an explanation—perhaps he didn't owe her that—but he should have at least come back to the Missionary Rest House and given her a chance to say her good-byes. But no, apparently, as soon as he learned of the whereabouts of a fisherman's dugout canoe, he braved the raging river so that he could race back to Luluabourg and catch a flight out of the country.

But what did this hurtful behavior have to do with a priest eating a priest? Was it a parable of some sort? Frankly, Madame Cabochon had always had trouble understanding the biblical parables. If Jesus had wanted to get his message across, why didn't he just come straight out and say it? Speak like an American! *Mon Dieu*, now she was going to have to go to confession again for thinking these blasphemous thoughts.

Nonetheless, this priest-eating-a-priest riddle was dangerous, salacious talk. It was just these sort of rumors that gave rise to new cults, and then those in turn gave birth to new religions that kept pragmatic folks, such as herself, in a constant state of turmoil. One was not supposed to find the answers, just to seek them.

Well, Madame Cabochon was in too much pain, and too confused, to care about sorting things out. Today, tomorrow, for the rest of her life, she would take in only good things; from now she would only enjoy. From this moment on, there was no room or time for ugliness, pain, or sadness.

"*Et, voilà!*" she said, as she pointed at the river. "There, you see? Already the river is building up a new island—branch by branch, mud bank by mud bank." She sighed deeply, joyfully. Nothing could dispel this mood. "This fills me with great happiness and hope. Listen, you despicable little wife-beater, go tell your wife, Hélène, that it will be my pleasure to take her to church with me today."

The OP stared up at her angrily. "Who are you to talk to me like that?"

"I am someone bigger than you, that's who, and if you don't get a move on, I will box your ears."

About the author

About the book

Read on

Insights,
Interviews
& More . . .

Meet Tamar Myers

TAMAR MYERS was born and raised in the Belgian Congo (now just the Congo). Her parents were missionaries to a tribe which, at that time, were known as headhunters and used human skulls for drinking cups. Hers was the first white family ever to peacefully coexist with the tribe.

Tamar grew up eating elephant, hippopotamus, and even monkey. She attended a boarding school that was two days away by truck, and sometimes it was necessary to wade through crocodile-infested waters to reach it. Other dangers she encountered as a child were cobras, deadly green mambas, and the voracious armies of driver ants that ate every animal (and human) that didn't get out of their way.

Penny Young

Today Tamar lives in the Carolinas with her American-born husband. She is the author of thirty-seven novels (most of which are mysteries), a number of published short stories, and hundreds of articles on gardening. ∾

Leopard Tales

LEOPARDS (*PANTHERA PARDUS*) were found throughout the Belgian Congo, where they were strongly associated with witchcraft and believed to be endowed with magical powers. Although much smaller than lions, leopards are incredibly strong for their size and capable of hauling antelope high into trees for safekeeping. They are solitary cats, which along with their spotted fur ensures that they are seldom seen by humans. As is the case with lions and tigers, there are confirmed cases of leopards becoming man-eaters. Black panthers are merely a melanistic form of the regular leopard.

In the area where I grew up, there were no large herds of herbivores such as one might see in East Africa. This was due in part to the practice of burning the savannahs once a year to kill game. As the herds of antelope and zebra were exterminated, the lions either met the same fate or else moved on. Some antelope species were better adapted to living a solitary existence, and each year enough of them survived to repopulate their particular niche.

The leopard, being much smaller than the lion and thus requiring less food, was also able to hold its own. When its delicate nostrils picked up ▶

the scent of burning elephant grass
at the end of the dry season, these
majestic spotted cats would slink into
the safety of the nearest riverine forest.
From where I lived, up on the high
savannah, it seemed that every gully
soon deepened into a tree-shaded
ravine that gave birth to a spring
of pure, untainted water. Follow
the spring, and one would surely
find a river and even deeper forest.

Therefore, it was the leopard that
reigned as King of the Beasts among
the people of the Kasai. Not only was
the leopard cunning, it possessed
certain magical powers. For instance,
a leopard had the ability to change its
shape. This attribute explained how
it was that an animal this large could
sneak into a village at night and leave
with a goat—or a person—and not be
seen.

As a living leopard possesses
magical powers, so too does a leopard
skin. For that reason, only a powerful
chief or king may wear a leopard skin.
Mobutu, who was the dictator of
Zaire (now Democratic Republic of
the Congo), wore a leopard skin hat.
If a village chief wanted to have his
subjects swear a loyalty oath, he
would have them kneel on a leopard
skin while they did so.

I was a child of missionaries who
never broached such talk with me, so

I must have heard it from my friends, or possibly from my "child-minders." Whatever the case may be, all these years later, I still feel uneasy around leopard-related items (although I have a cat who is part Asian Leopard Cat!).

For instance, I would not feel comfortable sleeping in a room that contains a leopard skin or a leopard skull. It doesn't make any sense, but there it is. However, I do posses a fabulous necklace, assembled for me by fellow author Faith Hunter, which is made from genuine leopard claws. I call this my "mojo" necklace, and I wear it whenever I speak about Africa, or when I need to call forth special courage.

The claws in this necklace come from a leopard that my papa shot sometime in the 1930s. The leopard had managed to break into our goat enclosure and had killed one of our goats. We kept the skin for many years, and I remember it draped over the back of our couch as late as 1960. By day the living room was exotic; by night it was spooky.

Somewhere along the line I became the keeper of the claws. I kept them in a box, out of sight, until I was almost sixty. When I first showed them to my friend Faith Hunter, she squealed with delight. There are eight of these enormous claws—think of your ▶

cat's claws made ten times bigger. I chose carnelian and black agate as the accompanying stones, and since the claws are hollow at the wide end we glued them to cowry shells. From the center of the necklace hangs an ivory amulet of the sort a witch doctor would wear. Knowing my papa, I wouldn't be surprised to learn that he actually bought it from a witch doctor. Do you see what I mean about this necklace having mojo?

My papa, may his memory be for a blessing, was a very interesting man. An inquisitive man. He is the only person I've ever met who used to rue the day that he passed up the chance to buy a drum that had a human navel on the drum skin (although perhaps not that many people have vendors showing up at their back door trying to sell them a drum with a belly button in the center).

My uncle Ernie, who was my mama's youngest brother, lived with us for a while when he was in his early twenties. The roads in our remote location consisted of two dirt tracks with a strip of grass growing down the middle. During the rainy seasons the roads became so washed out they became treacherous, and it wasn't uncommon to hear of a vehicle that had broken an axle. In the long dry season, the road would send up so much dust that I found it hard to breath because of a perpetually stopped-up nose.

Nevertheless, it was always exciting to travel at dusk, and then into the night. As the sun dropped low in the western sky, the francolins (a quail-like bird) would wander into the road, and whoever was driving would immediately stop so that the men in the car—or truck—could hop out and fire off a shot. If we were really fortunate, we'd run into a flock of guinea hens, which were much larger birds. Both made for good eating, just as long as Mama didn't serve you the piece that contained the bullet hole.

Also at dusk we stood a good chance of encountering jackals in the road. It must be said here that we were Mennonites of Amish descent, coming from many generations of strictly pacifist ancestors. However, our prohibition against killing did not apply to animals. On a number of occasions, I sat holding my breath as the Mennonite driver of our panel truck raced down our perilous roads trying to run over a jackal (sometimes even a jackal with pups at her side!). Why would a Mennonite man do this? For the thrill of the hunt, I suppose. Why did the jackal invariably run down the exposed dirt lane for a good bit before darting into the safety of ▶

the thick elephant grass that grew on either side? I haven't a clue. At any rate, if I remember correctly, the jackal survived about fifty percent of the time.

But it was when darkness fell that the fun really began. There is something to be said for the excitement generated by "safe fear": sitting out a bodacious thunderstorm in front of your fireplace, riding a roller coaster, or watching a horror movie. The headlights of vehicles were reflected by the animal life in the road, and the animals, confused and temporarily blinded, froze. Once, when Uncle Ernie was driving the panel truck and we three nieces were along for the ride, he struck gold. After all, how many young men back in Indiana get to claim that they ran over a leopard?

So Uncle Ernie pressed the pedal to the metal, and thanks to the headlights, he didn't even have to chase the cat. After admiring his trophy, he hoisted it into the back of the panel truck and continued on his merry way. The only problem was that the truck had only one bench seat up front, and it was already occupied by my parents. We three girls had been riding in the back, seated on our "sitters," as Mama called our behinds.

And now we were joined by a dead leopard.

Or was it dead? Its amber eyes were still open, and although its tongue hung out, its lips were pulled back in a perpetual snarl, the fangs clearly visible. What's more, with every bump generated by the hideous conditions of that road, the leopard's extended right paw would jiggle. In fact, there were times when we bounced so much the leopard appeared to lurch right at us. The combined shrieks of three girls aged eight, seven, and three were almost enough to make our uncle wish that he had politely honked and waited while the big cat came to its senses and slunk off into the bush.

The following year, with our uncle safely back in America with his precious leopard skin, we made a long trek to pick up my two oldest sisters from boarding school. Although there were very few roads, none of them were marked and there was never any traffic. A breakdown could mean a night spent in the bush without food or water (although we always tried to be prepared). At any rate, as were approaching the mission station with the boarding school, we somehow took a wrong turn. Because the trip had taken so long, it was dark by then, and "fun scary"—just as long as my ▶

Leopard Tales *(continued)*

papa didn't try to run over one of the world's fourth-largest cats.

All of a sudden, I heard him say, "This is the way to the leopard colony!"

"Are you sure?" Mama asked.

"Yes, it's all coming back to me. The last time we came here we almost made the same mistake. We were supposed to turn left at the crossroads, not right. The leopard colony is another twenty kilometers down this road. We're going to have to look for a place to turn around, which isn't going to be easy with all this mud. If we get stuck, you can count on spending the night in the truck."

"What about the leopards?" I whimpered. "I have to go to the bathroom, remember? You told me to wait, but I really, really have to go."

We jolted to a stop. "Crawl over the seat," Mama said gently, "and get out on my side. You can do it right here beside the truck. No one is going to see you."

"But the leopards will eat me!"

"*What?*" Papa said.

"That colony of leopards!" I began to sob.

"I think she heard us talking about the *leper* colony," Mama said. "It was foolish of Ernie to do what he did. I could just wring his neck. The poor child's been terrified of leopards ever since that night."

She was right; I had misunderstood. However, it would be another decade before I attended that same boarding school and learned about the leper colony. It was a special village where folks afflicted with this disease lived in total isolation, except for visits from medical missionaries. By then I was no longer afraid of lepers, but I was still terrified of leopards.

My parents had been pioneers, leasing land from the Belgian government and starting a brand-new mission. In the beginning, it was just us and Uncle Ernie. Then he left. But after a few years, we were joined by another family. Of course, we had no amenities out there in the middle of nowhere—no running water, no electricity on a regular basis, no telephones.

In the evenings, upon occasion, my parents wished to get a message over to the other missionary family. It would be dark, and the servants would have long since been dismissed for the day. For some reason, the task of delivering the note would fall upon me. It was something I dreaded, and I whined to get out of doing it. At night sometimes there were hyenas and jackals about, not to mention ▶

Leopard Tales *(continued)*

snakes, and of course there was always the matter of *the tree.*

The distance between the two houses might have been only the length of two football fields, but because of all the fear the tree conjured up, it might as well have been ten miles. There was nothing special about this tree; it didn't even offer shade. At night it resembled a child's charcoal drawing of one: a black stick with a black cloud for a top. What made it ominous to me was the fact that it had been left standing directly adjacent to the footpath that connected our respective dwellings.

I was always handed a flashlight and told to point it down toward the path and keep a sharp lookout for snakes. Instead, I kept it pointed at the tree's canopy—even when I was too far away to see anything. There was a leopard up there just waiting to pounce on me, clamp its jaws around my throat, and then pull me up into the inky darkness of the canopy. The next morning my parents would find the flashlight—and maybe a few strands of my golden locks—on the path below, but that's it. That would sure show them.

Still, as much as I wanted my parents to regret forcing me to carry a note under the "leopard tree" at night,

I didn't fancy having my jugular vein severed, or my innards pulled out, or the rest of me chewed up and swallowed by an overgrown cat. The entire distance between the two houses was too far for me to cover by running, so I walked. But I stopped walking just before I reached the spot where I thought the leopard might land on me. That's where I said my last "help me Jesus" prayer and ran like the Devil himself was after me. I ran until I nearly collapsed on the dirt path, which wasn't all that far. So, as soon as I could manage it, I looked behind me. Nope, I hadn't been followed. So far, so good. However, that was only half the battle; I still had the return trip.

"You didn't get eaten, did you?" Papa asked as he opened the door for me.

"Not *this* time," I said.

Papa chuckled. "I keep telling you that there is no reason for a leopard to hide in that tree and wait for days and days until the next time I need you to carry a message. Not with a forest full of animals just a kilometer away."

"Maybe it was a visiting leopard and didn't know about the forest." I had an argument for everything back then. My husband says I still do.

"If you want, tomorrow I'll post signs in *leopardese* informing ▶

Leopard Tales *(continued)*

visiting leopards of where they can hunt, and where they can't. And there is to be absolutely no climbing of that tree, and I'll be demanding a very strict penalty from any leopard that takes my pretty little girl out to dinner uninvited."

I tried to repress a giggle, so it came out as a snort, which caused me to giggle even more. "There is no such language as *leopardese*."

"That's what you say because you can't speak it."

"Can you?"

Papa nodded.

"Then say something."

"*Grrrrrrr.*"

Have You Read?
More by Tamar Myers

THE WITCH DOCTOR'S WIFE

The Congo beckons to young Amanda Brown in 1958, as she follows her missionary calling to the mysterious "dark continent" far from her South Carolina home. But her enthusiasm cannot cushion her from the shock of a very foreign culture—where competing missionaries are as plentiful as flies, and oppressive European overlords are busy stripping the land of its most valuable resource: diamonds.

Little by little, Amanda is drawn into the lives of the villagers in tiny Belle Vue—and she is touched by the plight of the local witch doctor, a man known as Their Death, who has been forced to take a second job as a yardman to support his two wives. But when First Wife stumbles upon an impossibly enormous uncut gem, events are set in motion that threaten to devastate the lives of these people Amanda has come to admire and love—events that could lead to nothing less than murder.

THE HEADHUNTER'S DAUGHTER

In 1945, an infant left inadvertently to die in the jungles of the Belgian Congo is discovered by a young Bashilele tribesman on a mission to claim the head of an enemy. Recognized as human—despite her pale white skin and strange blue eyes—the baby is brought into the tribe and raised as its own. Thirteen years later, the girl—now called "Ugly Eyes"— will find herself at the center of a controversy that will rock two separate societies.

Young missionary Amanda Brown hears the incredible stories of a white girl living among the Bashilele headhunters. In the company of the local police chief, Captain Pierre Jardin, and with the witch doctor's wife, the quick-witted Cripple, along as translator, Amanda heads into the wild hoping to bring the lost girl back to "civilization." But Ugly Eyes no longer belongs in their world—and the secrets surrounding her birth and disappearance are placing them all in far graver peril than anyone ever imagined.